A Dangerous Friend

BOOKS BY WARD JUST

NOVELS

A Soldier of the Revolution 1970
Stringer 1974
Nicholson at Large 1975
A Family Trust 1978
In the City of Fear 1982
The American Blues 1984
The American Ambassador 1987
Jack Gance 1989
The Translator 1991
Ambition & Love 1994
Echo House 1997
A Dangerous Friend 1999

SHORT STORIES

The Congressman Who Loved Flaubert 1973

Honor, Power, Riches, Fame, and
the Love of Women 1979

Twenty-one: Selected Stories 1990
(*reissued in 1998 as* The Congressman Who
Loved Flaubert: 21 Stories and Novellas)

NONFICTION

To What End 1968
Military Men 1970

A

DANGEROUS

FRIEND

WARD JUST

A Peter Davison Book

HOUGHTON MIFFLIN COMPANY

BOSTON NEW YORK

1999

Library of Congress Cataloging-in-Publication Data

Just, Ward

A dangerous friend / Ward Just.

p. cm.

"A Peter Davison book."

ISBN 0-395-85698-1

1. Vietnamese Conflict, 1961–1975 — Fiction. 2. Viet-

nam — History — 1945–1975 — Fiction. I. Title.

PS3560.U75D36 1999

813'.54 — dc21 98-50728 CIP

Printed in the United States of America

Book design by Robert Overholtzer

QUM 10 9 8 7 6 5 4 3 2 1

AS ALWAYS, FOR SARAH

And for David and JB Greenway,
thanks for the use of the library

CONTENTS

A Dangerous Friend

The Effort

I WILL INSIST at the beginning that this is not a war story. There have been plenty of those and will be many more, appalling stories of nineteen-year-olds breaking down, frightened out of their wits, or engaging in acts of unimaginable gallantry; and often all three at the same time. The war stories were from a different period, later on, when the war became an epidemic, a plague like the Black Death. Society was paralyzed by fear. Order broke down. Duty and honor were forgotten in the rush to survive. Commanders deserted their units, friends turned their backs. Among the population, individual burials were replaced by burials en masse. The American morgue was expanded again and again. Aircraft that brought fresh troops returned with coffins. I remember watching a doctor perform an autopsy while humming through his teeth, the identical note repeated monotonously. His fingers were rigid as iron.

When he saw me, he looked up and whispered, Bring out your dead.

But that time was not my time. That time was *later on*, when things went to hell generally, and the best of us lost all heart.

My time was early days, when civilians still held a measure of authority. We were startled by the beauty of the country, and surprised at its size. It looked so small on our world maps, not much larger than New England. We understood that in Vietnam Americans would add a dimension to their identity. Isn't identity always altered by its surroundings and the task at hand? So this is a different cut of history, a civilian cut, without feats of arms or battlefield chaos. If love depends on faith, think of my narrative as a kind of romance, the story of one man with a bad conscience and another with no conscience and the Frenchman and his wife who lived in the parallel world, the one we thought was a mirage from the century before, a bankrupt colonial milieu that offered — so many possibilities, as Dicky Rostok said.

We went to Vietnam because we wanted to. We were not drafted. We were encouraged to volunteer and if our applications were denied, we applied again. We arrived jet-lagged at Tan Son Nhut airport where someone met us and hurried us off to wherever we were billeted, usually a villa on one of the wide residential boulevards that reminded everyone of a French provincial city. Even the plane trees looked imported. And later that day we showed up for work at one of the agencies or the embassy or Lansdale's outfit or the Llewellyn Group and briefed — an exercise that had much in common with initiation into a secret society, Skull and Bones or the Masons. We learned a new language, one that excluded outsiders. We lived with one eye on Washington and the other on Hanoi, and the Washington eye was the good eye. The effort — that was what we called the war, The Effort — was existential, meaning in a steady state of becoming. War aims were revised month to month and often week to week, to keep our adversary off balance.

There were thousands of us recruited from all over the government, from foundations, think tanks, and universities, too;

even police departments. Sydney Parade had worked for a foundation while Dicky Rostok was a foreign service officer, as was I. A few of us went at once to the countryside, where we administered various aid programs in collaboration with our Vietnamese counterparts. We worked harder than we had ever worked in our lives, or would ever work again. We were drunk on work. Work was passion. We were in it for the long haul, and from the beginning we swam upstream.

We reorganized their finances. We built roads, bridges, schools, and airstrips. We distributed medicine and arranged for army doctors to vaccinate the children and conduct clinics for the sick. Our agronomists devised new ways to cultivate and harvest rice and then introduced a miracle strain that grew beautifully but did not taste the way Vietnamese expected rice to taste; so it was grown and harvested and left to rot or exported to India. We performed these chores every day, all the while trying to discover what it was that kept the war going, even accelerating, month to month. The success of the enemy seemed to defy logic. We had so much and they had so little; our nineteen-year-olds were supported by an arsenal beyond the imagination of the guerrillas facing them. Or so we imagined, as we knew next to nothing of their personalities, their biographies, where they had gone to school, where they were born, whether they were married or single, what animated them beyond the struggle for unification, a political ideal that could not account for their tenacious will; think of Brady's photographs of the Union infantry. So we wrote letters home describing Buddha's face. We described Vietnam as we would describe the character of a human being we had never seen but was famous nonetheless, an introverted personality replete with legend, rumor, and innuendo.

After a few months, friends and family dropped their pretense of polite curiosity. They had their own urgent inquiries. How are things actually? The reports on the evening news are so confusing, we can't make head nor tail of them. Are we winning this war or losing it? Give us your opinion. Your letters are ambiguous! Please give us the straight story, what's happening out there really? What's the story behind the scenes? And later still, We hope you know how much everyone here is behind you boys and what you're doing in Vietnam. It sounds awful. We all appreciate the effort. Is everything all right with you? Keep your head down. Hurry home.

Of course there was no straight story in the sense of a narrative that began in one place and ended in another. Nothing was deliberately withheld; very little was known. This was exhilarating, as if we were explorers in a land at the very margins of the known world. We argued all the time, unraveling the legend from the rumor and the rumor from the innuendo; and it was Parade who suggested that we were imprisoned in our own language, tone deaf to possibility. Parade thought the VC led the charmed life of the unicorn, the beast of myth that could be neither caught by man nor touched by a weapon. Rostok scoffed at that. There was no such thing as a charmed life. There was nothing on this earth that could not be tamed, given money enough and time.

We ventured far afield to discover the logic to events. Perhaps all occupation forces find themselves at odds with their hosts, knowing at once that they are but a veneer to another, more natural life, a life in-country that goes on as it has gone on for centuries, a life as teeming and fluid and uncontrolled as the life beneath the surface of the great oceans. We came to understand that there was a uniform world parallel to the artificial world we inhabited. Ours was swarming with shadows, dancing and fluctuating day to day while the parallel world was symmetrical and anchored, prophetic in a way that ours was not. It was this world we had to enter in order to discover the nature of the resistance, meaning a reliable estimate of the situation. We only wanted to know where we stood, not so much to ask.

In the meantime there was an infrastructure to be built and a bureaucracy to be put in place. The first was impossible without the second, and it was the second to which Rostok devoted his energies. He wanted his lines of authority to be unequivocal. Sooner or later, Llewellyn Group, generously funded, superbly organized, and staffed with the best minds, would discover a means to infiltrate the parallel world and decipher it — so many possibilities, as Rostok said.

He had a flattened nose, perhaps evidence of a youthful fistfight, and an unpleasant high-pitched laugh. He was always in motion, his hands describing arcs, his head turtling forward as he inquired, Huh? Huh? His memory was phenomenal, always an asset in management, but he seemed unaware that an overactive memory often blinded one to the circumstances of the present. Rostok was not at all bookish, but that's often the case with men of action. Those books he had read he invested with an almost mystical significance; probably he believed that the mere fact of his acquaintance gave them a kind of grandeur. Voodoo, Sydney Parade said.

One of his favorites was Joseph Conrad, not the Conrad of the African jungles but the Conrad of the open Asian seas, the coming-of-age Conrad who was always conscious of the shadow line between youth and maturity. Rostok believed that Conrad had a particular purchase on the delusions that attended men organizing themselves in difficult or dangerous situations. He liked to recall Conrad's story of the marvelous sailing ship *Tweed,* a vessel heavy and graceless to look at but of extraordinary speed. In the middle of the last century she bested the steam mailboat from Hong Kong to Singapore by an astounding day and a half.

No one knew what there was about the *Tweed* that accounted for her exceptional spank, perhaps the shape and weight of the keel, perhaps the placement of the masts, perhaps the ratio of sail to the length and breadth of the hull. She was built somewhere in the West Indies, teak throughout, the best of her breed and soon to be left behind by the iron steamers. Such was her fame, and such her mystery and allure, that officers of British men-of-war came aboard to look at her whenever they shared a port. They took meticulous measurements, they interviewed all hands, but no one ever discovered her secret.

The *Tweed*'s former skipper, Captain S——, thought he knew. When Conrad met the captain he had transferred from the *Tweed* to another ship, but his former command continued to hold his allegiance. Captain S—— told Conrad that she never made a decent passage after he left her helm. It was obvious that his superb seamanship was the reason for her great success and without him the *Tweed* was just another lumbering coaster. This was the mystical union between ship and skipper, each ennobling the other. Captain S—— looked on the sailing ship *Tweed* as Rodin looked on a fat block of granite.

Something pathetic in it, Conrad observed.

And perhaps just the least bit dangerous.

But Rostok held with the captain.

My first posting abroad was in the consular section, Saigon, and it was there that I met Dede Griffith, as she was known then. Dede was already seeing Claude Armand, in effect dividing her time between the tiny USIA office on Nguyen Hue Street and Plantation Louvet. When Claude was occupied I used to take her to dinner at Guillaume Tell or Ramuncho, and in due course we became good friends. Everyone liked Dede. When she and Claude were married, I gave her away — and never was a woman happier to replace one name with another. Thereafter she was Dede Armand and very quickly she dropped from sight, at least from the sight of the American community, growing each day. Of course I am the moron who failed to notify the lads upstairs when Dede came to renew her passport.

I knew the members of Llewellyn Group. It was hard to miss them, Rostok swaggering about the city like a Roman proconsul, though it was difficult to know exactly what he did, his specific brief, his place in the bureaucratic scheme of things. I got to know Sydney Parade very well because I was the one detailed to drive to Tay Thanh to tell him that his father had died. He was terribly upset at the news, it was obvious they were very close. Sydney had his father's photograph on his desk next to the IN and OUT boxes. He invited me to stay for a drink and dinner and we spent the evening talking about his father and about the Armands. In the course of that evening and other evenings, I learned what he and Rostok were up to. Sydney spoke openly with me, probably because I was a junior consular official with no friends in high places and no motive to tell tales; not that there were many to tell. Also, Sydney was short. When his father died, he had only one month remaining in-country. Or, as he peevishly reminded me, twenty-eight days, seven hours, and umpty-ump minutes. I was short, too, but I wasn't counting the days.

I returned to the State Department after three years in Saigon. And by 1974 I was back there, a little more seasoned now after tours in Foggy Bottom, Morocco, and the Philippines. I was assigned to the political section of Embassy Saigon — a kind of morbid practical joke, since by 1974 there were no politics, only the promise of more war despite the secretary's personal assurance: "Peace is at hand." In a way he was right, but it wasn't the peace he had promised and it wasn't at hand. At last, with American troops mostly withdrawn, the civilians were in charge once again. That meant we occupied the wheelhouse as the ship drifted toward the shoals.

It is the simple truth that I was one of the last Americans to leave from the roof of Embassy Saigon on April 30, 1975, our day of dishonor and of rough justice, too. We had been at it for so long, and when the end came it was almost with relief; we don't have to do this anymore. For as long as I live on this earth I will remember the bitter odor of smoldering greenbacks. I thought of burning fruit. I stood at the door of the strongroom watching an overweight marine sergeant feed the stacks of currency into a makeshift fire, the smoke of thousands of dollars filling the corridor. He whistled while he worked. I hoped the stench would reach Washington, D.C., and remain there for a generation. I remember the patience and courtesy of the staff crowded on the narrow stairs leading to the roof, the dark jokes and hesitant laughter, everyone listening to the crash of explosives advancing from the northwest. We knew we were present at the end of something momentous, and not only a lost war or lost innocence, either. That's a European idea, and they're welcome to it. I believe we knew on that day that our choices had been reduced to two: fear of the known or fear of the unknown, and for the rest of our lives we would fear the known thing.

Vietnam. You kept meeting the same people as you moved from post to post, diplomats you had served with, and of course the foreign correspondents. We were all connoisseurs of Third World adversity. I remember vividly a party I gave a few years ago. We sat up very late, about a dozen of us, diplomats and journalists; all of us had served in Vietnam during the early days. We made our bones in Vietnam, as American gangsters like to say — and none of us went home. It is equally true that none of our careers suffered, far from it. Service in the war gave you a leg up the ladder, even though, as seems so obvious now but wasn't obvious then, we were searching in a dark room for a black hat that wasn't there. And the same was true for the soldiers, at least for the officers. We survived and our reputations survived with us, and we, most of us, went on to succeed handsomely in the wider world. There is some irony here but no need to dwell upon it. The ironies of the effort are well known.

Yet for some of us the episode was only that, a brief wrestle in a dark room, a distant memory, so distant that whatever pleasure or pain there was has been forgotten. The foreign correspondents went on to other wars in other regions — and we, too. We were there with them. Some of them and some of us finally gave up on the Third World — we had been at the roulette table for too long, unsuccessfully playing the same number — and moved on to senior positions in London or Paris or Washington, or out of the business altogether, into banking or public relations, lobbying, consulting, where we could use the friendships we'd made and the valuable knowledge we'd gathered. The wars and famines were for younger men and women with faster feet and uncrowded personal lives and a powerful appetite for the unknown thing.

I was always surprised at those who were able to move on easily from Vietnam, the war one more experience in a lifetime of experiences, neither the worst nor the least. So vivid then, it receded, leaving only fugitive souvenirs and a few friendships. This was evident that night in my villa when we fell to talking of the early days of the Effort, the mid-1960s, before things went to hell and the plague arrived. Naturally we reminisced about our many blunders and about personalities, both the living and the dead. Six of us in the room remembered everyone mentioned, looks, job, eccentricities. Anecdote followed anecdote. I opened another bottle of cognac.

When someone said, Whatever happened to Dicky Rostok, I

did not reply. I wanted to hear what the others knew, because Rostok had gone to considerable trouble not to make himself the black hat in the dark room.

One of the journalists laughed, not unkindly. He said that Rostok had stayed on in Vietnam until early 1968. Then, with his usual exquisite sense of timing, he resigned from the foreign service and went home. About two days before the Tet Offensive. Can you believe it?

Yes, I said.

You mean he knew?

Rostok had a nose, I said.

I saw him in Switzerland not long after the war, the journalist went on. He was running some stock fund, living very well in Zurich. He tried to get me into the fund but I didn't have any money and told him so. Mistake, he said. His fund was one of the most successful in Europe and friends always got a discount. He said he had turned down an ambassadorship because he needed to make money. He had a new wife. And the new wife had expensive tastes. Then he went into insurance, selling life insurance to GIs, as I remember. But there was something not quite right about the way he went about it. There were complaints and an investigation. A congressional committee held hearings but nothing came of them.

Funeral insurance, I said.

Was it funeral?

Black limousines, a bronze coffin, a gravesite in the cemetery of your choice, a Spanish veil for your mother, and an entertainment allowance for the party afterward. There were other benefits but I forget what they were. He made a lot of money before the company folded, 1970 was a great year for him.

I don't know anything about that, the journalist said. I never knew him well in the war. But when anything hush-hush was going on I'd pay him a call and he'd give me some help. Dicky liked ink. Dicky had time for you. And that paid off for him. I was thinking that we all learned a lot in Vietnam, especially at the beginning when we pulled together, trying to find our way. No one wanted to be left behind. Rostok was good where it counted. I can't remember the name of that outfit of his —

Llewellyn Group, I said.

Yes, the Llewellyns. They were spooks, weren't they?

They weren't spooks, I said.

I thought they were spooks. They acted like spooks. Rostok had a deputy, wouldn't give us dick when we came around for information. What was his name?

Sydney Parade, I said.

Yes, Parade. Whatever happened to him?

One of the other journalists cleared his throat and said irritably, Who the hell was Sydney Parade?

Friend of Dicky Rostok's, I said mischievously.

I don't remember any Parade.

He went into teaching, I said. But I did not add that he'd retired and now spent his days alone on an island off Cape Cod, reading his books, watching the evening news, and sketching the pier that adjoined his house, one line drawing after another. Sydney believed in repetition.

The reporter shrugged; he had no interest in anyone who had gone into teaching.

Sydney was only there for a year, I said.

Just a bit player in the war.

So the end of my narrative has come at the beginning, as if you are standing at a distance and hear the echo of the bells and can only guess at their size and location. It is always necessary to look forward and backward at the same time. Only in that way can we preserve our identities and live truthfully. You know the end of things as well as I do. We cannot pretend not to know them or deny that they exist. When we relate events from the past we know the results and must acknowledge them, whether or not they bring us understanding, or consolation, or shame.

The year is 1965, before the Effort, begun so modestly, turned into something monstrous. Take the measurements, interview all hands, and there's still a mystery at the heart of it. Sydney Parade told me Rostok's version of Conrad's tale of the *Tweed* and her dangerous skipper, and some of the other stories that appear in this book. Sydney was not always kind to himself, owing to his bad conscience and, by his own admission, to his naïveté in the beginning. Rostok was usually straight with the facts, though his ego got in the way of everything he did and didn't do. I have always believed that a mountainous ego resulted from an absence of conscience.

I play no part in this narrative and will shortly disappear from it. I would not be writing it now except for my position in the middle of things. I was the only one in-country intimate with the four principals, Rostok, Parade, the Frenchman, and the Frenchman's wife — yes, and Gutterman, too. Do not forget for a moment that I was also present in Vietnam years later, when the country was unified by force, and Rostok and Parade were long gone.

The Family Armand

S YDNEY PARADE first learned of the intrepid family Armand
from his stepmother's sister Missy, who had lived with them in
France for a summer. Missy and the Comminges Armands became close that summer and subsequent summers, to the point
where she became a virtual member of the family and au courant
with its three branches, the Armands in Abidjan and Bangui and
of course the Armands in Xuan Loc. She spoke of them as if they
were characters in a nineteenth-century adventure novel. They
traveled widely and lived dangerously. They chose warm cli-
mates and colorful marriages. They described themselves as industrial ambassadors, supervising the twilight hours of the
French empire. Their specialties were oil, minerals, and rubber.

When Missy graduated from college, it was natural that she
return to France to live. Except for her sister, she had no family in
America; the Armands of Comminges were her family. Still, she
always managed a visit to Connecticut on Thanksgiving, and
it was at these family dinners with his father and stepmother
that Sydney learned of the brothers Armand in Abidjan, Bangui,
and Xuan Loc, how difficult and unsettled their lives were com-

pared to the Comminges Armands, Papa and Maman, their stone house next to a crumbling Roman wall on the edge of a medieval village, their three charming daughters, their devotion each to the others and to the land where they had lived, well, *forever.*

Missy was only a few years older than Sydney but he found her world adult and exotic — so close to Balzac, so far from Darien — though mysterious was probably the better word, for she never disclosed anything of her personal life, the pleasures and miseries of romance, or her work at the bank. Instead she rambled on and on about the Armands, so worldly, so cultivated, so diverse in their interests, so loyal to one another, so hospitable and droll. And you should taste Maman's lamb!

Where's Comminges? Sydney asked his father.

Foothills of the Pyrenees, his father replied.

And then, clearing his throat, he offered some advice. He said, Missy's promiscuous where France is concerned. She's become an expat, meaning she knows even less about her adopted country than she knows about this one. Thing about a foreign country, you never know what you don't know. Only a fool makes that mistake with his own. Then, because he was a great jazz fan, he muttered something about the Beale Street blues. She'll be lonesome her whole long life, he concluded cryptically.

For years Missy had urged Sydney to visit her in Paris. Every snake needed to shed its skin, often more than once; in that way you adapted to the environment. You can come any time, she said. Just give me warning. She had bought an adorable apartment in the rue du Louvre; there was a guest bedroom and a good museum across the street. The river was nearby. And if you come on a weekend, we can take the train to Comminges and you can meet the Armands at last. They'd love it. I've told them all about your family, Syd. What there is to tell.

For years plans were made and canceled, the occasion for

much amusement around the dinner table at Thanksgiving, his father loudly whistling the Berigan chorus of "I Can't Get Started" while his stepmother laughed and laughed. Then the gears meshed and one Friday morning in the early spring of 1965 Sydney arrived with his bags at the church square that introduced the rue du Louvre. For a long time he stood in the chilly early morning mist looking at the third-floor window, its blinds open, lights within. He was reluctant to intrude because he felt the slightest bit uneasy that he was there with his own ulterior motives of which Missy would not approve; and she would discover them soon enough, no matter the subtlety of his approach.

Sydney had been told that a successful meeting with the Comminges Armands would pay handsome dividends in the months and years to come. There was no logical reason why they would not want to cooperate. Cooperation cost them nothing, and French interests were involved, not to mention the man's brother. Everyone in the West was in the same boat, and they were in it for the duration.

So Sydney picked up his bags and walked into the building, aware of the fumes of diesel fuel mixed with freshly baked bread, a specific French anomaly that made him smile self-consciously, the smile revealing his nervous excitement at the task at hand. He was nearly thirty years old, a stoutish American tourist in an anonymous corduroy jacket, chino trousers, and loafers, no tie; even the look of relief was American, for in one year he had managed to shed two skins, a wife and a job, one after the other. His wife was an ocean away in New York. Their daughter was with her.

Missy was standing in her doorway, chic in slacks and a sweater. She had seen him standing in the square and wondered at his hesitation. There was only one rue du Louvre after all. Americans were always ill at ease in Paris, uncertain what to say or do. She waved at him but he did not see her. He was looking at the window on the floor below, a mistake they always made; such a simple thing that the Americans couldn't get straight. In France it went ground floor, then first floor.

She gave him a cup of coffee and a croissant and suggested a nap before the noon train to Comminges. The journey was hours long but they should be there in time for a late dinner. The Armands would be thrilled to meet him at last.

Aren't you jet-lagged? she asked.

I've only come down from Brussels, he said.

Brussels?

I've been in Brussels seeing friends, Sydney said vaguely.

In Brussels? Her tone of voice suggested that no good could come from any visit to the Belgians.

Some old school friends, Sydney said, wondering if Missy knew that one of the more obscure American military commands was located at Brussels. Probably the Pentagon would not be one of her interests. In any case, the commander's aide-de-camp was an old school friend of Rostok's. And the briefing had been useless.

He brought her up to date on family news — her sister had bought a Buick, and she and his father had won the Darby and Joan at Abenaki, two up — while she showed him around her apartment, spacious and done in the modern style, white couches against white walls, huge white lamps, abstract art on the walls except for a pastel Laurencin nude over the fireplace. Sydney handed her a box of chocolates and a bottle of Scotch, and a package of snapshots from her sister. Missy casually leafed through the snapshots — several of the Buick, several more of her sister in golf clothes — but stopped, frowning, when she came to the one of the family at Christmas.

She said, I'm sorry about you and —

Karla, he said.

Yes, Karla.

It was time, he said.

Missy raised her eyebrows as if to say, Time for what? She disapproved of divorce, preferring instead the many civilized alternatives. She said, You have a son, I remember.

Daughter, he said. She's fine. We're all fine. Sydney smiled to conceal the lie. His daughter was not fine. She was a three-year-old with a broken heart. But his stepmother's sister was not entitled to that news.

It's always good to take a holiday after emotional upset, Missy said, though Sydney showed no signs of upset. How long will you be in France, then?

I must leave on Monday, he said.

So short, she said, her tone of voice again disapproving; perhaps he had confused Paris with Philadelphia. Will you be returning to Belgium?

I'm going to South Vietnam, he said.

Oh, my goodness, she said. Why?

That's where I'll be working. It's all arranged.

I can't see you in uniform, she said. Then she remembered that he had taken some kind of degree in military history or the history of modern Europe and did speak some French, though with an execrable accent, painful to listen to.

No, no, he said. It's civilian.

She said, I don't know anything about it. We have troops there now, don't we? There was discussion in the senior staff meeting last week, an argument I didn't follow. I don't know the geography. The politics are a mystery to me. Is it about oil? Monsieur Pelliard thought the Americans were crazy to get anywhere near Indochina. He thought the Germans should be given that opportunity, it was their sort of thing. He was quite emphatic. All the senior staff agreed with him.

The Europeans aren't in any position to lecture us, Sydney said.

They don't learn from their mistakes, she agreed, bending forward and looking at him closely as if there were something she had missed. Except bankers, she went on. And my bank took a bath when the French were involved out there. We lost millions. So we're cautious.

Understandably, he said.

You didn't say who you'll be working *for*. Is it government? You're not with the spooks, are you?

No, no, he said, laughing though he disapproved of the word "spooks," signaling as it did a lack of respect for honorable men doing dangerous work. I'll be in the countryside, administering foreign aid. Building schools, getting the rice to market. Economic development, building democratic institutions. When she looked at him doubtfully, he added, We call it nation-building. Such was the word from Dicky Rostok when Dicky had recruited him in New York. Nation-building was the velvet glove that complemented the army's iron fist, and everyone knew that the war would be won or lost by the caress of the glove. In the last analysis, as the President said, the Vietnamese had to fight their own war. They were good people who needed help, not only on the battlefield against the Communist enemy but against poverty, disease, and corruption. Such a simple thing as getting the rice to market or the smallpox vaccine to the clinic would prove decisive. A stable currency was worth a regiment of marines. This was what Ros had learned after a year in-country. An unimaginably complex society, the experts said. You could never learn it all, and in the beginning you had to take care not to learn the wrong things. So much misinformation, so widely broadcast. That was why they had set up the Llewellyn Group, a group separate from the aid bureaucracy already in place, with its own mission and chain of command and communications with Washington. Llewellyn Group was both inside and outside the apparatus. It's important work, he said to Missy. And we'll make it succeed.

Missy put away the coffee things while she half listened to Sydney talk on and on, something about duty and responsibility. Her sister had told her about the breakup, a loose, painful, squalid, careless business. Sydney was not cut out for marriage. In that respect, her sister had said, the apple had not fallen far from the tree. And Karla was worse; but that was another story. Still, Sydney looked well. She thought he had filled out some since she had seen him last, at Christmas when his marriage was falling apart, but probably that was the masculine thrill of wartime duty. They loved it so. They loved it because the women were watching but not nearby.

I don't know anything about it, Missy said again.

While she dozed he watched the countryside slide by through dusty windows, the fields and farmsteads monotonous and unremarkable, the villages somnolent in the afternoon. The fields were utterly empty, as if a great epidemic had carried off the durable peasantry, leaving only farm animals and buildings behind. Stands of trees blocked the horizon, though now and again he caught sight of a château on its hilltop. These pastoral scenes unfolded like pictures at an exhibition, but pictures that gave no hint of the life beneath the skin of the canvas. Sydney had never been to Europe, in fact had never traveled outside the United States. There was always so much to see at home, a whole continent. He had let one opportunity after another slip by and was determined to seize South Vietnam.

He had no idea what to expect. The books he had read were written by Americans, French, and English. The Vietnamese in them were elusive, rarely speaking, seen in silhouette. The terrain itself was no less fugitive, seen through Western eyes. He imagined it now, closed in and thick with heat, its agriculture not far removed from the Middle Ages. The fields would bristle with human life. For Romanesque churches, Buddhist temples; for fields of grain, fields of rice stalk-deep in stagnant water. In Indochina time would be measured on an ethereal scale, and still important in the general scheme of things. A herd of cows, motionless in a flat field, appeared for a moment and then vanished as the train leaned into a curve. Suddenly he was in a tunnel and the train's wheels squeaked to a halt.

Rostok had made his pitch to the senior staff of the Foundation, everyone gathered around a refectory table with pads and pencils before them, carafes of water on a tray in the center. Sydney was invited because he was the director's assistant and because he was younger than the others; he was the youngest man in the room by twenty years, though this was not immediately apparent because he wore the same long face as the others. He knew Rostok through mutual friends, often dining together, Rostok running the table like a college professor turned talk-show host. He was then posted to the U.S. mission to the U.N., an institution he called The Building. A year ago he had been recalled to Washington and dispatched to Vietnam. Now he was back in New York, scanning the faces that were ever alert to nuance, the sweat and glitter of the well-polished fact that led to the rosy scenario; Rostok was looking for accomplices.

He was eloquent. Rostok began in a pessimistic vein and only got more so as he went along, stressing the novelty and mystery of the effort. Americans had never interfered in this way, except for a few small-scale operations, the Philippines, Central America, Cuba twice, never on a national scale, never in-country, hand in glove with the elected government. That was on the civilian side. On the military side the only comparison was to the Indian wars of the century before and that analogy broke down quickly enough, for a dozen reasons, not least the tenacity, skill, and coherence of the Communist insurgency in Vietnam. The Indians had no ideology, no Lenin, no Marx, no Hitler, no Ho, only Tecumseh and the various holy spirits that had let them down at important moments. The American Indians led a filthy life and could not see the future before them. They did not believe Tecumseh's vision of an entente cordiale among all the tribes; unite and prosper. All they wanted was to preserve what they had, forgetting that time never reversed itself, never, no exceptions. And on a more practical level there was the terrain. Vietnam was thickly forested, the forests broken here and there by rice fields; and the rice fields were bordered by wiry hedge-rows, ideal for ambush. And the allegiance of the peasants was in doubt, allowing the guerrillas a base of operations that rendered them invisible. They don't wear war bonnets. They don't carry bows and arrows.

Rostok paused for water, not a theatrical sip but one, two, three deep swallows, as if he were chugging beer. He smacked his lips and resumed, speaking of course without notes, moving his eyes to communicate with each member of the audience.

Along the spine of the Annamite Cordillera in South Vietnam the mountains were rugged and covered by triple-canopy jungle with ravines deep enough to conceal a regiment. He quoted from the great French sociologist Paul Mus. He quoted from Camus's *Myth of Sisyphus*. He quoted from General Vo Nguyen Giap's monograph on Dien Bien Phu, a document only recently available. *Our people's war of resistance was an all-out war waged by the whole nation . . . a protracted war full of hardship but . . . certainly victorious.* And as he looked out over the polished table at the fountain pens racing across the bone-white pads — the racing had begun with the words "novelty and mystery of the effort" and had not paused — he said quietly, But we are not French. We are not colonialists. We have no territorial ambitions. And if we do not hold in Vietnam, the dominoes will tumble from Danang south to Singapore.

Rostok wanted to give half a million dollars of the government's money to the Foundation for research into the psychology of the Vietnamese, independent research to ensure integrity, product the property of the government. Why was the Saigon administration unable to hold the allegiance of the people? The Vietnamese seemed unable to choose — and what was it about their anima that locked them in irons? The hearts and minds of the Vietnamese people were — terra incognita. Rostok gave an exaggerated shrug at the problem, mute acknowledgment that while solution was difficult, solution was also within grasp, given time and money and the sort of resources that the Foundation could bring to bear. We, too, require an all-out effort waged by the whole nation. He said then that what followed was classified; those who were taking notes must put their pens aside and agree to abide by the rules of deep background.

Rostok was a menacing figure, always disheveled. He gave the appearance of just having returned from some unspeakable bivouac, and of course his brain was stuffed with secrets, more secrets than it could comfortably hold, so it would not be surprising if one popped out from time to time, owing to inattention or simple forgetfulness. So the group assembled before him, many of them years older, quietly put down their pens and prepared to listen, though what had come before did not give them confidence.

He confided that the government had established a special group that was loosely tied to Embassy Saigon but not responsible to it. Llewellyn Group would report directly to the office of the secretary of defense, with a collateral brief from the office of the national security adviser in the White House. Obvious to everyone that the effort required a team outside the normal chain of command, not for intelligence or counter-insurgency —

the CIA already had more people than the embassy, and its plate was full — but for research and rapid reaction when the usual channels broke down. The bridge that didn't get built, the medical team delayed, the market terrorized, the road cut — and the research to determine the effect on Vietnamese morale. Half a million dollars wasn't so much, and the knowledge it would bring would be worth that regiment hidden in the ravine. Public money without strings was essential for an effort of this kind. It ensured independence at a time when everyone had an ax to grind. In another sense it ensured the integrity of the process; let the facts fall where they may. Universities were already collaborating in the common effort. The nation was reaching the hour of maximum danger, Rostok concluded, quoting the late President.

And then, before the polite applause had passed away, he made this observation.

You have no idea how little we know.

Sydney and the director spent an hour with him afterward. Rostok allowed that counter-insurgency in all its aspects was a slovenly business, not congenial to the straightforward can-do American spirit. Vietnam might well be a bridge too far, a war that could not be won by the means to hand. But that did not mean that the cause was hopeless. It did not mean that the war was not worth fighting. In fact, quite the reverse. What if it were the model for the future, in the way that Antietam was the model for the infantry tactics of the world wars of this century? And if America failed to learn its lessons, well then, America would fall behind. We'll see what we are made of as a people and as a government. Nothing in the national life was more important, nothing would have a greater effect on the generations yet to come. No less important was the confidence of the government *in itself* as guardian of the Union. We need the collaboration of the private community, its expertise and good sense. We need the best men, men who are unafraid of paradox, men who are eager to understand our Asian Antietam, and master it. Then Rostok had a fresh thought.

Our situation is the opposite of the northern armies, who sought to bleed the South white and reduce it to poverty. What did Sheridan say? Enemy civilians should be left with "nothing but their eyes to weep with." And who did he say it to? Bismarck. And Bismarck listened. As we have done. We are in South Vietnam for the protection of innocent civilians, and that is why we need your support, Rostok said, and was not at all surprised when Sydney Parade enthusiastically backed him up. Time for the Foundation to become *engaged,* Syd said, not from the sidelines but from the front lines.

But the director declined. He found Rostok — intellectually incomplete.

Not our line of country, Mr. Rostok.

The government would be grateful, Rostok said.

That's not our line of country, either, the director said. He wondered momentarily exactly how grateful the government would be, and how it would make its pleasure known. But he thought he knew the answer to that, and on the spur of the moment decided to hedge. He offered Sydney instead. He offered a year's leave of absence if Sydney wanted to see for himself the . . .

Modern world, Rostok said.

And report back, the director said.

Sydney agreed at once, with an alacrity that caused the director to look up sharply, the expression on his face so dismayed that Sydney was quick to assure him that he was fit, much fitter than he looked, and would be quite safe in the war zone, where the dangers were exaggerated.

I meant, I thought you'd want to talk this over with your wife, the director explained with a pained smile.

I will, of course, Sydney said. He was embarrassed at his

misapprehension. Karla will understand what all this is about. She'll get it right away. She's been through the mill herself.

That night he described to Karla what he was being called on to do, an odd locution but the one that had popped into his mind. He searched for words and was surprised at his incoherence. Such a simple matter and he could not find the proper thoughts, like he was some rattled witness at a congressional hearing. He looked around the living room, the heavy drapes and furniture, and Karla's Polish poster from the gallery two doors away, *Literatura i Plakat Socrealistyczny.* More agitprop, but that was the way of things downtown. Their building had a Stalinist feel to it, walls as thick as a fortress and as pleasing. He turned his back to the poster and looked into Karla's eyes. Certainly they loved each other and in a sense this mission was for them both, she would be with him in his heart. He mumbled something about the national security of the United States and the malevolence of Communist aggression against simple people who only wanted to be let alone.

He said, You understand that from your own life. You've been through it.

He watched her smile thinly, her eyes fixed on a point just above his head, and tried again, speaking gravely now, describing the war as Rostok had, a mighty effort that required the best men, educated men, civilian volunteers to support the boys in the infantry, you see. It's irresponsible not to respond. It's cowardly. There's an inequality, he said, not knowing exactly what he meant but believing he was close to a true thought. In any case, he believed the inequality of the sacrifice was immoral, a stain on the nation's honor. If you were in a position to help, you helped. Simple as that. I have to do it, he concluded.

Sacrifice? she asked.

Yes, sacrifice, he said.

For what?

For the *effort,* he said. In his mind he saw an infantry company motionless in a nameless field, providing security for medical teams as they vaccinated children, curious adults pressing close, worried at first and then grateful. Everyone was sweating in the terrible heat.

Involving the national security and the nation's honor.

Not only that, he said. Destiny was involved.

I want to make certain I understand, she said thoughtfully, because some of what you said wasn't clear. It still isn't. It doesn't add up. And it's unlike you to talk nonsense to me.

It's not nonsense —

She undid the ribbon in her hair and tossed it aside, facing him now with her hands on her hips, talking rapidly without pauses. She knew that one day he would leave her. That was what men did when they were thirty years old and working routine jobs without the promise of romance, or power or riches or whatever it was they wanted for themselves. Send me onto another path, this one is worn out. It won't take me where I need to go. They suddenly tired of domestic life. But she had never guessed that a war would be the reason he would leave. She had never guessed that, never in a thousand million years that — one day he would announce that he had heard an inspirational message from the government. A war was in progress and he was essential to the effort because he was uniquely unafraid of paradox and eager to understand the nation's Asian Antietam, which was somehow tied to sacrifice and destiny, the national security, and the nation's honor. And he called it the modern world.

She promised that if he chose to go to South Vietnam she would consider the marriage ended, kaput. She could never live with a war lover.

Send me onto another path, this one is worn out. He thought, Send me into another life, one with promise and desire. He remembered each detail of the argument that went on and on.

Their daughter, Rosa, fled to the television set, sitting curled in front of the screen holding her teddy bear, a splash of kinetic fluorescence on the furry surface of the bear. Tears streamed down her cheeks. When Rosa was disappointed her face knotted into obstinacy. He called her Rosetta Stone. When Sydney went to her she turned away and would not speak. When he pulled her close she froze, but he continued to whisper into her ear, Rosa-ta-ta Stone, describing the many marvelous animals in Indochina, elephants and stupendous tigers and black bears, and pythons and monkeys and birds by the gazillion. He would be back before she knew it. She sat with her thumb in her mouth watching a middle-aged man with a lampshade on his head. He knew that she did not understand things now but would someday if Karla did not poison her mind. Karla was capable of it, too, ruled as she was by her family's bitter and melodramatic history. He spoke a few more words, then left his daughter with her bear in the glow of the television set.

Karla demanded that he pack his bags and leave, he had done enough damage for one evening, talking to their daughter about the wretched war and its terrible consequences for humanity *and for this family.* Rosa had seen some film the night before and she had begun to cry then, too, because she had seen a photograph of a dead *child*, Syd, and that upset her — reasonably so, wouldn't you say?

He said, You shouldn't've allowed her to watch.

They broke into *The Flintstones,* Syd. So that three-year-olds could see for themselves what bastards the Viet Cong are. The government brainwashing three-year-olds. She opened her mouth to say something more, then turned away and began to fuss with the phonograph. She slid a record from its sleeve and stood tapping it on the edge of the old Webcor, some rhythm she was hearing in her head. When Sydney approached and put his hands on her shoulders she did not move or give any sign she felt his presence. She placed the record on the turntable and set the arm, but the volume was turned so low all he could hear was the undulating hiss of the needle. They remained like that for a minute or more, Sydney hoping she had somehow misunderstood the situation, that in his confusion he had not explained himself properly.

She said, You should go now.

I don't deserve this, she added.

It isn't what you think, he said.

Probably not, she agreed. Probably it's something else, something I haven't thought of or even conceived of.

It isn't a woman, he said.

It's only for a year, he went on. Rostok wanted to give the Foundation a half million dollars to oversee a project, I can't say what it is because it's classified, but we're equipped to do it. And that idiot director wouldn't take the money. Everyone else wanted to. Made me ashamed, sitting there and being asked to help and the director saying No, it's not our line of country. And when I spoke to him later he said Rostok wasn't offering enough, that if we waited he'd offer more and we could do the job properly, meaning properly funded, you see. Normally we design and fund our own projects and this would be a new thing, a sort of joint venture —

It's simple, she said. You want me and you want our daughter and you want to go to Vietnam to take part in your Effort, and when you're done you want us here where you left us, to welcome you home as if nothing had happened and you had never been away. Meantime, the peasants are dying by your hand. And you will die by theirs.

He said patiently, I'm there to help them. It's the Viet Cong that's killing them.

And in that year we will live in one universe and you in another and these will never meet. When you return to ours you will be unable to leave your own. It will be your prison. You will live in it forever and we will never understand what it is; and you will not be able to explain it to us any more than you can explain the workings of your own heart at this moment.

Her woodsy accent had returned, the voice of an educated country girl. In her utter anxiety she had returned to her previous life. Her lips barely moved and her eyes were hard as stones. He said quietly, That isn't true. And that isn't the way you felt about your father. He stayed behind. He's still there, twenty years after the war.

It took her a moment to answer.

My father fought Nazis, she said, her voice thickening with each word. In Czechoslovakia, his homeland. The Nazis had invaded, just as you are doing. Listen. My father was not on your side. My father was on the other side. He still is.

One of the commissars, Sydney thought but did not say. He had run out of ideas.

She watched the turntable move, listening to the hiss. She said, A few years ago a pianist came to my school for a master class. He was performing Beethoven's sonatas for violin and piano, all ten. He was playing in Brooklyn here and then going on to Boston and Chicago. He gave his class and then spoke about the sonatas and how, playing them, you could follow Beethoven's life, his loneliness, his bad health, his money problems, one domestic crisis after another, his deafness. Playing these pieces, the pianist understood that the composer sacrificed his life for his music, a succession of masterpieces. Triumphs of will. Triumphs of concentration, of inspiration, of unspeakable courage. Of devotion, yes. She looked directly at him and said no more.

He did not know what she meant. He murmured something about genius.

There are no Beethovens here, she said.

He shook his head, certainly not.

But I thought when it came time for you to give your life, you would give it for me.

He turned quickly and fetched his coat. When he looked back she had vanished. He let himself out, closing the door with a sharp bang. The neighbor down the hall stepped into the corridor, his face filled with alarm. When Sydney glared at him, he shrugged and stepped back inside. Standing in the bar on the corner, drinking one Scotch after another, Sydney thought about the kind of apartment building where raised voices were cause for concern. Everyone in the building had too much time on their hands, but instead of a devil's workshop they had created a police state where everyone knew everyone else's business and was quick to judge, and inform if need be.

She, too. Quick to judge and to set the ethical standards which all the world was required to meet, except her; like an absolute monarch, she made her own laws. But he had hurt her and she had hurt him back, and so that was that. The bar was dark, a family tavern with Rheingold on tap and pickled eggs in a glass jar and a silent white-aproned bartender with more troubles than you had. The place reminded him of the locker room at his father's club, the Abenaki, with its dark wood and odor of sweat and air conditioning, and the rustle of men's voices around the card tables near the fireplace, someone telling a joke and the laughter that followed. The bartender used an ivory spatula to clear the head from the beer steins. Sydney remembered languid afternoons with his father, the old man exhausted after eighteen holes and a hundred, hundred and five strokes, in and out of the rough. God, he was a terrible golfer but always cheerful, except the one time when he admitted that he hated not being able to keep up with his foursome. He'd played with them for thirty years. He didn't want to beat them, only keep up with them.

So she was born in Czechoslovakia, his father had said. My goodness, she's a pretty girl. And a musician? I don't know about

Czechoslovakia, he said, but I know about musicians. You'll have your hands full.

Now it was ended. He stared at the Rheingold sign back of the bar while he fought to keep his fear in check. My God, what have I done? But there was no going back, too much had been said that could not be unsaid. Sydney had difficulty assembling her many arguments; he had not listened carefully to her any more than she had listened carefully to him. But wasn't that normal, the way of the world? Of course people carried their baggage with them. If you were brought up in a Connecticut suburb — church on Easter and a Ford in the garage next to the outdoor grill and the golf sticks — you carried that. If you were born in Czechoslovakia and fled at the age of four with your terrified mother, leaving your father behind to fight Germans, you carried that. And later, if Czechoslovakia seemed to disappear into a kind of civic limbo, neither Czech nor Soviet, neither toxic nor benign, you made what excuses you could. The Nazis were defeated and the Reds in charge. It would take time for the Czechos to find their own way. Karla and her mother had the mentality of displaced persons, worried always that their papers were not in order or that their belongings would be confiscated or that their husbands would disappear.

He signaled the barman for a fresh drink.

Impossible to wind back the film. Not his, not Karla's. Nor Rosa's. If only Karla were different, he thought. She had no faith in the future.

In the beginning they never talked politics or worried about the fate of nations. When they met she was a struggling musician, trading as much on her looks as on her talent, which she had in modest abundance along with so many other young cellists. He saw her at an evening concert at one of the downtown churches. He was seated in a side gallery at the front, the musicians almost close enough to touch. The three cellists sat on low stools behind metal music stands, two middle-aged men in tuxe-dos and Karla in black trousers and a black turtleneck sweater with a long white silk scarf, the ends of it reaching to the small of her back. She had a wide forehead, her face divided by sharp planes, without doubt a central European, foreign born. Her hair was so blond it was nearly white and cut short with little re-verse commas where it touched her shoulders. When she leaned forward to arrange her score, her hair swayed with the move-ment of her fingers, the whiteness of her skin and hair brilliant in the glum light of the church. She wore high-heeled back leather boots and handled her cello as if it were featherweight. Her instrument was of a richer, darker wood than those of the men. They were cracking jokes in muffled voices, leaning back casu-ally on their stools as she bent forward; but they were looking at her provocative bottom, as purely defined as if she were nude. Sydney could not see the expression on her face but he thought she was smiling.

And then they began to play, gathering the instruments be-tween their thighs. Karla's right boot was planted on the floor, her left hooked on the first rung of the stool. Her legs formed a figure 4 and he thought her graceful as a dancer, disappearing into her music as a dancer disappeared into the dance. When the cellos were silent she wound her arms around the cello's neck, resting her fingers on the purfling. When she turned her head sideways, Sydney noticed no emotion in her face; and when things got off track in the fifth movement she neither frowned nor sighed, only stared at the score, ignoring the raised eyebrows of the musician on her right and the administrative yawn of the one on her left. The conductor seemed momentarily to lose his way, though he never looked at the score. The cellos came in again and she bent to her task, the fingers of her left hand throb-bing when she touched the heavy strings, the sound dense as the earth.

They were playing Brahms's grief-stricken German Requiem, the requiem in which, if you listen hard enough, you can hear the anxious souls beseeching God, struggling to enter the gates of heaven.

The applause was prolonged and when the orchestra was asked to rise and she slipped wearily off her stool, Sydney noticed that her sweater clung to her skin and her face glistened with perspiration, even though it was damp and chilly in the church. When she moved to pick up her cello she faltered, shivering. Now it had the weight of an anvil. She looked around but her colleagues were already gone. Sydney stepped forward to hand her his coat, which she accepted with a distracted nod of thanks, and then she disappeared into the dark space behind the altar where the other musicians were. The audience began to disperse. He waited for fifteen minutes but she did not reappear. The others said she had gone home. Karla always left at once when the concert ended. No, they did not know where she lived. Her address was never to be given out.

The next day she telephoned.

I seem to have your coat, she said.

How did you find me?

A letter in the pocket. Who's Babs?

My sister, he said.

Hmmm, she said, and laughed.

Well, he amended. She's someone's sister.

She signed it ex-ex-ex oh-oh-oh. What does that mean?

Hugs and kisses, he said.

She laughed again. She said, You were sweet to give me your coat. I'm afraid I forgot I borrowed it. At the end of these things, I'm out of it. I'm kaput. I don't know where I am. The church was so close, like a sauna. And the orchestra did not play well. The horns were out of sync. The baritone's voice was small.

The fifth movement, he said.

And the fourth and part of the third.

I didn't hear anything wrong, he said.

I did. Probably it was something only a musician would hear, things sort of collapsed. The tempi went haywire. Our conductor is very old and deaf in one ear, though he denies it up and down. But in the final movements he loses energy and then he loses his concentration. And last month he lost his wife. The requiem was for her. Did you notice, he had tears in his eyes the whole way through? I think he was pleased with the performance, on the whole. He said he was, and I suppose he wouldn't lie. He almost never does. Are you a musician?

Amateur, he said. Jazz trombone. Weekends I sit in with a band at a bar around the corner from my office.

Where's that? she asked.

Sixth Avenue, downtown. I work for a foundation.

Foundation? she said, as if she had never heard the word. What does a foundation do?

Gives money away, he said.

To anybody?

Irrespective of size, sex, race, or national origin.

Oh, she said, and fell silent. He could hear her breathing and wondered if he had somehow insulted her. Then she said brightly, Tell me when you're playing and where and I'll come by and listen a little and return your coat, Sydney.

Wasn't it bliss, that night and the nights following? Sydney played like a dream. Close your eyes and he might have been Jack Teagarden. He sang a solo of "Ain't Misbehavin'" and "Rockin' Chair" and Karla clapped and clapped. He persuaded the band to attempt a blues version of the first movement of Brahms One, the sextet, and the crowd loved it. Karla, too. Sydney walked her home and spent the night. They made love at once and talked until dawn, mostly about music and what separated the great from the good. Was there something in the German language that inspired musical composition? Later, he lay in her narrow bed and listened to her practice; ferociously, he thought.

He went to all her performances and many of her rehearsals, sitting in the front row where he could see her face as she played. She always wore black, and it gave him a kind of oily satisfaction knowing that she wore nothing under the trousers and black sweater. A month later they were married in a private ceremony, family only, with a reception at the New York Yacht Club — his father's idea, and not the success they had hoped for. The families did not get on, Sydney's father and Karla's mother separating after the first dance, Fred to the bar and Magda to the billiard room, where she challenged an aging member to a game of two-ball. Sydney and Karla departed the club in a shower of rice but no cheers. In the car Karla informed him that the quarrel had to do with politics, a mistake all around, but your father started it, she said, and wouldn't let go.

Magda gave as good as she got, Sydney said.

Not quite, Karla replied bitterly.

Sydney continued with his work at the Foundation, still the youngest man in the room with no retirements in sight. His father remarked that he was putting on weight; looking a little portly in your three-button suit, he said. Meanwhile, Karla had reached a plateau with her music. She compared herself to an athlete whose muscles were in the wrong places and no amount of exercise or training would improve them. If she were a miler she would clock in at four minutes, fifty seconds; that was the best she would ever do, owing to the muscles that were in the wrong places. She had always thought that desire was nine-tenths of the struggle. Desire could carry you over mountains. She knew that she would never be a soloist and it broke her heart; she had wanted it so badly, and still did. This, however, she kept to herself. When the baby arrived she took a year off, practicing her music on weekends. At least, she thought — at least she had a marriage that worked, with a husband who loved her.

Rain beaded the windows of the train, lumbering now into the grimy suburbs of Toulouse, row upon row of brick factories and lifeless streets with their cafés and boulangeries. The streets were narrow and without charm. Sydney thought they were as peevish and exhausted as the continent itself. Toulouse was the end of the line, and he imagined Comminges one step beyond that, a region more of the nineteenth century than the twentieth. He wanted this visit over and done with so he could get on with the business at hand. He ran a little riff on the window with his fingernail, then rested his head on the seat back and dozed.

A Child in Such a Milieu

*M*ISSY HAD NOT BEEN exaggerating when she described the charm of the Armands' stone house, a rambling affair with a flat tile roof and tiny windows set next to a second-century Roman wall, the wall damaged here and there but recognizably from antiquity. They were situated in a narrow valley overseen by towering hills, and a river was nearby. Monsieur Armand was as wide as a barrel with heavily muscled forearms and bowed legs. His wife was similarly built. They had greeted Missy with shouts and laughter, as if she were truly the fourth daughter. When she introduced Sydney they welcomed him cordially, happily accepting his gifts of smoked salmon and chocolate, purchased at the shop in the rue du Louvre. They insisted on showing him the house, each room including the wine cellar. The house was filled with heavy country furniture, crucifixes prominent in the bedrooms. Madame pointed out family pictures, her husband making jokes about the circumstances of the photography. Their English was poor and eventually they gave it up and spoke French, Missy translating when it was necessary.

Because the night was warm they sat in the garden. Monsieur

Armand poured red wine from a huge pitcher. Sydney sat back and listened to their animated conversation, first Missy's news — a promotion expected at the bank, a new carpet installed in the living room — and then the activities of the family Armand. The daughters had gone to Toulouse for the evening but would return the next day. There were frequent references to Abidjan and the oil business, apparently prospering. From time to time Missy turned to Sydney and translated, and he would respond with a question he hoped was intelligent and not too forward or intrusive.

How long have your brother and his wife lived in Abidjan?

Oh, many, many years.

Twenty years, Madame Armand said. They have a bungalow on the beach and fortunately servants are plentiful. They like the hot weather and swimming in the ocean. They own a small boat —

She had a face like a bun, pushed together, wrinkled and kindly. Her smile was beautiful to look at and she used it often. Sydney was beguiled despite his many reservations about the French and Europeans in general, often so resentful. Madame Armand turned to him frequently, making certain that his glass was full and that he was not too estranged from the conversation. And he managed to pick up bits and pieces, his university French returning helter-skelter. He was not paying close attention. The night was warm and Monsieur's wine tasty. He soon lost the thread of whatever they were talking about; in any case, it was Monsieur Armand's monologue, soft in the night air. Madame Armand excused herself to go into the house to see about dinner. Sydney relaxed and listened to the incomprehensible conversation and the buzzing of small insects.

Monsieur Armand suddenly leaned toward Missy and spoke rapidly, something about one of his brothers; and Sydney heard the words Xuan Loc, uttered with a discouraged shake of the head.

Sydney pulled his chair forward with a show of interest.

It's a town north of Saigon, Missy said.

One of my brothers lives there, Monsieur Armand said in English. It's a pretty market town. Then, to Missy: Tell him about Claude.

He's Papa's youngest brother, Missy said. He manages one of the rubber plantations in Xuan Loc district. He's been there, oh, fifteen years. But times are hard now. Production has been disrupted owing to the revolution. The Americans are bombing his rubber trees.

It's in a contested area, then, Sydney said.

Monsieur Armand erupted in a furious burst of French, Missy listening with a wry smile. When he was finished, she translated. Papa says it wasn't contested until the Americans decided to contest it. Everyone was happy working the plantation. The revolution had nothing to do with the rubber and everyone got along. Xuan Loc was always a quiet sector until the Americans invaded with their infantry and aircraft. Their artillery that fires indiscriminately at night. Until the Americans arrived, Xuan Loc was as tranquil as Comminges, Papa says.

This is true, Madame said from the doorway. We visited Claude and his wife four years ago. We remained two weeks and traveled everywhere with no difficulty. We went to Saigon for the shopping and to Cap St. Jacques on the sea. The people were always friendly and many of them spoke French. Of course there was politics. There's always politics, isn't that so?

One artillery shell can ruin a dozen trees, Monsieur Armand said.

Yes, Sydney began, but —

And the production's ruined.

Yes, Sydney said.

It's a very old plantation, very dependable.

The Viet Cong, Sydney said.

Monsieur waved his hand, a gesture of contempt. Pah! he said.

Still, Sydney said, and tactfully did not mention Dien Bien Phu.

The real war, Monsieur said sharply, the war with the Viet Minh, the war we fought for twenty years, that was serious. And we understood them, too, what they were capable of, because we had governed them for so long, since the middle of the nineteenth century. In the North they are serious people with a serious army. These people in the South are not serious. The government isn't serious, either. And the Americans are too serious.

Sydney smiled at that.

It's a bad thing for the population, Monsieur said.

I agree with you there, Sydney said.

They should be left in peace, therefore.

Tell that to the Viet Cong, Sydney said.

Syd's going to South Vietnam, Missy put in.

She translated while Sydney explained about the Llewellyn Group, a benevolent arm of the government wholly separate from the Pentagon. The two were as different as chalk and cheese. An enthusiastic, public-spirited Congress had appropriated two billion dollars for the improvement of roads and bridges, the security of the market, and new schools and clinics equipped with the latest medicines. All this to get South Vietnam on its feet once more, the government functioning both in the capital and in the provinces, the countryside pacified. Then the population would rally to the Saigon administration. The Communists would be licked, deprived of their base of support . . . As Sydney spoke, he felt the power of the logic. Of course he was describing an illusion, but men died for illusions, at Thermopylae or Antietam, or Verdun. Illusion was another word for ideal, something serious and altruistic, neither heartless nor selfish. He was conscious of speaking with the authority of the government itself, and then he remembered something Rostok had said.

It's a matter of hearts and minds, you see.

In the sudden strained silence it was obvious that Monsieur did not see; and Missy was looking at him strangely. Sydney knew that he had failed to make his point. The French had a specific way of looking at things and always through the prism of their degraded colonial past. But their capacities were diminished. Their view of the world was no wider than this valley in Comminges, and now that he thought of it Sydney decided that the analogy would be to the not-much-of-a-future-but-oh-what-a-past American South, the cavaliers so backward, broken down and sentimental. The French were conscious of being on the fringes of things and without influence. No one cared what they thought or did beyond a few cineastes who thought the silver screen a reliable mirror of the world's injustice. The French couldn't hold Indochina and they couldn't hold Algeria, no matter what General de Gaulle promised. Probably even Bangui would be lost to them, so they lived in a threatened might-have-been world.

Yet this much was also true. Those few French who remained in the various colonial outposts would have valuable insights. You would have to look from their prism into your prism. Rostok was quite emphatic about it, intrigued as he was when Sydney described the Armand connection. Claude Armand could be very helpful if he chose to be. He would have friends, and the friends would have friends. And from Claude and his friends and the friends of the friends, Sydney would learn the lay of the land, the solidarity or lack of it among the colonials, and their relations with the government and the government's enemies. What did these colonials want for themselves? And when they peered into the future, what did they see? Rostok knew without a doubt that they saw a future identical to the past, a plantation life that flourished without regard to the politics that surrounded it. They saw themselves as a still center inside the vortex, and as long as they moved with the vortex, the center would remain — still.

The administration at Saigon or Hanoi would have no more effect than a hurricane to a bottom-dwelling fish.

Discover what you can, Sydney.

That's your first assignment.

First question: How does a plantation operate effectively in the middle of a war when the enemy controlled the countryside, provided the security, and collected the taxes? Rostok had offered the obvious answer: They paid off the Viet Cong in Xuan Loc as forty years before saloonkeepers in the Loop paid off Scarface Al while the police looked the other way; and the police, too, were rewarded for their trouble. The American ambassador had a theory that the so-called insurgency was little more than simple banditry, a convenient way to make a living in uncertain times. A Chicago shakedown racket, the ambassador called it — and perhaps Claude Armand would offer a disinterested view of this theory, or at the least the view of the saloonkeeper.

This was Sydney's first intimation of the parallel world, and what he saw in his imagination was an ambiance not far removed from that of the Abenaki Club, well-tended gardens surrounding a graceful, low-slung bungalow with a swimming pool and perhaps a croquet court in the shade of a great Asian sandalwood, dogs and children underfoot, white-coated servants passing cocktails and canapés on silver trays in an atmosphere as tidy and civil and sound as safe Switzerland.

He did not mention this vision to Rostok, fearing that it was out of date. Rostok believed that if Syd used his wits, became friendly with the Xuan Loc Armands, perhaps did them an unbidden favor, they would be eager to share their insights and information, perhaps introduce him to other French expatriates living between the lines, trying to make ends meet. These French would be mindful naturally that the Americans controlled the

South Vietnamese. The Americans would have to be taken into account, lest the Americans become thoughtless.

Sydney was dismayed that the discussion had turned into an argument and wondered now how he could make amends.

Monsieur muttered something to Missy in French.

He said to Sydney, More wine?

It's very good, Sydney said. It's excellent.

It's ordinary wine, Monsieur said.

A breeze had come up and the night was no longer so still, dry leaves clattering now in the trees. The temperature had fallen. The snow-furred summits of the mountains at the head of the valley glittered in the yellow moonlight. One of the peaks looked like a miniature Mont Blanc. Sydney felt the old man's eyes on him, an ominous measurement. He looked into the darkness and tried again.

Perhaps you're right about the situation in Vietnam, he said. I've yet to see anything firsthand. I've never been in-country. It would be logical, though, that each nation's experience there would be unique, owing to the circumstances of the arrival and the nature of the occupation. Sydney waited while Missy translated, staring all the time at the thumb-sized peak that changed color while he looked at it. He said, It's obvious that we'll profit from the French experience, unhappy as that experience turned out to be. All of us are interested in any information. Insights. Into the lessons learned by the French in Vietnam during the many years of struggle. I do know we're in it for keeps, win, lose, or draw.

It won't be a draw, Monsieur said.

No, certainly not. And it'll take time, we know that.

D'accord, Monsieur said.

They're resilient people, determined and resourceful. We don't know much about them, actually. Sydney smiled wanly and shrugged; so much to learn, so little time. Briefers in Washington had told him they knew nothing of the personalities on the other side. Except for Ho and Giap they were faceless bureaucrats and guerrilla commanders in the field. Many had been trained by the Russians at their secret base in the Ukraine. The briefer described the base in meticulous detail, the course of study, the weapons, and the commander and his deputy, apparatchiks from Kiev; when you had so little information of immediate value, you dispensed what you had, so the briefer went on and on about the installation near Kharkov; and there were Cuban observers as well.

Unsettling, Sydney said, knowing so little of a man's past, his family circumstances, where he went to school, his quirks and prejudices. In the real war, Allied intelligence knew everything there was to know about the Wehrmacht, from Jodl, Canaris, and Rommel down to regimental commanders, which ones were Nazis and which weren't. There were British officers who had gone to school with some of them, for Christ's sake. And we didn't even know for sure where Ho was born. For the longest time we thought he had been a chef at the Paris Ritz when actually it was the Carlton in London.

We're fighting ghosts, Sydney said with a little strangled laugh.

They're difficult to know, that's true.

They're excellent fighters, Sydney said.

Yes, Monsieur said. The Communists are.

In the last analysis, it's their war.

It certainly is, Monsieur said.

President Johnson made a speech about it the other day.

Monsieur Armand looked at him suspiciously and took a mouthful of wine. A speech to the Vietnamese?

No, no, Sydney said. The American Legion.

Missy translated, taking her time, and when she was finished the Frenchman was smiling broadly.

They're finally beginning to focus in Washington, Sydney said. Monsieur nodded. Is it really two billion dollars?

That's this year, Sydney said. More next. And the year after, more still. We're going to spend this war to death, deep-sea ports for ships and airfields for the biggest jets. And add to that the bridges and roads and so forth, and technical assistance for the government ministries so that taxes can be collected and budgets balanced, little Vietnam will be the most modern country in Asia. It'll have the infrastructure, you see. It'll go from the Middle Ages to the twentieth century in five years. It'll look like California. There'll be an economic boom, even agriculture, the rubber plantations, for example. It's a small country after all, think of two billions this year and more next and the year after. When Monsieur smiled, Sydney wagged his finger and said, Oh yes, the rising tide raises all the boats.

All that money, Monsieur said.

And know-how, Sydney said.

Of course, Monsieur said. I'd forgotten about the know-how.

It's the most important thing, Sydney said. And then he thought to add, So that Citroëns can ride on Indochinese rubber once more.

Citroëns, Monsieur said.

And Renaults, too, Sydney said.

And the troops —

At least three divisions by the end of this year, that's confidential. Our people think three will be sufficient.

Monsieur rolled his eyes and chuckled.

Then we'll send more, Sydney said blandly.

To table! Madame Armand called from the doorway.

They ate in the kitchen at a round wooden table with a bowl of flowers in the center. The table, each place with its cluster of glasses and flatware and red napkins, looked almost as appetizing as the food, a steaming stew served from a heavy tureen. Madame Armand urged Sydney to taste the water, the purest in all Europe; the source was only a few miles up the valley. Missy and the Armands were talking family business, something to do with the eldest daughter, who had a serious beau. Sydney ate and listened, looking up now and then to inspect the kitchen and its old-fashioned equipment. The hearth looked a hundred years old and the firearm hanging above it about the same. Pots in a dozen shapes and sizes hung from the whitewashed walls.

On the wall next to the cupboard were photographs of the colonial Armands, Hubert in Abidjan and Claude in Xuan Loc; the picture of Felix in Bangui was last in line and obscured by shadows. Hubert and his wife and children were photographed on the beach, a sloop bobbing at anchor behind them. The sloop was framed in such a way as to suggest it was theirs. The French tricolor fluttered above the transom. Hubert was recognizably Monsieur Armand's brother, a muscular, thick-waisted brute with a mat of coal-black hair on his chest and a serpent tattoo on his forearm. His wife was short and stocky and the children were stocky, too. All five were deeply tanned, and all five wore dinky bikinis and white rubber swimming caps on their heads. They were squinting in the glare, their expressions sullen, impatient in the African heat. All in all, Sydney thought, a family to avoid.

Claude and his wife were photographed on the long verandah of their bungalow in Xuan Loc. The time appeared to be late afternoon, for the rubber trees behind them cast weak shadows. Vietnamese workers could be seen here and there in the distance tending to the trees, aligned in rows. They carried long machetes around their narrow waists. These Armands were seated comfortably on a rattan sofa, a coffee table in front of them; they would not have been out of place in Darien. Claude's hair was red and curly and cropped close. He wore wire-rimmed glasses. He was slender and appeared very fit, looking into the camera's lens with a relaxed half-smile, not giving much away, a smile that suggested private amusement, some worldly absurdity in the day's affairs. His left hand was raised tentatively, as if he were trying to summon a lost memory. Sydney thought he was about forty, old enough anyway to have elusive memories. His wife looked at him with the most open affection — perhaps at that moment he had murmured a droll endearment as he sought the thing that was out of reach and the photographer said, Hold it there, perfect. In his white ducks and short-sleeved shirt, Claude might have returned from the golf course minutes before. His wife was as slender as he was but not as guarded, obviously aware of the camera but indifferent to it; she was the sort of woman who took a good photograph. She was fine-boned with almond-shaped eyes and a provocative lift to her chin. Her skirt was bunched up around her knees. No doubt she was waiting for a breeze in the thick stillness of the late afternoon. The couple — they were indisputably together — appeared entirely natural and at ease waiting for the photographer to make the picture. A glass pitcher of iced tea, a package of Gauloises, and a brass lighter indicated end-of-the-day domesticity. Books were stacked on the coffee table along with editions of *Paris-Match, Le Nouvel Observateur,* and *Life.* Sydney wondered when the photograph was taken. Nothing in it identified the year, even the magazine covers were generic: Princess Grace, a burning building, LBJ. Behind the sofa was a Matisse poster, long-stemmed red and yellow wildflowers adumbrated by the picture frame.

Claude and his wife, Madame Armand said.

They're very attractive people, Sydney said.

He's a devil, Madame said, laughing. He can be naughty. Dede keeps him in line, though.

I imagine she does, Sydney said.

Everyone likes Dede, Madame said.

I can see that, Sydney said. When was the picture taken?

Only last year, Madame said. And then, as if to explain the timing, she added, Dede is an American.

Sydney said in surprise, She is?

Oh yes, Madame said. She worked for your embassy. Claude met her on the tennis court at the Cercle Sportif. It was a thunderclap for them both. Dede — and here Madame began to laugh loudly — is from Chicago!

Rat-a-tat-tat, Monsieur said, moving his hands as if he were firing a machine gun.

And she is just pregnant, Madame said. Pregnant only three months. We had a long letter from them last week, they're so thrilled. Five years they've been married.

And now they have decisions to make, Sydney said.

Decisions? Madame said. What decisions?

Why, where to go now. I mean, where to live. Vietnam's no place for a French family, and it'll only get worse.

They will stay, Madame said. Why wouldn't they? They have everything they need. They love their house, it's very spacious, and Dede has furnished it nicely in the French manner. She has her birds and a beautiful garden. In that wretched climate, everything grows. Claude manages the plantation well. He enjoys it, even though things aren't as they were. Claude went out there for Michelin when he was young, barely twenty. My husband did not approve. Claude was the baby of the family and headstrong; and Felix and Hubert were already gone. My husband thought everything was finished in Indochina. But Claude did not listen. He went away and did very well for himself and soon met Dede. She worked for the cultural section of your embassy but gave it up when she married Claude and went to live in Xuan Loc. They've been happy on the plantation and even now Claude tells us not to believe everything we read in the newspapers. The reality is always very different, isn't it? Of course there's uncertainty, the American bombs and the general insecurity of the countryside. It's no longer safe to drive after dark and the bomb-ing seems to have gotten worse but nobody bothers them in Xuan Loc. Why would they?

The bombing could be stopped, Sydney said.

Madame was silent a moment. It could?

Sydney felt the wine rush to his head, and now he smiled warmly. If they're American bombs, it can. I can stop it.

Missy and Monsieur Armand were listening hard while they ate, Missy now and then contributing a phrase in English when Madame lost her way. Now they were silent while they consid-ered what Sydney had said. Monsieur poured the last of the wine from the pitcher and refilled it from the cask on the sideboard. Sydney said nothing further and looked again at the photograph on the wall, allowing the silence to gather. It was no doubt true that they led a pleasant life on the plantation with their servants, birds, and garden, and untrustworthy newspapers for consola-tion. Claude Armand did not look headstrong, though; not that casual photographs ever disclosed much. Sydney knew now that he was not forty years old but younger. He was one of those men who looked forty whatever his age.

Madame glanced at her husband, then cleared her throat. She said, Are you married, Sydney?

I was, Sydney said. We're separated now. She'll be filing for divorce . . . And then he paused, wondering if Karla would go through with it. Perhaps not, and then when this was over —

And do you have children?

My daughter lives with her mother in New York.

A daughter, Madame Armand said. What a pity.

No, she's a wonderful child, Sydney said. She's doing fine. He was mildly offended at the intrusion.

I mean the divorce, Madame said pleasantly. It's so hard for the children. In France it's very difficult to secure a divorce. The state discourages it. And the church. It's better to stay together and make do the best you can. There are always alternative arrangements. Naturally each situation makes its own demands, that's well known. And now you've left them both to serve your government in Vietnam. No doubt it's for the best. Still, young children —

She's fine, Sydney said shortly.

That's what worries me, she said. A child in such a milieu.

Sydney nodded. He could not imagine raising a child in the middle of a war.

I thought you said you weren't military, Monsieur Armand threw in.

I'm not, Sydney said.

Yet you can stop the bombs.

Sydney said, The civilian representative has authority in his own sector. That's the way it's set up. Not in all circumstances at all times, but in some circumstances at specific times. Each situation is judged on its merits. Its contribution to the overall effort. As I said, I'll look into it when I get there. And I'll do what I can. Naturally Claude would like to — get on with his business without interference. If he intends to continue, as you say he does, with his wife and child. And perhaps there are ways he can help us out. It's a common effort after all. We're on the same side. And no one wants the Communists in charge. How many Vietnamese does he employ?

Monsieur hesitated, apparently making an effort to recollect. This was unsuccessful, for he shook his head at last and said, I have no idea.

A dozen? Two dozen? One hundred? It's a large plantation and would require many workers. A serious payroll.

I have no idea, Monsieur repeated.

But you were there, Sydney said softly.

For two weeks only, Monsieur said. We went to the beach at Cap St. Jacques. Dede took us into Saigon for lunch and sight-seeing. We bought souvenirs. We went to the zoo. We didn't talk business.

Rostok had warned him that the interview would be difficult. They're not like us, Ros had said. They're not straightforward. They're not aboveboard. They're not interested in product, they're interested in logic. And when an idea visits them, it never leaves. When they have a grievance they'd rather nurse the grievance than settle it. With the French, everything was personal.

So there are all these factors, Sydney said. He took another swallow of wine.

In what way would Claude help you out? Monsieur said slowly, an edge to his voice. How would Claude fit into your war from his plantation? What do you expect Claude to do for you? He watched his wife rise and begin to collect the dishes, Missy moving to help her. But Monsieur put his thick hand on her forearm, indicating that she should remain to help with the translating.

I have not thought about that precisely, Sydney said. But it's not only our war, it's your war, too.

We are finished with it, the old man said.

But it's back, Sydney insisted. It's at Claude's doorstep whether he wants it to be there or not. And we're in it together.

Monsieur Armand hesitated, and then he said, You would expect him to collaborate, then? As a friend and ally.

Be helpful, yes.

Claude and the other plantation managers?

If they wished, yes.

And in return you'd stop bombing his rubber trees.

We're getting ahead of ourselves here, Sydney said.

Monsieur Armand allowed himself a wintry smile. You *wouldn't* stop bombing his rubber trees?

I would speak to the military command after I had the facts. And after Claude and I had a talk.

About how he might be helpful to you, Monsieur said.

Yes, Sydney said, thinking that he had gone further than he intended. His plan was to take things step by step but the old man across the table was intent on forcing the issue. So he decided to bring the conversation into more neutral territory, no more talk of collaboration. He thanked Madame Armand for the meal, superb in every way, surely superior to anything he would find in Vietnam —

Thank you very much, she said, but Vietnamese cuisine is excellent, especially the fish.

You seem to have given quite a lot of thought to my brother, Monsieur said abruptly.

Missy has always spoken warmly of your family, Sydney said. I mean lately.

It would be a pleasure to meet Claude, Sydney said.

No doubt, Monsieur said.

Perhaps he wouldn't want to, Sydney said thoughtfully. I suppose I can understand that. It could be awkward for him. Perhaps risky, depending on the circumstances. He has a wife. And soon he will be a father. He would not want to expose himself more than necessary. The Communists were ruthless and adhered to the old rule, My enemy's friend is my enemy. Sydney took a swallow of wine and observed that it would take courage to meet openly with Americans, the occupying power; and the moment he said the words he knew he had blundered, the phrase all wrong. Monsieur Armand grew red in the face and bellowed a furious burst of French, and then he threw down his napkin and left the table. When Sydney asked Missy what he had said, she blushed and shook her head. But she was smiling.

Tell me, Sydney said.

Papa said Claude has balls to his knees, Missy said.

*

Monsieur Armand did not reappear, and shortly Madame followed him to bed. Missy and Sydney did the dishes, not talking
much. They both knew he had made a careless error. He had
committed a simple mistake of language, wanting to move back
from the precipice only to discover that he had been walking a
high wire, the old Frenchman willing him to fall. Certainly this
would not have happened if there had been a common language
along with ordinary common courtesy. And Missy had been no
help at all, her loyalties lay with the Armand family. But he had
a better idea now of just how suspicious the French were, and
how determined to preserve their — he supposed the word was
neutrality. He wondered if Dede had the same instinct. Dede
from rat-a-tat-tat Chicago, wife of devilish, naughty, balls-to-
his-knees Claude. In a rational world Dede would be eager to
confide in a compatriot, but Sydney knew now that the world
was not rational.

Probably you should leave tomorrow, Missy said.

I'm sorry about it, Sydney said.

Yes, she said. So am I. There's a morning train.

God, they're stubborn, Sydney said. They get an idea —

They're very nice people, Missy said.

— and then they try to nail you.

I think you were trying to nail *him*. He just got there first. If
you had told me, I might have been able to help.

A mistake all around, Sydney said.

What did you want from him actually?

A friendly letter of introduction to his brother. Something that
said I was a friend of the family. Didn't have horns and a tail.

I could have given you that, she said.

You could?

Yes, of course. You still don't understand. The Armands are
my family.

It's obvious now, he said.

She shrugged and turned away, drying her hands on a towel.

So how about it? Sydney said.

Not now, Missy said. Now that I know what you want.

I don't want so much, Sydney said.

You want Claude to collaborate. That word has a particular meaning here. Don't you know that?

We are not Nazis, Sydney said evenly. *We're not Nazis.*

I don't know anything about it, Missy said.

Whose side are you on? Sydney demanded.

Not your side, Missy said.

The clock in the hall chimed midnight. Sydney stacked the dishes and carried them to the cupboard, looking again at the photographs of the Abidjan and Xuan Loc Armands, Dede so openly American and relaxed as she stared into the camera's lens. He wondered who or what had brought her to Embassy Saigon, a hardship post half the world away from the Near North Side, Astor Street, North Dearborn, one of those probably — or a suburb, Winnetka or Lake Forest. He knew she was a country-club girl by looking at her, the shape of her chin and the way she held it and the way she did her hair, no different from the girls around the tennis courts and paddocks of Darien in the summer. Smith or Vassar, a degree in art history or English literature; he'd stake his life on it. Yet she had married an expatriate Frenchman and was living in no man's land, a war zone no longer under embassy protection.

I'll find a way to meet her, he said to Missy.

I'm sure you will, Missy said.

And in the shadows, the Bangui Armands standing in front of a filthy gray Land Rover, lush jungle all around. Felix wore a djellaba, his wife a long flowered dress. Two small children peeked out from behind her skirts, the children round-faced and the color of café au lait. Their mother was black as oil, a kind of luminous silky blue-black. Felix looked unnaturally white beside her, his pale skin suggesting exhaustion or illness. Her hand rested heavily on his shoulder. She was the one with the authority, or perhaps it was only local knowledge. Sydney stared at the photograph a long time, wondering at the story behind their courtship and marriage, and how Felix had adapted to an unfamiliar continent. He wondered what urge had sent Felix to Africa and into the bed of a native woman, and how that had changed his life. Perhaps it hadn't. He would be an outsider in Bangui regardless of his living arrangements. Sydney had forgotten now what it was that Felix did. It was either mining or farming. But he did not look like a miner or farmer. He looked like a drifter, a nomad despite the Land Rover. Bangui seemed a very long way from this village in the Pyrenees, farther even than Abidjan or Xuan Loc.

Sydney shivered in the sudden chill. He wondered if a spring snow was on the way and looked out the window, to the Roman wall and the high hills beyond it. The wall was bathed in pale moonlight, its contours crisp and indomitable. Sydney turned to say something about it to Missy but the kitchen was empty. She had gone upstairs without another word, leaving him to find his own way.

Dacy

DUSK AT PARIS-ORLY. Someone had given him Malraux's early Cambodian novel for the long flight east but he could not read it, and he set it aside somewhere over Switzerland. The references escaped him, the sentences too zealous in the antiseptic atmosphere of the Boeing, its dull-blue cabin a world apart from the earth below. The plane was half empty. Sydney dozed between fitful passes at *Fortune* and *Time* and an unsuccessful attempt at conversation with the businessman across the aisle, a Lebanese en route to Singapore via Bangkok. The Lebanese was either buying a ship or selling one, it was hard to tell which. His language was as dense as Malraux's, and when he learned that Sydney was going on to Saigon, he lost interest.

Dawn in Delhi, where they were brusquely offloaded to wait for hours in the damp heat while a labor dispute was adjudicated. Families lay sleeping in every corner of the terminal shed while a clamor rose in waves; all flights were delayed. Aloft again, mountains were visible in the far distance, and then Sydney realized they were the foothills of the Himalayas. The time was early morning when they arrived in Bangkok, but the relief crew was still at the hotel downtown, so the plane was delayed hours more. Lifting off on the final leg, leveling at fifteen thousand feet, Sydney looked out the window to observe Cambodia below. The land of a thousand elephants had every aspect of the Mississippi Delta, just as Rostok had said.

The Boeing was noisy now with Americans returning from a holiday in Bangkok. Only a few of the Paris passengers remained. Stewardesses hurried up the aisle with trays of bloody marys; drink fast, boys, the flight's short. But the Americans knew that. Sydney, glass in hand, looked down to South Vietnam, villages here and there, narrow rivers, roads with traffic. Beneath the green fields, water glittered like a spray of diamonds. He thought of veins under the skin. When the plane banked, he was momentarily blinded by the sun and moved to shade his eyes with Malraux's novel. Probably the Frenchman was lucky to have discovered Indochina in the 1920s when it was not far removed from Conrad's day, time measured by the thrust of a prow, Saigon sleepier even than Singapore, the interior as remote as any interior on earth; yet in the villages a revolution was struggling to be born. When the plane touched down at last it rolled past scores of American military aircraft, fighters, helicopters, olive-drab Pipers, burly transports. Soldiers lounged in the shade of the wings. When the Boeing halted in front of the terminal, the Americans erupted with a loud sarcastic cheer; one of the stewardesses took an exaggerated bow. The raucous laughter and conversation reminded Sydney of the atmosphere in a fraternity house the night before graduation; the last carefree hours before the serious business of earning a living.

The stranger next to him yawned and shifted his body. He had not bothered to cinch his seat belt over his vast stomach for the aircraft's descent. He turned and said, New here?

Sydney nodded. First time.

Well, he said. Good luck.

You too, Sydney said.

Yup, the stranger said, finishing his drink and tucking the plastic glass into the seat pouch, the plastic cracking with the sound of crumpled paper.

Been here long?

Ten months and thirteen days. He looked at his wristwatch. And eight hours and thirty-five minutes, give or take. Six weeks to go.

You're short, then, Sydney said.

No, no, the stranger said emphatically. I'm not short. You're not short until you're a week or less. It's bad luck to talk about short when you're long. Jesus Christ, don't talk about short. That's asking for it. He scowled at Sydney, then rapped twice on the wooden handle of his valise. Remember that, he added as he moved ponderously up the aisle.

When Sydney cleared customs at last, Dicky Rostok was nowhere in sight. Tan Son Nhut was quiet at midmorning, poker-faced Americans arriving on one side of the sawhorse barriers and resigned Vietnamese leaving on the other side. He was startled by the whispering of the Vietnamese, an incomprehensible seven-toned murmur of women; the men were mostly silent. The uniformed officials at passport control handled each Vietnamese travel document as tenderly as a purloined love letter, weighing it in their palms and thumbing each page, looking from the traveler to the photograph and back again, and then once more, sniffing and squinting to make absolutely certain — while on the arriving side of the barrier the scrutiny was routine, almost apologetic, the green passport opened, the visa located, the stamp applied, the passport returned with a blank administrative smile. Meanwhile, the Vietnamese inched forward and the murmur continued to rise and fall in the long lines that reached from the interior of the terminal to the teeming sidewalk outside.

Sydney stood alone in the vast open-air lobby feeling the

heat and the press of humanity, the Americans so large, bull-like shoulders bulging under short-sleeved drip-dry shirts, the Vietnamese dressed up and brittle as birds, shy in the muscular ceremony of arrival and departure; and just then he understood that he fit both categories, arriving in one sense, departing in another. He had only made landfall. His journey had yet to begin, and until it did he would remain as much a part of America as the Boeing he had just left. This airport seemed to be as much American as Vietnamese, the local police standing about with the authority of cocktail waitresses in a gambling casino. He wondered at the identity of the Vietnamese travelers, as many women as men, grinning and nervous as they made their way slowly to passport control. They would be traveling to Hong Kong or Bangkok, to shop or to transact business, perhaps to emigrate. In any case they did not seem reluctant to leave.

The Americans were obvious enough, construction workers and government officials, crew-cut soldiers in mufti. He recognized someone from the State Department, a deputy assistant something or other who had conducted one of the endless briefings, and a woman who worked for one of the think tanks, Hudson or RAND. He remembered her from a conference at NYU. Mr. Ten-months-and-thirteen-days-and-eight-hours-and-thirty-five-minutes was nowhere in sight. Sydney recalled a photograph he had seen of the Gare du Nord in the spring of 1940, soldiers leaving for the front, civilians returning, the picture's texture dark and grainy, somber in the filtered light. Paris had never recovered from its abrupt defeat. In 1940, no one knew who was in charge and the future was in doubt. The Germans were invading once again and there was no animation or confidence in the faces of the French, one more difference between Paris then and Saigon now; and no one doubted who was in charge here.

Those few departing Americans were provided a special gate, *U.S. Personnel This Way.* When Vietnamese approached this gate they were coolly waved away. Military policemen loitered close by, visually inspecting each departing American; and if there was cause for suspicion he was pulled from the line and asked for his passport and exit visa, and if the answers were unsatisfactory the suspect was moved against the wall and searched without delay, the questions suddenly official and specific, and before you knew it there were four military policemen, not two. Sydney watched the little drama unfold, an unshaven middle-aged man shaking his head no, then sighing, staring at the floor, explaining something without looking up, extending his wrists as if he expected to be slapped or handcuffed. The MPs conferred among themselves, one of them consulting a thick blue book, apparently a roster of names.

Sydney heard the MP say, Get the hell out of here.

Yessir, the suspect said.

Don't come back, the MP added.

Why would I come back? the suspect said, and moved along to Vietnamese passport control, where he was waved through. Sydney watched him hurry into the lounge, where the bar was doing an energetic pre-lunch business. So Vietnam was like Puerto Rico, as easy to slip into as it was to slip out of, so long as your papers were in order and your name absent from the roster of suspicious characters.

Noise drifted from the bar to the terminal area. Sydney was surprised to see young Western women among those three-deep at the bar and at tables, everyone laughing and toasting each other. The women were tanned and attractive, in their close haircuts and short skirts looking like coeds on spring break, the last fitful hours before the long flight north. The atmosphere was one of high impatience, a kind of nervous flutter. Through the wide window back of the bar, Sydney could see a flight crew strolling to the Air Vietnam Caravelle waiting on the tarmac. Suddenly one of the women threw her arms around the neck of the man standing next to her and kissed him deeply; the others applauded, even the unshaven middle-aged man, who stood on the fringes of the group drinking beer from the bottle. And then Sydney realized he had misunderstood the ambiance. It was not impatient or nervous. It was festive.

Annoyed, he turned away, looking left and right, uncertain where to go. Of course Ros had better things to do than wait for a morning at febrile Tan Son Nhut, but surely he would leave a message. Sydney watched a television crew being greeted with shouts and handshakes, Vietnamese scurrying about to load the heavy equipment into a white van with a network logo on its side panel; and then the van hurtled away into traffic. He had the address of Llewellyn Group House, Tay Thanh district, but he had no idea how far it was and whether it was safe to travel by taxi. The little blue and white Renaults did not look roadworthy, either. So he marched to the sidewalk where he stood with his suitcases in the damp heat, the sun ferocious but ill defined in the thick diesel haze, and wondered about the reliability of the taxis.

When a Vietnamese approached and tried to hand him a card, Syd shook his head.

You come, the Vietnamese said.

Go away, Sydney said, but the Vietnamese was insistent, shoving the card in front of his eyes and jabbing at it with his finger. Syd saw that the writing was in English, introducing the bearer as the faithful Minh, who would drive him to Tay Thanh. *Welcome to the war. See you for dinner. Rostok.*

Tired and disoriented — the dregs of the bloody mary had left a rancid lemony taste in his mouth — Sydney stowed his luggage in the back of Minh's Scout. He stood swaying in the heat while Minh patiently held the door, waiting for him to climb inside; he did not fail to notice the ideograph drawn on the door, a pair of clasped hands. The Scout stumbled into traffic and turned away from the city. Saigon's anonymous suburbs unfolded, one following another, indistinguishable villages, each with its market and roadside kitchens and stagnant river, some viscous tributary of the Saigon. Traffic began to thin, sedans yielding to trucks and trucks to Solex motocyclos, rickshaws, and pedicabs. Ordinary bicycles were everywhere along with foot traffic, mostly old women with bundles and children. Every few moments Minh would tap the horn but always moved respectfully to the side of the road when a military convoy needed to pass. When the convoy was American, Minh gave a smart salute.

And suddenly they were in the country and alone on the road. The air was sour. The fifteenth century began just beyond the broken asphalt, water buffalo hauling wood plows, a weary farmer leaning on his plow. Beyond the field was the rain forest, dense and mysterious, feral, sickly green in the midmorning light. In the far distance low hills were visible through the haze. Here and there in clearings were temples where Buddhist monks in pumpkin-colored robes moved aimlessly about, apparently in contemplation. The temples seemed in no way distinguished architecturally, and Sydney was put in mind of the makeshift shrines beside roads in rural America commemorating the dead in a traffic accident. Mongrel dogs prowled the perimeter.

They passed a guard tower surrounded by barbed wire, causing Syd to wonder whether the wire was there to keep the guards in or the enemy out; in any case, he could see no guards. He closed his eyes, sweating in the heat, his shirt stuck to his back and chest. He was unable to assimilate the environment. Eyes closed, he sensed the world turning and he was turning with it, molecules rearranging themselves as he sat dumbly in the front seat of a government Scout with its symbol of hope, clasped hands. He would never again travel this road in exactly the same way; the vacant guard tower would soon be as familiar as the stone bridges on the Merritt Parkway. No doubt at that hour momentous decisions were being made elsewhere in the world, in conference rooms in Washington or Moscow. And in due course a bomb would fall or not fall in his vicinity or someone else's and the war would creep forward, as promised.

Minh let him out in the courtyard, fetched his bags from the rear of the Scout, and drove away. They had not exchanged a word since "you come" and "go away." The front door of Group House was not locked, yet there was no one present. The place had an abandoned look, as if it had been evacuated in the course of a hasty retreat. Typewriters and filing cabinets were intact but paper was loose everywhere on the floors and the ashtrays were filled to overflowing. Framed photographs of the ambassador and the President were askew on the wall; someone had drawn a moustache on the President, giving him a resemblance to Stalin. Sydney wrestled his bags upstairs to the living quarters. The bed in the big room was unmade, the towels in the bathroom mildewed. An empty whiskey bottle was lying in the tub, and women's underwear was draped over the single chair. Two more empty bottles filled the plastic wastebasket, along with discarded toothpaste tubes, aspirin vials, shaving cream, mosquito repellent, hair spray, deodorant jars, and Kotex cartons. Above the bed were various *Playboy* centerfolds, haphazardly taped to the plaster. An army-issue .45-caliber pistol was lying on the bedside table, the pistol as forlorn as everything else in the room. A wobbly message was written in lipstick on the mirror: *Im a prisoner in the Vtnamese laundry and need help now, D. D.*

Dacy, Sydney said aloud. That bastard Dacy.

Tony "Dicey" Dacy had not worked out. Dicky Rostok had said that Sydney would have some public relations work to do with the staff and some of the local people in Tay Thanh. Dicey was a handful. Nice enough fellow, Ros had said, but not suited to the environment. Dicey lacked tact. Dicey went over the edge as some do here because of — the situation.

I suppose he was scared to death, Sydney had said.

Scared? Why no, Ros had said. He wasn't scared. There's nothing to be scared of, if you keep your wits about you, use common sense. Meaning a sense of proportion. Dicey Dacy liked to drink and he also liked to chase women, in more or less that order. He especially liked to chase women when he was drinking, and he was drinking most of the time, maybe remembering the fifty-year-old wife he left at home in Modesto with the Chevrolet and the children. Dicey was having the time of his life in Tay Thanh. He was just a little round guy with a fringe of frizzy black hair on his bald head, looked like Kukla. This was his first trip outside the United States, except for Vancouver once over Labor Day. So we had complaints from the village elders and the staff, and it became necessary to let Dicey go, reluctantly because he was damned good with accounts; and he wasn't happy about it because of the fine life he'd found here, but the other choice was the stockade. We can't tolerate fuck-ups, Syd, because fuck-ups tend to get into the newspapers and the supremos back home don't like it, town-gown embarrassments in the middle of a war while our brave soldiers are getting shot at. So we fired him. Gave him a week to get out of the country. Last I heard he was holed up somewhere in Saigon, incognito. Dicey loved life in Indochina. Dicey said he found the fountain of youth in Tay Thanh. Truth was, he found himself. Dicey grew into himself right here.

And I'm cleaning up, Sydney had said. And apologizing to the staff and squaring things with the elders.

That's right, you are, Ros had said. That's your most immediate assignment, to restore some trust between us and our plucky little allies. This won't be easy. I try to look beyond their eyes into their brains. To see what's bothering them beyond Kukla fucking their teenage daughters, because there has to be something more to it, the way they're behaving. Most uncooperative lately, a kind of slowdown such as the UAW used to orchestrate on the line at River Rouge come contract time. They're difficult people. It's like looking at the Mississippi Delta from thirty-five thousand feet, one big river and a hundred tributary rivers, itty-bitty towns and fields and then a boat with a wake behind it. You know there's life, you just can't see it. They believe in magic, you know. Magicians and sorcerers and astrologers and numerologists. God's there somewhere, along with the usual sins and virtues and ways of redemption. But it's hard to see the unity, other than the big river itself; and you can't see where it begins and you can't see its end, either. I think they're trying to figure out why we're here. I think geopolitics doesn't have much meaning for them in Tay Thanh. So we must want something from them and they don't know what it is unless it's their souls. That's what the Christian missionaries wanted, and how far removed are we from them? Different uniform. Different Antichrist. We're practicing salvation, Syd, not in the hereafter but in the here and now. And the Vietnamese are wondering what the price is, and they're guessing it'll be high. What we want really is their loyalty, and is that so much to ask? Do you see the fine line we're walking here? We've got to do our level best and Dicey Dacy isn't our level best, so we've defrocked him and sent him on his way. And you're nominated to clean up his broken dishes.

Sydney began to smile.

I'm not joking, if that's what you're thinking, Rostok said.

Tell me this, Ros. Where did you find him?

He was a policeman, Rostok said. And a friend of his congressman. So he had superb references and we thought we were lucky to get him, experienced man, streetwise, as they like to say. But not everyone fits in here, no matter what their résumé says or what they promise. Matter of restraint and a sense of proportion. Matter of modesty, a sense of where you are and a sense of how much is too much. You can drive over to the PX in Saigon and buy Johnnie Walker Black for about two bucks and Beef-eater gin for half that. A man can live like a rajah in South Vietnam. And you can buy French perfume and hair spray and nylon stockings and Winston cigarettes and Playtex bras and those little gold Seiko wristwatches that the young girls like because they don't have those goods over at the Tay Thanh market. And the girls will do almost anything to get them, too, because they don't have much in their lives to look forward to. Their boyfriends are on the other side, living God knows where in serious danger. The girls are bored and frustrated and adrift and naturally look to us for support. Why wouldn't they? We're the future. When they look into the new year, who do they see? They see us. And the year after that for as many years as it takes. We're cocks of the walk here, Syd, but there are ways and means of living a reasonable life without turning Group House into a god damned bordello.

Understood, Syd had said.

I knew you would, Ros replied.

Sydney dumped his suitcases on the bed, washed his face, and walked downstairs to his office. The walls were bare except for Stalin-LBJ and the ambassador on one wall and an enormous map of South Vietnam on the other, Tay Thanh district outlined in red, the province in blue. Someone with coral-colored lipstick had kissed Saigon. The lipstick had begun to flake but the intent was clear enough. When he switched on the overhead fan a wisp of smoke fell from the gears and after two momentous revolutions the blades feathered to a halt with an end-of-the-world finality. The air thickened. Sydney opened a window and watched a brilliant yellow bird nose here and there in the bougainvillea. Its beak was the size of a toothpick and it poked among the leaves as if it were writing messages on them, and then it flew away.

Waiting for him on his desk was a large oblong carton

wrapped in silver paper that squeaked when he touched it. The return address was his parents' place in Darien. He recognized his father's spidery handwriting. The note inside said, "These will be as valuable to you as life itself and unless I miss my guess they will turn out to be life itself. Happy birthday, Sydney. Love, Dad." He had forgotten that it was his thirtieth birthday next week, whichever day it was; he had lost track of dates along with everything else.

Sydney looked at the shape of the carton and knew at once that his mischievous father had sent him his prized shotguns, the twin Brownings he had won in a poker game at the club but unused for many years because of the old man's failing eyesight and newfound reverence for animal life; he had always kept them cleaned and oiled, however. Naturally the old man would not know, and if he did know wouldn't care, that sending firearms through the APO system was strictly forbidden, punishable by a fine together with a sharp letter in your personnel file, a career-threatening letter depending on the title beneath the signature. Definitely bad news and Tay Thanh was already on the list of problem districts, thanks to Dicey Dacy. So his first day in-country was already compromised. Sydney supposed that his father, in his infinite capacity for fantasy, imagined him suiting up on lonely weekends and driving to the Camau peninsula or the central highlands to gun for mallards, a battalion of ARVN airborne deployed for security. But the box inside the carton was unopened.

The Brownings were wrapped together in heavy butcher paper, sealed with duct tape and secured with thick twine, wound to within an inch of its life and knotted with some arcane sailor's hitch such as you would use on a foundering vessel. Taking the box apart was like unraveling chain mail but at last his father's handiwork was exposed: not firearms at all but two intricately carved boxes, each ten inches by fourteen inches, one marked IN and the other marked OUT in deep curving script. The old man could be very droll. He knew that the IN and OUT boxes were the maneuver battalions of bureaucratic existence, now forward, now back, now concealed, now full, now empty. They were the yin and yang of a life inside the government; in fact they were, as the old man said, life itself, its tact and proportion, its essence. IN and OUT boxes were the guardians of the language; language was action. So in a sense they were weapons of a specific lethal sort.

The old man was a woodworker in his spare time and these boxes were lovingly crafted of walnut, tongue-and-groove joints and each with its own delicate design on the sides along with the intimidating script in front. God knows how many hours he had devoted to them, using his platter-sized magnifying glass in order to cut accurately. At work, he could be mistaken for a master jeweler. His concentration was so complete that when you came upon him in his shop in the basement it was wise to tread loudly in order not to startle him, especially when he was using the knife, his phonograph cranked up high, Billie Holiday or Louis Armstrong keeping him company. He worked in the brilliant light of four lamps, his hands steady enough, perhaps not as steady as they once were.

Was it a subtle change in temperature or a small noise or a sixth sense? Just then Sydney knew he was not alone in the office. When he turned he saw a young Vietnamese woman in the doorway. She was staring at him incuriously, her arms at her sides; and then he saw that she was not looking at him but over his shoulder, as if she did not want to appear too forward.

He said, Hello.

Hello, sir, she said, her voice very soft and strained.

I'm Sydney Parade.

I know, sir.

I'm the new coordinator. Then he added, with a note of disapproval, Mr. Dacy was fired.

She nodded.

I just arrived. Minh brought me from the airport.

Yes, she said.

And your name?

Mai, sir, she said. Office manager.

He looked at the papers on the floor and nodded.

Mr. Dacy, sir.

Made this mess?

She was listening carefully, then seemed to nod. Her hard little eyes were following him now as he moved behind the desk to straighten the President's photograph and collect the papers scattered beneath it. He gathered them and placed them in the OUT box. She did not move and he guessed she was waiting for instructions.

He said, Well, Mai . . . He began slowly to explain about Dicey Dacy, how his behavior had been found to be intolerable and the government had removed him from Tay Thanh. He was on his way out of the country, never to return. Criminal charges would no doubt be filed once the facts were assembled. Of course she would have an opportunity to testify if she so desired. Counsel would be provided at no cost to her. Sydney apologized on behalf of Llewellyn Group and Mr. Richard Rostok personally. They were mortified in Washington, always recognizing that mistakes were often made owing to the enormity of the undertaking, reconstruction of South Vietnam. Literally hundreds of jobs were open and the security procedures regrettably lax. He said, You yourself were not — molested?

She moved her lips fractionally and seemed to shudder but her shy smile told him the answer was no.

He said he was glad to hear it. That god damned Dacy, he said. He would make every effort to undo the damage that Dacy had done to the image of Llewellyn Group. Thank God the scandal hadn't reached the newspapers. Meanwhile, he wanted a full bill

of particulars, specifically any loss of government property together with any personal complaints of the staff. In any case,
they would all start afresh at once. Dacy was gone. Dacy would
not return.

He paused then, watching her stand motionless, her gaze still
over his shoulder. An unwelcome thought forced itself into his
mind.

He said pleasantly, How old are you, Mai?

She said, Yes, sir.

So she had not understood one word. He had been talking
into fathomless Asia itself, and she had let him do it. And it had
served him right, trying to pass off Dicky Rostok's public relations homilies as honest concern. He had not failed to notice the
little gold Seiko wristwatch, either. Sydney smiled warmly and
with the universal gesture let her know she could take the rest of
the day off.

And Mai — she smiled, too, nodding gravely and backing out
of the office that still stank of Dacy and whiskey. She knew the
smell would never leave it. Even the geckos refused to inhabit
this room, no matter how often it was scrubbed. This new man's
voice had been harsh, similar to Dacy's. It was an American
voice without lilt or feeling. At least with the French she heard
some rhythm, some small change of tone that let you know what
they were feeling when they spoke. With Americans you had to
listen very carefully and watch them closely; their gestures often
gave them away. This American was not filthy like Dacy, and
that was something. Perhaps he was not quite as coarse, though
his language was thick with gutturals, the sound of gears in a
machine. In the lower register he sounded like an animal. He had
a full head of hair and a softer manner than Dacy. But Dacy had
been gentil on first meeting until he laughed, and then she knew
he was common, a vulgar type. Dacy's booming laugh was cruel.
She watched this Sydney moving the carved boxes left and right.

The boxes seemed to have some meaning for him and surely in time she would discover what the meaning was. With the dark circles under his eyes and his stubbly beard, he resembled the construction workers she saw at the installation near Xuan Loc, the radar; they were always leering and making crude gestures. She would have to be patient and see what this one wanted and what he was prepared to give for it. He did not seem to regard Dacy as a friend. He seemed to understand that Dacy was a pig. This Sydney did not look like a drinker, either, though you could never be certain. Dacy often drank alone when he thought no one was looking. He should have known that someone was always looking. Americans did not notice what went on around them, as if their own field of force was sufficient protection from the world. They did not know that you must become one with the world; you did not escape it, you disappeared into it and at that time you discovered what was required of you. With his gray face and slumping shoulders, this Sydney looked like any exhausted round-eyed traveler in a shapeless suit, discouraged at the asymmetry he found. Now he was pawing through the desk drawers with his thick fingers. He was perspiring, too, and the smell annoyed her, yet another manifestation of egoism and immodesty. He muttered something she could not make out. He shook his head and cursed, as Dacy often did with the thick growl of a dog. It was evident then that he had forgotten all about her. Mai had ceased to exist.

Goodbye, sir, she said softly from the outer office.

'Bye, Sydney said without looking up because he had found a photograph stuck between the drawer and the desktop, a picture of Dacy and a young girl. She wore an army-issue helmet so large that it covered her eyes and nose, giving her the comical appearance of a lascivious doll or warlike Lady Godiva astride her man-stallion in brilliant yellow sunlight. She was sitting in Dacy's lap, her legs spread, her fingers cradling his balls. The rest of him was erect. They both faced the camera, the girl grinning and Dacy grinning, too, except his grin was blissful and hers was indecipherable, detached as it was from her eyes. Her glossy hair spilled over her shoulders. She was small and looked like a child atop Dacy's bulk, his heavy thighs and fleshy knees. In her tiny fist, his erection resembled a giant plum-colored acorn. Dacy's half-lidded eyes gazed triumphantly into the ecstatic future, one golden afternoon following another, golden afternoons without end in a distant country with infinite patience and possibility, where everyone knew the value of a dollar.

Sydney stared at the photograph, wondering about the preparations for it, the helmet and the time of day, the camera's timer set and then the scramble back to the chair. He looked more closely now and saw that Dacy and the girl were sitting in the desk chair; and the camera must have been placed in the low bookcase, the one beneath the photographs of the President and the ambassador. So Dicey had a sense of humor, making unwilling voyeurs of their excellencies. Sydney did not fail to notice the gold Seiko on the wrist of the hand that held the erection, and the rhinestones on the fingers, and Dacy's fat thumb resting on one of the rhinestones.

Dacy was bald with a fringe of hair that resembled the puppet Kukla, exactly as Rostok had said. His jowls were unshaven, and unless pictures lied Dicey Dacy was the suspect Sydney had seen at the airport, the one briefly detained by the MPs and then sent through passport control, "and don't come back." The one who had scuffed his feet as he looked at the floor and shook his head no, extending his wrists to receive the handcuffs. Dacy did not look like a man familiar with remorse. It was his last desperate bid to remain in the country of his dreams. Any jail cell in Saigon was paradise compared to the split-level in Modesto. A man like Dacy could not grow into himself in sunny California, altogether too American, too strait-laced and composed, a soul-killing domestic milieu.

Sydney moved to replace the photograph, forgetting for a moment that the desk no longer belonged to Dacy. He saw then that there were dozens more photographs, Dacy and the girl on the floor, in the bed upstairs, in the bathtub, on the sofa, perched on the edge of the desk itself, the poses identical, the girl's detached grin and Dacy's busy fingers and glazed ecstasy. Sydney thought, The answer to chaos is repetition.

Getting Used to It

NIGHT HAD FALLEN when Sydney and Rostok settled in at the café across the street from the police station at Tay Thanh. The café was without walls, open to the night air. The fluorescent lamps cast a fitful light, buzzing all the while; insects collected around them, crashing into the glowing tubes. Sydney was alarmed by a teenage boy crouched in the corner. He had the unpredictable look of a wild animal, his neck disappeared into his shoulders, his head forward, his legs splayed awkwardly on the wooden floor. He rocked slowly on his knuckles, keeping time to some inner rhythm. One of his legs was infected with elephantiasis, a formless limb below the knee. The leg looked like an elongated balloon filled with water, flopping this way and that. At the waiter's command the boy rose to scatter the insects around the lights. Then he fetched a pitcher of water, the useless leg dragged behind him like a tail. The foot was huge, the size of a man's thigh but without sinew.

Food's good here, Ros said.

The boy filled their water glasses, concentrating hard. Up close he did not look like a wild animal, merely an undersized boy performing a simple task. Sydney turned away, filled with pity. What a ghastly combination of bad luck, bad genes, infection, and Third World medicine. What sort of life would this boy know? And would it be better or worse than the life of the girl in the helmet? And just then Sydney thought he had seen enough of Vietnamese youth for one day, his first in-country. Part of him was still in New York and another part in Comminges.

The boy finished pouring water and then limped away, his heavy foot making a silky sound as he dragged it across the floor. Sydney wondered if the boy was in pain. He didn't look in pain.

Don't drink the water, Ros said.

I don't intend to, Sydney said. The boy —

His name is Cao, Ros said.

Maybe one of our medical specialists, Sydney began.

Ask them, Ros said. They like unusual cases.

I will.

You'll have some trouble with the family. They like Cao the way he is. Cao panhandles our soldiers, earns more than his father. Cao's the only asset that family has, so he's worth something the way he is, and not worth much if he's just like everyone else. You dig, Syd? Don't look so surprised. They're only trying to get on, like most of us.

When the waiter arrived, Rostok ordered beer for them both and noodle soup and cracked crab. He spoke in Vietnamese and the waiter replied in kind. Ros listened patiently while Sydney told him about Mai, the office manager who did not seem to understand English and was distant in other ways, though she could be excused given her experience with Dacy. The office was filthy, official papers scattered everywhere. Fortunately none of them bore a classification stamp. One of the filing cabinets was broken, apparently by a crowbar or rifle butt. The air conditioner in the bedroom was broken. The bathwater was lukewarm. The refrigerator leaked. And someone had drawn a moustache on LBJ's face, giving him the most uncanny resemblance to Dzugashvili in his youth. Sydney noticed Rostok's glower and began to laugh. He decided at that moment not to describe the photographs, Dacy and the girl in the helmet.

So I didn't get what I was promised, Mr. Dicky, and now I want a plane ticket back to New York.

Fuck you, Ros said.

Did Dicey actually do any work?

Rostok thought a moment, hand to mouth. There was a bridge out near Bien Hoa. Needed repair so Dicey saw to that. And then the VC blew it up and Dicey lost interest. Short attention span for a police officer. He was only here for six months, but that was about five months too long. Fair to say that he didn't get into the swing of things, at least the way we'd hoped.

I know what you mean, Sydney said mildly. Still. Six months.

We used to let people alone out here. Let them do their jobs, and if they had a problem to let us know and we'd try to fix it, and if we couldn't fix it we'd cover it up. That was back when we were lean and mean, everyone a serious volunteer and eager to take part. Then we got much bigger, budget and personnel both. Things got away from us, fair to say. So it took us a while to — figure Dicey Dacy out.

That was it, one bridge?

Civic action and reconstruction and development weren't Dicey's long suits, as we found out. He didn't understand the concept of nation-building, thought it was bullshit. He liked doing the accounts. Good at it, too. Dicey was a wizard with the adding machine. They loved him at headquarters because his paperwork was always complete and on time. You'll find the Tay Thanh accounts in excellent shape, simply excellent. There aren't a better set of books in all of Three Corps. He was even able to account for the bridge, the concrete and the iron.

Sydney watched the boy scooping rice from a bowl. When he

finished he put the bowl in front of him and looked tenderly at the waiter. In the shadows with the bowl the boy again resembled an animal.

That was a barter arrangement with the Army Corps of Engineers, Rostok went on. Dicey knew someone over there. They got something they wanted in return for the iron. I didn't ask what it was because I didn't want to know. Ros craned his neck and slapped at a mosquito. Look, Syd, he said. Everyone liked Dacy. He was so pussy-struck. It was funny. He was just having a good time, away from Modesto and Mrs. Dacy and the kiddies. I think he'd never had any fun in his life. Then he began to drink and it wasn't so funny anymore because one night he hurt one of the girls, broke her arm. He didn't know how to drink. He was just a dumb small-town cop who knew a congressman. Someone took a shot at him one night and from then on he always carried a weapon. And that wasn't funny either because he was always drunk. He got to thinking he was entitled to something because he was a volunteer in a war zone. At the end he was begging for it from any girl who would give it to him.

Was the girl badly hurt?

Simple fracture. We paid her off. And her family.

You know, Sydney said, Mai has a little gold Seiko.

Not from Dacy, Ros said. Mai has a special friend.

Mai has a history, then?

Syd, for God's sake. She's a human being. Of course she has a history.

Is the special friend one of theirs or one of ours?

Here's our beer, Rostok said.

Beer arrived and they both drank. There were two other tables of Vietnamese and a third of two Americans alone, speaking in conspiratorial whispers. One of the Americans moved the palms of his hands over the table as if he were summoning the Ouija spirits. Everyone was eating soup and cracked crab and drinking beer. Sydney remembered a quiet restaurant on the wharf at Mystic; that restaurant reminded him of this one, a place for locals only where everyone minded his own business. In the summer the windows were thrown open to the sea air, the Atlantic breeze as thick and used up as the inland air at Tay Thanh.

Had your shots, Syd? Malaria, hepatitis, plague?

Those and a few more. One other, I forget. Hurt like a bastard. Cholera.

That was it.

Never, ever drink the water under any circumstances.

I know, Ros. And never drink Coke without checking for ground glass in the bottle.

Where did you hear that?

Washington. The briefing. They said kids ground up glass and put it in the Coke bottle and then resealed the cap. Bad news.

It's bullshit, Ros said. The mamasan with the grenade in her underpants? That's bullshit, too. And the fifty-seven varieties of clap? That's bullshit.

They mentioned the clap, too. They devoted an hour to the clap.

They're idiots. They don't know anything so they invent stories, as you do with a child at bedtime, not knowing you're scaring him to death. Or maybe you do know. Anyhow, forget them. Just don't drink the water, and if you're making ice, use bottled.

Aye, cap'n, Sydney said.

I'm tired, Ros said. I'm as tired as I've ever been in my life, eleven hours of meetings today and there'll be eleven more tomorrow and the day after. And for the rest of the month, probably. You'll be in those with me from now on. And you keep your own counsel for a while, don't say a word until you get the feel of things. It won't take long. There's a special vocabulary you'll have to learn, god damned acronyms up the ying-yang. Fingerprints of our secret handshake, Syd. MACV, JUSPAO, USAID, ARVN, and the others, all used commonly. The one that isn't used commonly, except among ourselves, is CAS, Covert American Services. They don't use CIA in-country, and if anyone does use it the boys leave the room, like they were members of Skull and Bones. So you don't use CAS with journalists or the other tourists who arrive to judge things.

Cass, Sydney said.

That's it, Syd.

Thanks for letting me know.

Always at your service, Rostok said.

You'll have to make your own way, he went on, just as I did. Except I'll be better with you than my master was with me. Because he thought I was undermining him. He thought I wanted his job.

Llewellyn.

Boyd Llewellyn, Rostok said.

Sydney smiled. But you did want his job.

And I got it, Rostok said. But I didn't undermine him to get it. I outthought him and outfought him. Boyd's paranoid like most superior bureaucrats. Stands to reason, the product's so intangible, it's hard to know who deserves credit for it, or blame if things go the wrong way. Boyd knows how to move paper. He moves paper as well as anyone alive and his fingerprints are never anywhere near the bad news. The bad news was my news. His news was the bridge that Dicey built. When the VC blew it up, that was my news. Then, before you knew it, Boyd was bye-bye, his year was up and he was back home at headquarters telling everyone how fucked up things were, the effort going nowhere, not much money, so little experience, no direction. How none of us knew how to do our jobs and therefore we were caving in to the military, taking orders from majors when we should have been giving them to brigadier generals. And the solution was to strengthen the reporting procedures. Meaning tighter control in Washington. At God knows what cost in man-hours and distraction from the job at hand, nation-building and hearts and minds. Boyd wanted more paper to push. The more paper he was given, the more indispensable he would become.

Not stupid, Boyd. Man's a Heifetz of the filing cabinet. You want to know the location of the IH Scout, serial number 9847t92635h, Boyd could find the paper on it. He has a pretty good feel for the waste, too. The leakage. The medicine that never arrived, the bulgar rice that disappeared. The trucks hijacked at Saigon port. Boyd told Administration that it was only a matter of time before a committee of Congress got wind of things and then — we were all fucked. Televised hearings, witnesses under oath. So the wise thing to do was increase the paperwork, cover your ass in triplicate.

Rostok sighed and leaned across the table. In the dull sideways light his features seemed haggard, dark circles under his sad eyes, his skin slack. He needed a haircut. He tapped his fingers together and began again.

Meanwhile, we're trying to control the military. Keep the heavy war away from the civilians we're trying to protect. So we insist, No H-and-I at night. He looked at Sydney and gave the explanation. H-and-I means harassment-and-interdiction artillery fire. They load up the artillery and fire shells into the rain forest helter-skelter. It's like the lottery for a millionaire. They have plenty of shells and once in a while they're bound to hit something of value and in the meantime they're killing animals and an occasional civilian. And when they finish up they send someone around with the solatium payments, so much for a water buffalo, so much for a chicken coop, so much for grand-dad. They send teams around with satchels full of money. Each team has a lawyer because the peasants are shrewd. Granddad dies of a heart attack, everyone stands around weeping and wailing, accusing the Americans of murder. It's the lawyer's job to make certain that Uncle Sam isn't being shaken down. They've got quite a law firm over at MACV, bright lads skilled at interrogation. Naturally they depend heavily on their interpreters. Who are Vietnamese.

Sydney looked up at the sound of thunder in the distance.

Artillery, Rostok said. H-and-I.

The soup and cracked crab arrived and Ros ordered two more bottles of beer. The thunder receded. One table of Vietnamese left and another arrived. The soup was good and the cracked crab very good. Sydney was struggling to orient himself; barely seventy-two hours before he had been saying his awkward goodbyes to Missy in Comminges. He wondered what it was that had attracted the French to Indochina beyond plunder, unless it was only that. He had read somewhere that the central highlands were reminiscent of the foothills of the Pyrenees, if you could forget the elephants. Opium played some role, according to Malraux, who ought to have known. Probably the heat and the beauty of the women had something to do with it, too.

See those? Ros said. He nodded at the table of newly arrived Vietnamese, thirtyish men except for the one in the shantung suit. Traders, Ros said. Motor scooters, gasoline, television sets, weapons. The suit divides his time between Saigon and Bangkok, with side trips to Taipei.

Big for a Vietnamese, Sydney said.

That's because he's Chinese.

The table suddenly erupted in giggles, the Vietnamese covering their mouths and the Chinese in the shantung suit gesturing and grinning, bringing the joke to its conclusion. The waiter arrived with a bottle of Chivas Regal. The table continued to giggle while the waiter filled glasses with ice and poured the Scotch. Rostok signaled for more beer but the waiter somehow failed to notice and glided off into the kitchen with his empty tray.

The little shit, Rostok said, loud enough so that one of the Vietnamese turned to look at him, and then smiled in recognition. Rostok smiled back. He said to Sydney, That one used to be aide-de-camp to the Three Corps commander. They were distantly related. Not a bad aide-de-camp, energetic, spoke good English, very good with our people. He always had excellent idiomatic explanations why the time was not right to draw the enemy into battle. "Their backcourt's better than ours this season." "We'll roll when we get the tune-up we've been promised." He bought his way out of the army and then set up this place. With seed money from the Three Corps commander, who should be along any time now.

As you say, Sydney said. Everyone has a history.

Not everyone, Rostok said sourly. That Chinese, for example. We know his name but we don't know who his principals are. We don't know anything about his family. We don't know where he does his banking. We're not sure of his nationality. Sometimes he's Taiwanese, other times Malayan. He's whatever his passport says he is, and he has more than one passport. He says he's on our side but I bet he says that to all the girls.

Sydney bent over his cracked crab and watched the Chinese, fastidious as he slowly lifted the glass to his mouth and set it down again. His companions were jabbering and he appeared to listen to them; but Syd thought he was far away inside his own nocturnal world, thinking whatever rich traders thought at such moments. His suit was beautifully tailored and his tie knotted just so. His loafers were polished and he wore no socks. When the Chinese turned to look at them his hand moved to his throat, adjusting the knot; and then a smile, one of utter indifference, a smile for the record only, a notice-the-Americans smile. Whatever his nationality, wherever his true home, he seemed completely at ease in Tay Thanh.

Sydney said, I thought the Vietnamese hated the Chinese.

They do.

But not this one?

Sometimes they make exceptions, Rostok said.

They were silent a moment, eating, listening to the murmur of conversation and the buzz of the fluorescent lights. Sydney felt the thickness of the rain forest, and somewhere in the vicinity the movement of the river. Now and then a motorbike clattered in the street. For the moment there was no distant thunder. He imagined activity in the forest, from the river beside the café all the way to the Cambodian border, patrols moving, supplies moving, lines of wiry men hurrying along the trails, the night silent except for the creak of their gear. They would speak only in whispers. Everyone would be listening hard for the whoosh of the artillery shell, the one-in-a-million shot that actually found its target.

Rostok scraped back his chair and rose. He walked slowly to the kitchen and peeked in, said a few words, and returned to the table. After a while the waiter arrived with two bottles of beer and fresh glasses, muttering something that sounded like an apology. Rostok watched him with a half-smile, following him with his eyes all the way back to the kitchen.

Sydney's attention had begun to wander at the solatium payments, and the bureaucratic mumbo-jumbo that went with it. This was not the Dicky Rostok he remembered, the one who could see around corners and knew what you were thinking before you thought it, the Rostok who believed in thorough preparation and displayed always a sunny pessimism toward the way of the world, a mysterious passage always beyond reach, though not beyond bluff. Yet the Dicky Rostok before him sounded now like the branch manager of a tight-fisted savings and loan association waiting for the examiners to show up; and then he remembered the hard little eyes of Mai at Group House, her eyes comprehending what her ears couldn't. And Minh, too, stubbornly silent as he piloted the Scout from Tan Son Nhut to Tay Thanh, dodging American convoys. Probably it was only jet lag but Sydney did not feel entirely in the picture. He was looking hard at it but he wasn't in it. He was aware suddenly that Ros had stopped talking and was looking at him with a sympathetic smile.

You'll get used to it, Syd. It takes a minute. Of course you need a lust for complexity. You need ambiguity in your heart. But there's a kind of romance to life here in-country. Anyhow, it's what we have. We didn't get to choose, it's our secret reward. So we work with it, best we can. Hope for victory. Make it happen. Rostok began to laugh, turning to watch the commotion at the door. A slender Vietnamese in a pale blue ao dai made her entrance, hesitating, then floating to the side of the Chinese businessman. He rose with the others at the table, bowing formally. She had left two men at the door and now, at her nod, they disappeared into the darkness. The woman sat and poured tea from the pot on the table. Sydney guessed her age at somewhere between thirty and fifty; almost certainly an entertainer, and a successful one from the look of her. She wore huge rings on her fingers and a gold chain circling her throat, a presentation vaguely French, as if she had just arrived from a cabaret somewhere in Montmartre. It was hard to tell at that distance, but the watch looked like a Rolex.

He said, Who's that?

Madame Le, Rostok said. A singer. Everyone's friend.

I wonder if she needs a sideman.

I forgot. You play, don't you.

Trombone. I doubt if she needs a trombone. There wouldn't be a trombone in her ensemble.

Your wife played the cello.

Yes, we were a musical family. Same tunes, different instruments. Sydney shook his head as if to clear it. I can't remember what I expected to find in Tay Thanh. I've been here less than a day, it seems like a century. But I don't think it was this. I don't think it was her, Madame Le. Or the Chinese in the shantung suit. Or Cao.

Ros pushed his plate away and leaned back in his chair, nodding at a new arrival who stood importantly in the doorway. He said, You have to remember that ordinary life goes on here as it does everywhere else. Forget everything you've read or been told by the briefers, who're only interested in their war, their American dream where everyone's either shooting or being shot at. Truth is, children go to school. People go to church, love each other, even in this situation. People quarrel and gossip and have dinner with their friends. Mow the lawn. Listen to music. And here he is now.

Rostok rose and shook hands with the new arrival, then introduced him, General Binh, the III Corps commander. The general's face was perfectly round and unlined, his hand soft as a child's and carefully manicured. He and Rostok talked sotto voce, alternating English and Vietnamese, something about an "incident," the incident unspecified but apparently not serious, for the general was smiling benignly. After a moment he joined the other table, laughing at something Ros had said. Sydney saw that another bottle of Chivas Regal had materialized with a fresh glass for the general.

That's a general? Sydney asked.

One of the better ones, as a matter of fact, a product of our own National War College. He's quite an expert on the Napoleonic campaigns. Normally I like to talk to him in his office, a more private venue. But he often isn't in. Or isn't in to me. So I take my opportunities where I find them.

He doesn't look like a general, Sydney said.

Neither did Bonaparte.

Rostok thumbed a cigarette from the pack in front of him,

then patted his pockets unsuccessfully for a match. Instantly Cao was at his elbow, producing a Zippo, lighting it, waiting for Rostok to inhale. He tapped the Zippo on the tabletop and pushed it across to Rostok. This is Mr. Parade, Rostok said.

Cao nodded and shook hands.

Mr. Parade will be helping me in Tay Thanh.

Welcome to Tay Thanh, Mr. Parade.

Thank you, Sydney said.

You need anything, you ask me, Cao said.

I will, Sydney said.

I am always here, Cao said. He stood lopsidedly with both hands on the table, palms down to steady himself.

Sydney said, When did your foot become infected?

Cao looked questioningly at Rostok, who translated.

Many years, Cao said.

Have you seen doctors?

It's congenital, Rostok said. He pocketed the Zippo and handed Cao a wad of piaster notes.

Or a parasite, Cao said, and with a nod he was gone, scuttling crabwise across the floor, the useless leg swishing behind him.

He's well spoken, Sydney said. He did not want to admit that he had thought the boy was retarded, incapable of speech or much else; and he was not a boy, either, but a man nearing middle age.

Yes, well spoken. Cao — finds things. Things go missing and Cao finds them, a jack for your car, a deck of cards, a pound of sugar. Cao and Dacy were great friends until Dacy crashed. Rostok started to say something more but signaled for the check instead. He began to drum his fingers on the table, looking sideways at General Binh and the Chinese deep in conversation. Madame Le had disappeared. The table of Americans had departed also and the restaurant was so quiet Sydney could hear the rustle of the river water outside. Rostok sighed and flexed his fingers.

Marriages are going to hell everywhere, he said suddenly.

Sydney looked up but did not reply. He was watching Cao in the corner, counting the notes Ros had given up. He was not interested in discussing marriage. Ros often employed the creative non sequitur to keep people off balance or to fill dead air when he became bored.

I don't mean you, he said.

It's what happens, Sydney said.

I don't know how happy Janet is in Hong Kong. Rostok again began to drum nervously on the table. The apartment's nice and we have it cheap. Janet has friends. But she's been talking about going back to Virginia and that's all right, too, if it's what she wants to do. She doesn't care for Asia. She doesn't like the food. She doesn't like the heat. She says she's lonely. It's harder and harder for me to get away for long weekends, and when I'm there she complains that I'm really still here, and that's a low blow because I make a hell of an effort, getting away. You can't just leave a war whenever you want to. Women have a hard time putting themselves in someone else's shoes, don't they?

Rostok sighed and rapped the table sharply.

He said, Strange thing is, in the year we've been here, she's aged ten. You can see it in her face and the way she moves, her conversation. She's gained weight. She's careworn. She hates the war because I'm in it. She thinks I'll be hurt and that's reason enough to get out. She spends too much time at the press club playing bridge, listening to the horror stories. They don't know anything, you see. The newspaper people look at our war zone through a telescope and they think they know what it is because they see the outlines of a hill or a valley. Sometimes they see the dimensions of a human being. But they can't know what it is really because they're not invested. They're bystanders, note-book people. They're defeatists and Janet's defeatist, too. She expects the worst, and when she doesn't get it she thinks it's a trick they're playing. Janet used to look for things out of life. We always knew there was a jackpot somewhere and if you wanted it badly enough and were willing to work hard enough you'd find it, or it would find you. That's what drew us together, the idea of the jackpot. My God, we're still young! Or I am. She isn't. Suddenly she's a defeatist and prefers Virginia to Hong Kong.

Sydney was silent. Janet Rostok was always the quiet one at the table, chain-smoking Pall Malls and nursing a single high-ball. She was known as a good sport who excelled at tennis and bridge, utterly without personal ambition — and then Sydney realized he had no idea what her ambitions were. Whatever they were, she never spoke of them. She seemed to be focused on tennis and bridge and, by general agreement of their friends, on Rostok. He often said he could not survive without her.

Gutterman manages it, I don't know how. Or rather I do know. He's married to a slope, has been for years. You'll meet him tomorrow, my deputy Pablo Gutterman. But you'll never meet his wife because she lives behind the scenes, strange-look-ing woman, refused to speak English the one time I met her, strictly by accident in the central market. Pablo was buying shoes and she was choosing them, as if Pab didn't have sense enough to find the right ones. I didn't recognize him. I stood next to him for the longest time and then he said something and I looked up. He went red in the face when he saw me. He tried to escape but saw he was trapped and forced to introduce his wife. She's a dumpy thing, middle-aged like him, eyes too big for her head. She offered her hand, almost weightless but hard as stone. And after a pleasantry they were gone, like *that,* disappeared into the crowd. Damnedest thing, Pablo looked like the others, all the other men in the market, so I didn't recognize him.

And that's how he manages? Sydney asked.

I suppose it is, Rostok said. Buying shoes in the market with his frau, and then a cup of tea somewhere, and a game of mahjongg at the end of the day, after he mows the lawn. I don't think Pablo knows where he is. My God, this is the adventure of a lifetime. I mean in the sense of a long sea voyage, the ship alive under your feet, strange ports of call, an untested crew, a skipper who never shows his face, and nasty weather all day long. He laughed loudly, savoring the caprice.

Maybe it isn't her adventure, Sydney said. Any more than it is Janet's.

It's everyone's adventure, Rostok said. You'll discover that there aren't enough hours in the day to do what you have to do, and at the end of them you'll have energy left over. You'll have energy to burn, more energy than you know what to do with because the war doesn't take. It gives and gives and then it gives again. It's like being plugged into an iron lung, Syd.

The waiter arrived with the check and Ros threw down another wad of piasters.

So I suppose it's finished, he said.

We married when we were young, he added.

Before Sydney could make the pro forma protest, Rostok was out of his chair and walking toward the door.

Let's take a walk, he said.

The street was dark. Even the forest seemed to sleep, the only sound the swish of water somewhere. Stars were visible overhead but the constellation was not familiar. The fetid odor of the forest was not familiar. A vast anonymity seemed to settle over the street, the wooden shacks on either side of it, and the forests and hills beyond. They began to walk in the direction of Group

House — his house, Sydney thought, his private address now. He thought of the IN and OUT boxes on his desk and the work that would begin tomorrow. Down the street a dog barked twice and was silent.

I love it, Rostok said softly. I love this place.

Why, Ros?

He stretched his arms wide, looking at the sky and the blurred stars. I love the freedom, he said. I love not knowing. The shape of things in the morning.

And being in charge, Sydney said.

Yes, that, too.

They walked on. Far in the distance they heard the chop-chop of a helicopter. A light flared in one of the houses nearby, and as suddenly went out. Rostok began to laugh quietly, muttering something about night sounds in the countryside, everyone gets used to them and when they're absent, you miss them.

Do you ever dream, Syd?

Now and again. I don't remember them, though.

Rostok cleared his throat and said, I receive Ho Chi Minh in my dreams. He visits me often, though not in the form you might think. He's in the kitchen of the Carlton making pastry under the direction of the great Escoffier, bending over the marble counter with his poche à douille filled with batter. He makes cygnes en pâte à choux, the swans reminding him of the beautiful birds on the Petit Lac and the Red River at Hanoi. He squeezes out teardrops of batter, all the time remembering the lake and the river, and Trotsky's teachings and the cruelty of the French and the titanic struggle for doc lap, independence, a struggle that he knew would not be won in his lifetime but was inevitable. He must give his life to it. Meanwhile, he has his patriotic pastry to attend to. I watch him. He never says a word, never looks up from his pastry table. His hands are frail. His skin is the texture of old paper. He never smiles, never looks up as he continues to squeeze the pastry bag, replicating one swan after another. And when I wake up, he remains on the margins of my vision. When he vanishes at last, I am sorry to see him go. But I know he will return, in that form or in another, chef or president. And in time these dreams will have meaning for me as they did for Goya, who described his subjects arriving when he was asleep; and when he woke he drew them exactly as he remembered them, his sueños. They are most detailed, most suggestive. They are among his finest works. Still half asleep, Goya made extensive notes on a pad he kept on his bedside table. In the morning he went to work, bringing his sueños to the canvas. And I do the same, make notes when I rise, and one day I will bring them to life.

Rostok's voice had fallen to a whisper, and then died away. Sydney waited for more but Rostok had said what he had to say and now was silent. He imagined his friend's nightstand filled with wild jottings, descriptions of Ho at the pastry table, patiently counting swans while he imagined the revolution to come. Probably he thought of the birds as so many expendable infantrymen, fragile as meringue.

They walked on, Rostok lost in thought. Mist was rising from the forest, wispy vapors that seemed to take one shape, then another, vanishing and gathering again in the heavy air. The village was behind them now. Rostok said softly, Tell me what you can about the Armands. What did you learn?

Sydney hesitated, then explained about Missy and her apartment in the rue du Louvre, the long trip south from Paris, the stone house and the Roman wall, the heavy meal and the raw wine, and the four Armand brothers, one in France, two in Africa, one in Indochina. He related the conversation as best he could recollect it, Missy translating, the old man belligerently staring across the table, his heavy arms across his chest. Suspicious old bastard, wouldn't give an inch. He thinks it's dangerous for his brother to meet with Americans. Meet with Americans, share information with Americans, that might mean you're choosing sides. Plus, we've been bombing his rubber trees.

So you didn't get the letter, Rostok said.

I got the back of his hand, Sydney said.

Nice place they have?

Stone house in the mountains. Second-century Roman wall in the back yard.

Rostok stopped to light a cigarette, blowing a smoke ring that hung stubbornly in the mist. Did you tell him that you could do something about the rubber trees? That Claude's rubber trees were under your supervision? That you had authority and could do something about the bombing?

I did. He didn't buy.

Rostok kicked at a stone in the road and muttered something.

He thought I was too dangerous for his brother.

People are going to have to choose sides. Even French people.

They think they know more about it than we do.

Everybody thinks they know more about it than we do. But that's not the point. Cooperation's the point. Choosing sides is the point.

They don't forget their experience any more than we forget ours, Sydney said. We think we're back in the European theater in War Two. We want to bomb. We think if we turn Haiphong into Hamburg we'll break the spirit of the population. We think there's a Rhine somewhere, and if we can find it we can cross it and occupy the enemy's heartland, and then old Ho will retire to his bunker with his mistress and commit suicide. And the French don't want to fight at all. Why would they? Where did fighting ever get them? In this century it's one catastrophe after another, from Verdun to the Maginot Line to Dien Bien Phu. So I don't think we ought to count on them, Ros. It's really only us here on the ground. And that's what we've wanted all along, isn't it? We've wanted to be the sentry on the bridge. And now we are.

There are ways and means, Rostok said vaguely.

Did you know Claude's wife is American?

Rostok muttered something noncommittal.

She worked for the embassy. She was Cultural Affairs. What do you suppose she did in Cultural Affairs? Bring jazz bands to Danang? *West Side Story* to the opera house in Saigon? Maybe university professors to lecture on myth in William Faulkner. What do you suppose she did as cultural attaché?

I think she ran the USIA library.

I saw her picture, a good-looking woman.

That's what they say, Rostok said.

There must have been people who knew her, embassy people. Our people. She must've had women friends, people she went to lunch with. She must have had a roommate before she married Claude. They're the ones who ought to make this approach, if you want to go ahead with it. Seems useless to me.

It was a while ago she worked for the embassy, Rostok said. Anyone who knew her has been rotated home. And when she married Armand she disappeared into Xuan Loc, and that's an insecure sector, has been for years. She even stopped going to the Cercle Sportif. Last time anyone saw her was when she showed up to have her passport renewed. That was routine, no one thought anything about it. She was in and out in thirty minutes and the moron on duty didn't have the sense to check her out and get a message upstairs. He did notice that she had nice legs and freckles. At that time we thought we had things in hand and no one cared about an American living on a rubber plantation, unless she was in danger; and if she was, she didn't say so. None of our people have even met Claude Armand. Two of the lads went out to the plantation a few times, made the courtesy call, anything we can do for you, Dede, and by the way, how's the security situation in your sector? But no one was at home and the servants weren't talking. And then they realized they were at the wrong plantation. So everyone forgot about them. Except me.

I think they're unimportant, Sydney said. They're two people holed up on a rubber plantation, and who cares?

Let me tell you something, Syd. Hard to succeed in this business. You've got to have something that no one else has. MACV has the army, the navy, the air force, and the marines. The spooks have the money and the confidence of the people who count. The embassy has the State Department, and their teletypes connect to Highest Levels. What do we have? We have a few smart guys and an ambitious charter. They're hoping Llewellyn Group can make some difference but they have no idea what that difference might be. So our great task is to have something that no one else has, and when we get it we'll be listened to, and if we don't get it they'll collapse us like a tin can. What that thing is right now is knowledge. We've got to know things that the rest of them don't know from a source of information they can't figure out. If they do figure it out, they'll steal it, especially CAS. Then we're out in the cold. We want a source of information that's ours and ours alone. They'll have to admit, Rostok has that information. He's the only one who has it and he's holding it tight, because he's a son of a bitch. So ask him nicely and give him something in return.

Rostok paused, suddenly alert. Then he lowered his voice.

And then Llewellyn Group will count for something. Not before. It's information we're after and I'm not even certain what information, what it is that I need to know. I don't even know what I don't know. But I intend to find out. And I have an idea that Monsieur Armand and his American wife will be able to help me. I'm highly confident, Syd. And I have confidence in you, too. It all fits in.

Then he was quiet, listening.

Shut up now, Syd.

They moved, crouching, into the shadows of a sandalwood tree. Rostok dropped his cigarette and stepped on it. It was so quiet Sydney could hear the ticking of his wristwatch; then he realized it was not his wristwatch but something else, a mechanical click-click of something in the road ahead, and mixed in with it a strenuous vibration, the pulse of bodies moving. When they came out of the mist they were elevated and as clumsy as camels, their heads forward, bodies swaying, humpbacked, moving in a single-file caravan. They were slow. The bicycles lurched this way and that, avoiding the ruts in the road. The men did not speak and glided like ghosts in the swirling mist. Three feet separated each bicyclist. Sydney counted six, and six more, then stopped counting because Rostok was breathing so heavily he thought the troop would surely hear them. Each man carried a slung carbine, a backpack, and a long black sock that looked like a bandolier but was filled with rice. Their uniforms were black and their faces camouflaged. They came on and on, never speaking, as much a part of the night as the dead air that surrounded them. Rostok had begun to tremble and when one of the guerrillas turned to look at them, Sydney held his breath. The Vietnamese wore little wire-rimmed glasses that had slipped to the end of his nose. His expression was blank. In his exhaustion and myopia he saw nothing and in a moment was gone; and then they were all gone, leaving Sydney and Rostok in a state of silent terror. When Sydney put his hand on Rostok's back it came away wet with sweat. Rostok stank. His face seemed to glow in the dark. And then they were talking at once.

God almighty.

Did you see that one look at us? *Right at us.*

Ugly little bastard, blind as a bat. That's as close as we'll ever come, Syd. God almighty.

Did you see the bikes? They looked fifty years old.

God almighty, Rostok said, and began walking.

Five minutes later they were in the driveway of Group House. Rostok opened the door to his Scout and heaved himself inside. He took a revolver from the glove compartment and laid it on the seat beside him. He sat for a moment, thinking, his hands at two and ten on the steering wheel. He was gripping it so tightly his knuckles were white. He started the engine, the racket shattering the evening stillness. He lit a cigarette and watched the smoke drift away out the window.

Our lads caught a couple of youngsters last week, he said thoughtfully. Infantrymen from the Something regiment that operates around Tay Ninh. They were just peasant boys from the North. The interrogator had a bright idea. Instead of asking them the usual questions about troop strength, operations, and so forth — which he knew he wouldn't get answers to anyway, until he went to the screws and the water pail — he asked them questions you might ask in a high school history exam. Turned out they didn't know the simplest things. They had only the vaguest idea who we were and where we came from. They did not know we occupied a continent half the world away. They did not know the simplest facts about the twentieth century, Hitler and the Second World War. Eisenhower and the D-day landing. They did know about Stalin and they knew about the Bomb. They had never heard of Roosevelt or Truman. Drew a blank on Winston Churchill. They did not know where Australia was. Of their own revolution they were similarly ignorant, except that it had to be done and it would succeed, thanks to Ho and General Giap and the example of Dien Bien Phu. Think about that, Sydney.

Sydney grunted. His mind was back somewhere on the road with the silent bicycle soldiers.

Nothing to fear from them, Rostok said. Knowledge is power and they're ignorant, so in the last analysis they're powerless.

Nothing to fear from the Armands, either. They're marginal people. They won't last. They've been in Vietnam for so long they can't imagine the shape of the modern world, its conscience and direction. They're not stupid people. They're people who are unaware. They're people who have been left behind. The world has moved on but they have not moved on with it. So they're incomplete. They choose to be incomplete, so the hell with them.

Sydney tapped the hood of the Scout. Bye-bye, Ros.

When you find Claude Armand, let me know at once.

Rostok gunned the engine, then turned it off and got out of the Scout. On second thought, he would not attempt the drive back to Saigon. He was tired. He reached through the window to fetch the revolver. If Sydney's spare bedroom was free, he'd take it.

A Shooting in the Market

*F*OUR MONTHS IN-COUNTRY, dreamless at night, Sydney Parade was the happiest he'd been. In the mornings he spread the huge map of Vietnam on his desk and memorized the villages in his sector, some of them inaccessible by road. The army provided a helicopter for a reconnaissance by air, but that was useless because the landmarks were unfamiliar and distances seemed not to correspond to the map. Yet he believed he had entered into the modern world at last, the one that floated unmoored on the surface of a vast windless mirrored ocean, the horizon forever out of reach. The journey mattered more than the destination, which remained undefined. Whatever it was, they were making progress toward it.

Llewellyn Group lived in flux, the days changing and dissolving, marked only by the accumulation of facts, data assembled from a thousand collection points — rice distributed, vaccinations administered, dikes repaired, roads and bridges built, schools refitted, reports filed. Numbers were fundamental to the estimate of the situation. They tried to build a narrative from the numbers, numbers doing the work of verbs and predicates, numbers supported by instinct, instinct supported by numbers. These were the facts of the matter. As Rostok said, It all adds up.

In his letters home, Sydney attempted to put a human face on the statistics — the resigned look of schoolchildren as they stood in line waiting for polio vaccine, the patience of farmers as they listened to an agronomist explain the miracle of pesticides, the surprise and pleasure on the faces of the local militia when an army unit arrived with a Rome plow to build a soccer field. He imagined himself undergoing a kind of conversion, from apostate — though he had never had great faith, so there had been precious little to renounce — to believer. If these small actions could be duplicated in the countryside every day, would not the Vietnamese people rally to the cause of the government? The revolution offered only hardship and danger, of living like a hunted animal without adequate provisions and with no furloughs, ever, only funerals in absentia. What sort of life was that? Meanwhile, the American arsenal grew and the infantry divisions kept coming.

And the revolution did not hesitate. It grew along with the American arsenal, and the raids and subversion and sabotage grew as well. None of this activity was justified by the statistics, so painstakingly assembled.

The country team was drawn to extreme analogies in attempting to explain the flux of the facts. Preparing for bed in the thick heat, elated at his own good fortune, Sydney began to think of them as believers in the occult, the veneration of the Virgin or of the Cabala or of ordinal numbers or strange beasts, unicorns or Chimeras, invoking the spirits of the dead or the white magic of theurgists. Often he thought of Ho Chi Minh's pastry swans afloat on a silver platter, decorated with confectioners' sugar dust and angels' hair; how disconnected from the revolutionary world the kitchen at the Hotel Carlton must have seemed to the young revolutionary, and how tyrannical old Escoffier in his toque and white apron stained with the blood of young lamb.

They sought only to arrive at an estimate of the situation, the subterranean as well as events in front of their own eyes. The ground shifted as they watched, each day a discrete unit unconnected with what had gone before or what would come later. Far from giving a sense of possibility, the fitful days seemed accidental and baffling, somehow perverse. Parade was the same person. The world was the same world, yet unfamiliar day to day as if each milky sunrise brought forth a new narrator with a fresh tale to tell and a special way of telling it. Naturally some narrators were less skilled than others, hence the tortuous path to an agreed-upon estimate of the situation. And that was what the authorities in Washington demanded and would have. Washington sought a novel angle of vision, a way of looking at the facts that eliminated utterly the bias of the observer. The idea was to quantify progress in such a way that no one could dispute it. What must be done? Where do we stand in this war? How tight do we draw the tourniquet? Not simple questions at all. Perhaps not even the right questions. But their world turned on the answers.

In that general spirit Sydney Parade went in search of Claude and Dede Armand.

No one knew the precise location of the Armands' plantation. It was not marked. The Americans said it was in the vicinity of Xuan Loc town, either north or south off Highway 1. However, it was reckless to drive too far north of town, where the government's writ did not run; south was the better bet because the road was secure, at least in daylight when the militia's guard-posts were occupied. Sydney enlisted Mai's aid, but she turned up nothing. At the café he received only puzzled stares, except for Cao, who said he was unable to help.

None of the village elders had the vaguest idea of any rubber plantation under the supervision of a Monsieur Armand. That name was entirely unfamiliar. Of course SIPH and Michelin and the other rubber companies had vast holdings from the century before, from Xuan Loc south to Vung Tao on the sea. SIPH alone had eighteen thousand hectares under cultivation. But always there had been a manager in charge of the whole. He lived in Cholon and was habitually unavailable, often traveling in Malaya and Cambodia. Individual managers had responsibility for their own fields but, alas, they were uncommunicative. They only wished to keep to themselves, for the good of the production.

The local prefecture was no help either, for taxes and general oversight were the responsibility of the ministry in Bien Hoa, well known for its secretiveness and hostility to any sort of inquiry. Each plantation was its own authority, sufficient unto itself. The government had no reason to interfere. The planters were good citizens, and the rubber industry the keystone of the district's economy.

Why do you wish to see this Monsieur Armand? the priest asked.

His wife is American, Sydney said. And I bring greetings from his family in France. I would be grateful for any assistance. Perhaps if I gave you a note, you could pass it on when you see him.

I have never met him, the priest said.

They were sitting in the front pew of his church, Father Nguyen looking old and worn out, his withdrawn eyes and shaved head giving him the aspect of a Buddhist venerable rather than a Catholic priest. He wore a black short-sleeved shirt and absently fingered the small ivory cross that hung from his neck on a silver chain. His English was slow and precise, his voice hesitant; but that could be the strain of violating the Ninth Commandment. This priest was no stranger to false witness.

Yet Monsieur Armand has lived here for years, Sydney said.

I did not know his wife was American, the priest said.

An American from Chicago, Sydney said, adding a smile.

Chicago? the priest said, shaking his head. His expression was bemused, as if he suddenly had had a vision of the Wrigley building or the stockyards. He said, How do you suppose she found her way from Chicago to Xuan Loc? It's the other side of the world, Chicago. Life must be very strange for her now, so many of her compatriots in Vietnam. And in uniform.

They did not attend mass, then?

I am sure they have not, the priest said. He looked vaguely scandalized. He thought a moment, then continued, Surely I would have seen them, a Frenchman and an American woman from Chicago. They would be conspicuous, no one could miss them. They would be noticeable, yes?

One would think, Sydney said. He let his eyes wander over the interior of the church, the threadbare carpet and the chipped feet of the plaster Jesus on the cross behind the altar. One of the windows in the choir was broken and here and there the roof sagged.

Your roof needs repair, Sydney said.

Yes, the rains last year damaged it badly.

Not war damage?

No, the priest said. Xuan Loc is peaceful.

I would be honored if you would allow me to have the roof fixed, Sydney said. Perhaps work could begin as early as — next week. It's only a matter of scheduling one of the construction battalions. Major Buszcynski would be only too happy to help. He's a fine craftsman and his men work quickly.

Sydney waited while the priest thought. He rubbed the ivory cross between his thumb and forefinger as he scrutinized the ceiling, the wood flaking, infected with dry rot. The entire structure was unsafe, had been for years, a fact he had repeatedly warned the diocese about, but the archbishop had other uses for church funds. Now this American walked in and offered one of his battalions — next week! Of course there was risk, a troop of foreign soldiers occupying the church. Repairs would take time. Inquiries would be made, and if his answers were not correct, trouble would follow. Still, if he refused and the archbishop found out —

Yes, the priest said at last. It's very kind of you. Perhaps you know someone who can fix our organ.

Alas, Sydney said. But I'll inquire.

Thank you, the priest said.

My pleasure, Father. I will call on you next week.

I am always here, the priest said. Somewhere behind them a door opened and closed.

In the meantime, I will continue to search for Monsieur and Madame Armand. I know he is eager for news of his family. And she might enjoy speaking with a compatriot. And if by chance you should discover the precise location of the house, perhaps you would be good enough to let me know. In confidence, of course.

The priest smiled distantly, rising to shake hands with Sydney. Then an elderly woman was at his elbow. She was obviously distraught. She took his hand in both of hers and whispered a few words in rapid Vietnamese. The priest stepped back, alarmed. The woman moved closer to him and spoke again, motioning urgently with her hands and beginning to wail. The priest put his arm around her and, facing the altar, genuflected. They remained a moment, heads bowed. Then he took her arm and they hurried off together, leaving Sydney alone near the altar.

At the side door the priest paused and looked back.

There has been a shooting in the market, he said, and was gone.

*

The market was on the edge of town, a sprawl of low wooden stalls. There were no American vehicles, no ambulance nor any sign of military activity. Acrid smoke from cooking fires hung in the hot woolen air, merciless at noontime. Water buffalo stood motionless in the marshy field next to the market while tree sparrows and small woodpeckers flitted here and there. Vultures swung in lazy circles overhead. When Sydney arrived in the Scout he was aware at once of the vacancy and the silence and the nonchalance of the women behind the long tables laden with foodstuffs and clothing; their expressions were unreadable. The market was usually crowded at midday but now it seemed forlorn. The police the Americans called White Mice for their milky cotton uniforms appeared to be in charge. They were standing in a circle with their hands on their leather holsters chatting among themselves. One of them saluted when Sydney approached, then waved listlessly in the direction of the interior stalls. He said there had been shooting and people injured. He did not know how many injured, or who did the shooting, or why. He and his squad had arrived after the fact and no one seemed to know exactly what had happened. Those responsible had disappeared.

A local matter, he said. A feud between families, a girl in trouble, an unpaid debt, this was common in the countryside —

VC, Sydney said.

Not VC, the mouse said, shaking his head vigorously. This was not a political matter but something personal. There were no VC in Tay Thanh. VC were not involved.

American soldiers, Sydney began.

This is a Vietnamese affair, the mouse said. American soldiers do not have jurisdiction here.

Where is Father Nguyen? Sydney asked.

I have not seen him, the mouse replied.

Are there doctors here?

They are en route, the mouse said, shifting his eyes in such a way that caused Sydney to doubt the information.

He turned and walked off between the stalls of clothing, straw mats, cheap wristwatches, coconuts, live chickens, pots of pho, and contraband from the American PX. He was calculating the distance from the market to the army clinic at the firebase south of Tay Thanh, a half hour or more. A small crowd had gathered at the back of the market. There were many more women than men, their voices high in the leaden atmosphere. Sydney walked slowly and with caution because he was not armed and did not know what to expect. He had no confidence in the White Mice, who were surely lying about the VC; the commissars were involved in every aspect of the market's operation. He moved to the edges of the gathering and gently pushed people aside, very conscious now of his size and awkwardness, a round-eyed foreigner in their midst. He was unwelcome.

A Vietnamese woman in filthy pajamas was bending over one of the injured. She was holding his hand and staring dully at his ribs, the bones exposed through torn flesh. The ribs were white as ivory. The young man's eyelids fluttered as he whispered something to the woman. Sweat jumped to his forehead as he spoke and still no one moved to bandage the wound or otherwise offer succor. The wounded man was dying by inches in front of their eyes, already entering the shadow realm; and no doubt these spectators recognized the privacy of the situation because now they began to withdraw, leaving the wounded man and the woman attending him in a specific zone of intimacy.

Sydney had never watched a human being die. This one let go of things with appalling patience, his spirit struggling, then relaxing, then struggling again until the tendons in his neck pulled taut like ropes. His skin had a glassy sheen. All the while he was whispering to the woman as she gripped his hand, her palm pressing his knuckles. When at last she eased her grip, he nodded. Palm to palm she pushed his hand back as if they were arm-wrestling in pantomime. His spirit ceased to struggle. She dropped his hand on his chest and his eyelids ceased to flutter. Ebb tide, Sydney thought, the instant when the ocean's motion was suspended, the shoals exposed, dead low water awaiting a fresh surge. The wounded man stared straight ahead and died with one last word on his lips, though Sydney had no idea what it meant. The body seemed to rise and then it fell back. The woman got slowly to her feet and vanished between the stalls. Sydney stepped back and turned away, suddenly ashamed for his useless witness.

Then a small boy was tugging at his shirt.

You come, you come.

One more sight to see. They began to walk together around the deserted perimeter of the market. The White Mice appeared to have departed but the vultures still swung in the heavy air above the forest. The ground was soft underfoot. Bits of paper and cloth were scattered about, evidence of disorder and flight. The boy indicated one of the stalls, larger than the others. When he put his hand out for money, Sydney handed him some piasters and told him to go away. Then he stepped into the stall where half a dozen Vietnamese men were gathered in the shadows arguing. They looked at him incuriously. One of the men had a carbine slung over his shoulder. No one seemed to be in charge. On a pallet in the rear a woman lay groaning but when the man with the carbine attempted to touch her, she moved his hand away, complaining weakly in Vietnamese. He bent to look into her eyes, murmuring and shaking his head. She did not reply, and Sydney noticed her foot twitching. The Vietnamese shrugged and rejoined the incomprehensible argument; and abruptly the men began to laugh, a kind of mirthless giggle.

They reminded Sydney of adolescent boys in a locker room,

taunting one another before they turned on the outsider. The carbine was the rolled-up towel. One of them nudged the woman with his toe but this time she lay still and did not respond. He and his friends moved back into the shadows and resumed their argument. They were shoving each other and talking at once. Violence gathered decibel by decibel. The woman said something in Vietnamese, her words soft and hesitant. She was asking for something but the men paid no attention to her. Whatever she wanted, she would have to wait for it. The one with the carbine was face to face with a black-eyed teenager with a little feathery goatee and a black beret, the goatee doing most of the talking, his hands moving in agitated arcs.

Sydney stepped forward into the interior of the stall. Along the sides he saw tins of tomatoes wrapped in ammunition bandoliers. There were jerry cans of — he supposed they were filled with water. On the edges of his vision he saw the small boy peeking around the corner of the stall, his eyes wide with — perhaps they were wide with anticipation, perhaps something else.

What happened here today? Sydney asked, and at his voice, loud in the closeness of the stall, the woman seemed to flinch.

The one with the carbine answered in Vietnamese, a long, unpleasant sentence, apparently an explanation of some kind. He waved his weapon threateningly. One of his friends seemed to object but was quickly silenced. Then the one with the goatee stepped forward, looking closely at Sydney, at his face and his clothes, his shoes.

Che gha, he said, followed by a long line of syllables. And again, Che gha, che che che. And finally, American?

When Sydney said yes — he answered softly, as if he were in a classroom and did not want to call attention to himself — Goatee broke into an approximation of a smile and turned to his friends with a nonchalant movement of his fingers that said, plainly, See? I'm right. But the one with the carbine was not convinced.

Che gha, Goatee said again.

And from her pallet at the rear of the stall, the woman said in an infinitely weary drawl, The idiot's asking if you ever met Che Guevara. He thinks that since you're an American and Che's an American you might have met, perhaps at one of the demonstrations at the university. The University of Havana at Miami. He knows that Che is a revolutionary hero in America and speaks often at university rallies and in Washington. He knows you would be sympathetic because you're wearing blue jeans and your hair's over your ears. Perhaps you've heard Che and shaken his hand. And if so, he is wondering what Che is like to meet. And shake hands with.

Goatee listened to the woman with evident satisfaction.

Sydney said, Only once, when he addressed the joint session of Congress.

The woman said, Don't be a fool. I will not translate that.

What should I say?

That you have not had the honor. Che is very important to this boy. Do you understand? Che is a god to him.

I can pretend I met Fidel, Sydney said carelessly, trying to enter into the spirit of the occasion.

He doesn't know who Fidel is. He knows Che.

He's probably heard about the women, Sydney said. Che's a true Latin lover. Girls love the beret and the machine gun and the cigar. When she did not respond, he added, What will get them out of here? So that I can get you to the hospital.

She said a few words to Goatee, smiling as she said them. When she finished she was breathing heavily but Goatee was nodding, apparently satisfied, motioning Sydney forward. There was blood on her clothing but she had ceased to heave and lay now with her face turned to the wall.

Sydney said, How are you injured?

I am not injured, she said. She gave a long sigh and added, as if by afterthought, I am having a miscarriage.

When he approached, she shuddered. The one with the carbine turned to his friends and grunted something, gesturing at the woman. Sydney saw then that she was greatly pregnant. He touched the canteen at his belt and wondered if it was safe to give her water. He knew it was necessary to get her to the army clinic but did not want to leave her alone with these Vietnamese. He heard movement behind him and then silence. When he turned, he saw that the stall was empty. He watched the men hurry across the field, the one with the carbine in the lead, Goatee close behind. The small boy trotted after them. They entered the forest in single file and vanished. He was alone in the stall with the woman, who stirred again, groaning and holding her stomach with both hands. He wondered suddenly about her husband.

He unhooked the canteen from his belt, having difficulty because his hands were shaking. He had not been frightened while they were there, but he was now that they had gone. He was undone the way anyone is after a near miss. He waited a moment to allow things to settle. Voices came to him from outside the stall, the market resuming its natural life. He supposed he had taken courage from the woman, who had spoken sharply to them, giving nothing away but not allowing them any liberties, either. There was some familiarity in her manner and now he remembered the sly smile that accompanied her words to Goatee, a smile that suggested complicity, even affection. She was injured but stubborn and unafraid, contemptuous almost.

He said, I have water here.

She muttered something he could not hear.

She said, Can you help me?

He said, The army clinic in Tay Thanh —

His voice sounded strange, even to himself. She had flinched when she heard it moments before, but seemed calm enough now. He noticed the thin gold chains around her swollen ankles and the gold crucifix at her throat. He wished the priest were there with him. When she moved to look at him, he wet her lips with water. Her eyes were filled with mistrust as she stared at him, moving with difficulty, rising painfully from the pallet. She held her stomach with both hands and stood swaying. When he put his arm around her shoulder she gasped as if all breath had been torn from her lungs, then murmured something through clenched teeth. She said, Slowly please.

Sydney said, Where is your husband, Mrs. Armand?

She said, Haven't you caused enough trouble?

Ten minutes later he returned in the Scout. A crowd had gathered in front of the stall. Two peasant women assisted Dede Armand into the car, laying a blanket so that she could lie down on the cramped rear seat. She was explaining something to the women, who nodded reassuringly. From her pocket she extracted a pencil and paper and wrote a number, her fingers unsteady on the page. She offered the women money but they politely waved it away. She said something that made them smile, then fell back on the seat and closed her eyes, her hands crossed on her belly. Her dress was stiff with blood. She moved then from shadow into sunlight, raising her chin defiantly — and he remembered the woman in the photograph, her long neck and arched upper lip, her freckles and almond eyes, gazing at her husband with the most open affection. She was not at ease but she was very pretty, even in extremis.

Sydney steered cautiously around the perimeter of the market, the Scout laboring in four-wheel drive. When he drove over ruts in the field he heard her sharp intake of breath. But she did not cry out and did not speak at all until they were out of the field and well along the highway heading to Tay Thanh.

Not your American clinic, she said at last.

It's close, he said. It's a good clinic, really, our own doctors and a full pharmacy and operating room —

No, she said firmly. She needed to go to Saigon and named a private hospital. She gave the street, ninety minutes' driving time if he maintained good speed. She could hold on for ninety minutes, more if necessary. The worst was over now. She was no longer bleeding as she had been and the pain was not so bad. It was tolerable. But God, she said, it was very bad in the market. She woke up feeling queasy. She was stupid to have gone to the market. My own fault, she said. Not that it makes much difference now.

She was beginning to ramble, and he decided that if she fainted he would take her to the clinic in Tay Thanh whether she liked it or not.

My doctor is there, she said. He knows me. He will do what he has to do. Anyway, I trust him. It's bad to go into something like this with a stranger you don't know or trust. He's a friend of my husband's. They used to play tennis together.

Try to rest, Sydney said.

I'm resting, she said.

I mean sleep.

It's all a matter of faith in any case. Her voice broke then and she murmured something under her breath, evidently a prayer for she was holding the crucifix next to her cheek. She said, Are you religious?

He said, No.

I wasn't until I came here.

He smiled into the rear-view mirror. No atheists in the fox-holes?

When I became pregnant, she said.

I'm sorry, he said.

She was quiet a moment, staring out the window at a pagoda. She said, There were plenty in Winnetka.

What did they believe in Winnetka?

She shrugged, still looking out the window. They believe there is safety in numbers. The higher the number, the safer it is.

Money, he said.

Not only money, she replied.

I know about Winnetka. I grew up in Darien.

There was a country club in Darien.

Several, he said. But the one you mean is the Abenaki Club.

Yes, that's it. I used to date a man in Darien. Todd. We'd go to the Saturday night dances. They called them supper dances. Todd used to say, God, it's nice at the Abenaki Club. And it was, too.

Probably we bumped into each other.

Probably we did, she said. They were sort of twin cities, Darien and Winnetka.

I would have said, Excuse me for stepping on your foot. And you would have said, That's all right. And then you would have turned to Todd and whispered, Who's the oaf? And Todd would have said, That's Sydney Parade. Stay away from Sydney. Sydney's bad news. God, it's nice at the Abenaki Club when Sydney's not around. His name was Todd Blanksomething. Blankenwhip, Blankenwheel.

She said, I've forgotten.

We had a fight when we were teenagers.

Keep your eyes on the road.

And I know what he believes in. He believes that a seven iron gets you from tee to green on the short par three.

She closed her eyes, still holding the crucifix. A column of Vietnamese soldiers was sprawled along the side of the road, taking a siesta. Their weapons were spilled carelessly around them. Substitute golf bags for weapons and the scene was reminiscent of the caddy shop at Abenaki. Sydney slowed, concentrating on his driving. The road was thick with local traffic.

I don't know Saigon, he said at last. I mean the streets.

I know it, she said, her voice strong again. She raised herself on one elbow, looking around at the carts and animals that clogged the road. She described the approach into the city, street names that meant nothing to him. Then she described the hospital, small but efficient and well equipped. French doctors were in charge. The hospital was a few blocks from the Continental Palace Hotel and its world-famous terrace where everyone gathered after work for drinks and intrigue. The hotel was a landmark, sort of like the Paris Ritz. Everyone stayed there.

You'll have to direct me, Sydney said. And then he added, You're making a mistake, this French hospital.

Not a mistake, she said.

American medicine, he began.

Is no better or worse than French medicine. It's all the same medicine. There's nothing that can be done anyhow. The baby is dead. After a pause she repeated herself, The baby is dead. And I do not know why that should be.

Where is your husband?

Claude will be there, she replied quickly. The women at the market will telephone him and he will know where to go. She was silent a moment. He could hear her breathing, shifting position, pulling the blanket more tightly around her. I hope he is there. I cannot bear this alone.

Sydney attended to his driving. The road had cleared and he was able to accelerate. In the distance he saw the road that would have taken them to the army clinic. The wise move would be to take her there whether she wanted to go or not. But she was very determined, and her husband would be on his way to Saigon.

You almost got us killed back there, she said. Those boys were nervous. Someone told them a round-eye in blue jeans was in the market and they thought you were Claude, even though Claude has never worn blue jeans in his life. Then, when it was obvious you weren't Claude, they didn't know what to do. They didn't know who you were. They have an idea that the American people support their war. Movie stars do. So there was that interval of — self-criticism. That's what they do when they don't know what to do, criticize themselves in order to find the true path, that is, act correctly. In the end they decided that you were not against them.

Sydney watched her in the rear-view mirror. The moment she had turned toward him in the stall he had recognized her. But she looked nothing like her photograph now, her face drawn and yellowish in the midday light.

She said, They have their own discipline. You talked too much and they did not like your tone of voice. But you did not challenge them directly, and that was wise. So thanks for that and for not arguing too much now.

What were they doing in the market?

The usual, she said. They argued with the merchants. One thing led to another. They're just peasant boys, really, far from home. They were hungry and demanded rations and money. Someone fired a weapon, I don't know who. You know how these things are. My bad luck that I had come in off my stake for a Coke. They were there, ordering everyone around. So there was shooting and one of them was killed. And the wife of one of the merchants. Everyone began to run and I was knocked down and began to bleed. Gosh, it hurts.

My clinic is only a few minutes away.

Don't start that again, she said. Don't be tiresome.

I'm worried about you, he said.

Keep driving, she replied.

He was making what speed he could, using the horn, passing rickshaws and motocyclos. But traffic was heavy again and now he saw an American military convoy ahead; and just then he passed the road to the clinic.

He said, So they were VC, back there.

Local cadre, she said. Harmless.

Harmless?

Usually harmless. Someone decided to challenge them, and that's always a mistake. Almost always.

And they knew you and your husband?

She did not reply to that. He watched her raise her eyebrows as one does at a slow-witted or naïve remark. He pulled to the side of the road to allow the convoy to pass, four army trucks with jeep escorts fore and aft. The jeeps were mounted with machine guns, the guns manned by GIs in flak jackets and steel pots. They waved and he waved back. The convoy was traveling much too fast for the condition of the road but that was not his affair. When they were past he started up again, the Scout bucking now in the uneven road. They were almost at Tay Thanh.

They drove in silence for a time and then she said, I haven't thought about the Abenaki in years. They always had pretty flowers for the dances, and lights in the maple trees.

They still do.

Roses and chrysanthemums.

I don't remember the species, Sydney said.

I was there once or twice in the summer, making the rounds the year I came out. My roommate and I had our own dances in Winnetka and then we went to Grosse Pointe and Rye and ended up in Darien and Westport. That was the summer of 'fifty-three, all those country clubs before I went off to Smith. I remember dancing outside at Abenaki. You could smell the flowers and the mown grass of the golf course. People would wander onto the fairway with their drinks. Wasn't there a famous occasion when two of them were found sound asleep in a sand trap the next morning? It was a scandal because they were married but not to each other. Probably every club has its own morning-after sand-trap story, not only Abenaki. They were lying in the sand trap with empty glasses, quartered limes in the sand . . . She had begun to talk rapidly, her voice losing strength and focus, trailing away.

I'm better now, she said after a moment.

It helps me to talk. Was I making any sense? Tell me when I stop making sense.

Perfect sense, he said. What happened after the sand trap?

She said, What are you doing in South Vietnam, Sydney Parade?

I run one of the aid programs.

Is that what Llewellyn's outfit does?

That and other things, Sydney said.

I know who you are. I know who you work for. You're a brass band in Tay Thanh, making your inquiries about Claude and me. No, I mean why here instead of Latin America or Africa or other places where Americans go to spread the word. What encouraged you to come *here?* Did you have a marital breakup? So many do. They come here to get away from the missus and the children underfoot. They come here like they used to come to Havana. The girls are cheap and the whiskey's cheap, too. It's hot. And it's better than Havana because your army's here to protect you and you don't have to worry about courts of law, like that dreadful character who ran things in Tay Thanh, Dacy. They were ready to kill him. They would have if he hadn't wised up and gotten out of the district. Claude says he's holed up somewhere in Saigon with a teenage whore. If you're in touch with him, you'd be doing him a favor to tell him to go back to America. Be doing us a favor, too, not to mention the Vietnamese. Where do you get them from, Sydney Parade? Where do you *find* people like Dacy? Or do you think South Vietnam's like Australia a hundred years ago, a place to dump your incorrigibles.

She hesitated, trembling, her hand on her forehead.

She said, Am I still making sense?

I suppose you are, he said.

Because I need to rest for a while. Let me know when we pass the airport and I will direct you from there. Better hurry. Her voice wavered as a fresh spasm rippled through her body. But please if you could watch out for the potholes.

Assimilate or Disperse

FIFTEEN MINUTES from Tan Son Nhut she asked if she could have some water from his canteen. He passed it back and she drank a few sips while she raised herself to look into the rearview mirror. God, she whispered. I look a mess. Poor Claude, only last evening talking about the unpredictability of the revolution and how we would have to be more careful. Her voice wandered, as if her thoughts were blown off course by errant winds.

The day had begun so well, she said. A café crème and a brioche on the verandah, listening to short-wave BBC. Do you listen to the BBC, Sydney Parade? You should. The news is reliable. And most of it isn't from here.

I'll remember, he said.

Then she had taken her binoculars and field guide, *Les Oiseaux de l'Indochine Française,* and staked out the grove of firs at the western edge of the plantation, enjoying the company of the birds and a trillion murmuring insects. The forest was dark even at midday, and a patrol had passed within a hundred meters of where she stood. They moved gracefully and quietly with a rhythm like dancers. And at once she saw a fire-backed pheasant and a red junglefowl, all in the space of fifteen minutes.

A wonderful morning, she said.

It was so rare to see them together. The point of bird-watching was to discover disparate species in the same area, and when you did it was cause for rejoicing. There were the normal wood-peckers and sparrows but she had not expected the junglefowl and the fire-backed pheasant — to be absolutely official about its identity, "Diard's Fire-Backed Pheasant, *Lophura diardi* (Bonaparte)." Not the emperor, surely, but a relative. It would be hard for the emperor to keep track of birds with all those corpses on his hands. Birds would not *count,* would they? On the other hand, the emperor was a hunter and the bright red face of the fire-backed pheasant would attract him, no? Probably it was named in his honor after one of the great bloody victories, Austerlitz or Jena; the bright red face would remind the ornithologist of Austrian blood, or the feather in the emperor's cap.

Sydney said, You were bird-watching?

Of course, she said. You have no idea how many species there are on the plantation, Sydney. Vietnam is an aviary. You could spend your entire life cataloging the birds in *Les Oiseaux de l'Indochine Française* and never see them all, until one day you would find a species that had never been recorded and then you could name it after someone, Gray-faced Buzzard (Dacy). She laughed hollowly and then fell silent, idly watching the motorcycles and taxis, stalled now in the traffic jam around the airport. Helicopters thumped overhead, the sound blending with the roar of commercial jets. The air was thick with the stench of kerosene.

He said, Isn't it dangerous?

Why should it be?

As you said, "the revolution."

They're not interested in birds or the people who watch them.

She leaned forward, resting her chin on the seat back. She said, Go straight here until you see the cathedral, then turn left.

If I see a military jeep, I can get us an escort.

No escorts, she said.

Sydney drove through a high iron gate into a courtyard bounded by low stucco buildings with louvered windows open to the air. Large-waisted plane trees shaded the courtyard from the afternoon sun. Among gnarled stone sculptures of the Cham, patients in blue pajamas sat in twos and threes on wooden benches attended by nurses who stood apart chatting among themselves. The hospital had its own specific ambiance, like that of a campus or religious retreat far from any commercial or civil authority. When Sydney turned off the Scout's engine the place was quiet and cool under the huge leaves of the plane trees.

Then two doctors were opening the passenger door and lifting Dede Armand from the back seat, speaking to her calmly in French. Two Vietnamese orderlies stood nearby with a stretcher but she paid no attention to them and broke away from the doctors. With a sharp cry she spilled into the arms of the gumbooted stranger who had come up behind the doctors. He half carried her to the stretcher but she refused to lie down. She was laughing and crying at once, saying she did not want to leave him for the stretcher or for anything else, everything would be fine now that he was here at last. He whispered into her ear and kept whispering as his hands caressed her hair and shoulders, though his eyes were fastened on her bloody dress and the belly beneath it. Finally he picked her up and hurried her into the hospital like a bridegroom crossing the threshold, the doctors giving what assistance they could and the orderlies bringing up the rear, everyone talking now until the French doors slammed and the courtyard was as before, peaceful, with only the vague hum of traffic beyond the stone walls. The patients in blue looked on

from their benches before returning to conversation or their newspapers. Somewhere a radio played American pop from the
armed forces station; and then as Sydney strained to listen he
realized it was not American pop from a radio station but *La
Bohème* from a phonograph.

He took a long swallow of water from the canteen and lit a
cigarette while he strolled the courtyard, admiring the stone figures of the Cham, animal deities. The Cham were a Muslim tribe
that had refused to assimilate. Now there were only a few iso-
lated communities, mostly in central Vietnam. They had held out
for three hundred years, like the American Indians, except the
government did not care where they went or what they did and
offered no sympathy, or employment either. Assimilate or disperse. These sculptures were very old and represented what was
known of Cham culture, at least to Westerners. No doubt the
Cham had their own view of themselves and perhaps the sculp-
ture meant no more to them than golf to a Connecticut squire,
something they did in their spare time as recreation. At one of
the briefing sessions in Washington Sydney had shared notes
with the provincial-representative-to-be in Qui Nhon, who had
announced his intention to make friends with the Cham and
discover what animated them and what they valued, if anything;
and if they had any insights into the progress of the revolution.
They were a subjugated people, after all. The briefer had laughed
and said, Good luck.

How distant all that was, the blackboard and chalk, the maps,
the charts and bar graphs, the briefing books and the lectures of
experts. Nothing in the briefing books about a shooting in the
market at Xuan Loc, a séance with the local VC cadre, and
a ninety-minute drive to a private hospital in Saigon with an
American woman in the rear seat of the Scout, her dress soaked
with blood, haranguing him for a general lack of subtlety and
tact. And that was why, when she heard his Sousa voice in the

stall, she flinched — appalled at the impulsive American official come to violate her neutrality. She was one of those who lived between the lines in South Vietnam, living as if there were no revolution and no reason to choose sides, happy to pursue her bird-watching from a safe haven on her husband's rubber plantation. Forget the revolution and she could have been one of those who fled the big city for rural Connecticut. Simplify.

Sydney watched an elderly monk step through the French doors, his arm in a black sling, an IV hanging from a wheeled steel tree. He moved carefully, favoring the arm and his right leg, awkwardly gripping the tree with his free hand. The other patients looked up and nodded respectfully, offering a palms-together Buddhist greeting. None of them rose to speak to the monk, who acknowledged them with a benign dip of his chin. His saffron robes were brilliant in the monochromes of the courtyard. He made a dignified figure as he shuffled along six inches at a time. Sydney wondered if this monk was the one injured in the bomb attack at the temple a few blocks from the American embassy. A number of religious had been killed or injured including a radical, a monk controversial within his own sect and a danger to the government. Sydney could not remember his name — it was Thich Tien Something, a stubborn opponent of all Vietnamese factions, particularly the government faction. The bomb at the temple was an outrage condemned by the various parties, except the Viet Cong, which did not issue communiqués. Because no one had claimed responsibility, the government was free to denounce the Communists — in the guise of monks more radical even than the old man shuffling along the perimeter of the courtyard, pushing his steel tree. He turned now to look at Sydney, his expression perfectly bland. It would be too much to call it serene. When Sydney nodded, the monk appeared to return the nod and after a moment continued his circumambulation of the stone path beneath the windows of the low buildings, the path guarded by the stone deities of the Cham.

La Bohème ended. Sydney sat comfortably on a bench under a plane tree and lit another cigarette, watching the French doors and wondering how Dede Armand was faring inside. He remembered the threadbare gloom of the New York hospital where his daughter was born, the plastic furniture and the month-old magazines, the waiting room filled with men. Karla was in labor for eight hours, and when he was allowed to see her at last she could only murmur, I've been in a train wreck. The doctors in New York were hurried and irascible, behaving as if they had been somehow inconvenienced by the long labor and delivery. These French doctors seemed sympathetic and capable and Claude Armand very capable. Sydney had never seen a woman drop into a man's arms as Dede had, falling from the highest precipice without fear, knowing she was safe now with her husband, his eyes wide open with relief.

If Claude was horrified at her condition, he betrayed nothing, continuing to whisper into her ear and comfort her with his hands, while she held on. And then he picked her up and carried her into the hospital because the stretcher was too impersonal for a woman with blood on her dress and a child in her belly, the child growing inside her these many months but still now. It was obvious they meant everything to each other. Living between the lines in dangerous circumstances would give them a special connection, like living on a fault line or under a volcano. They could trust no one but themselves; or blame no one but themselves. In Vietnam they were without allies in a milieu overturned by revolution and that was no part of their life together. The war was one thing, the plantation another, as distinct as Darien and Harlem. Sydney remembered that Karla had looked at him that night as she might a stranger, and then she asked him to leave the room, she was so tired. But he stayed, and when she woke up an hour later she was so happy to see him. She made room in the bed so they could hold each other.

He watched the French doors open and Claude Armand step into the sunlight, his hand on his forehead. He took a step and sagged, steadying himself on one of the Cham deities. When he looked up he saw the monk creeping toward him, pushing the IV tree. Claude went at once to the old man and they embraced, the Frenchman towering over the old Vietnamese. His khaki shirt was stained with his wife's blood. They stood talking a moment, Claude explaining something, shaking his head with infinite melancholy. Then he spat a furious sentence in Vietnamese, causing the monk to put a finger to his lips, leaning close now, speaking directly to him in a soft purr. Claude nodded wearily and looked around. When he heard a helicopter's chop-chop he stared at the sky with loathing. There were two of them flying over the hospital, side by side. Claude said another few words to the monk, all the while scuffing the toe of his shoe on the gravel.

He started when he saw Sydney on the bench under the plane tree. He took the monk's free hand with his own and spoke urgently a minute more, nodding his head in Sydney's direction. And then he looked back at the French doors and the darkness within the hospital. No one was visible through the open windows. This seemed to be a moment of indecision for him. Claude stood motionless, then turned and said goodbye to the monk and walked across the gravel to the bench where Sydney sat.

He said, I want to thank you for what you did.

Sydney said, It was nothing. How is she?

You didn't have to do it.

She is an American. Of course I would help her.

The Frenchman looked at him strangely, pursing his lips as if measuring the value of an American soul against a French or Vietnamese soul. He said, She needed to be brought here, where she knows the doctors. Where they have the proper facilities. Where she feels comfortable.

I understand. I offered the army clinic because it was closer, but she insisted.

It would have made no difference, Claude said.

Sydney nodded, afraid now of what he might hear.

The babies were stillborn.

Babies?

Yes, twins. A boy and a girl. Both dead. We had no idea there were two.

And your wife?

He paused before answering, and when he did his voice shook. They're not sure. They think she will be all right but they need to wait before they're sure. It's the way of doctors, isn't it? They always make you wait before they tell you something you don't want to hear. He slowly knocked his fists together while he looked at his muddy gumboots. She's under the anesthetic now.

I know she'll be fine.

There was an ocean of blood, Claude said. He looked sky-ward where two more helicopters were idling. I have never seen so much blood.

She told me that the hospital was excellent. Sydney thought to add, As good as anything in France.

It's an ordinary hospital, Claude said. But she knows the staff. She has confidence in them.

She told me you play tennis with the surgeon.

Claude smiled. She said that? It's true. He's a better doctor than he is a tennis player.

Well, Sydney said. They breed confidence in Chicago. It's one of their natural resources, along with money.

And at that, the Frenchman laughed. She has plenty of the first, not so much of the second. Her family did not care for it that she came to Vietnam with the embassy. And then when she married me . . . He shrugged. Perhaps they had someone picked out for her. Do you suppose that was it?

Probably they thought Vietnam was dangerous. Or they were opposed to the war.

They liked the war, Claude said. They didn't like her in the war. They don't understand what she is doing with her life.

What does she say?

She laughs and says they are her family and are entitled to their opinions. Claude smiled at the monk, who continued to circumambulate the courtyard in six-inch steps.

Who is he? Sydney asked.

Claude replied that he was the monk injured in the explosion at the temple. They had rushed him at once to this hospital because they feared for his life in the Vietnamese hospital, where accidents had been known to occur. The American military hospitals were impractical. He is a bonze with many enemies, Claude said, some known, some not known. He was active in the demonstrations that caused annoyance. So they brought him here, where he would be safe. This hospital — and here the Frenchman paused fractionally — is neutral. It is like Switzerland in Europe. But he is not recovering as rapidly as they had hoped, so they are making arrangements to move him. There are many offers from overseas, eminent surgeons in eminent hospitals. But he thinks that if he leaves Vietnam he will die. Separated from his ancestors, his temple, and his prayer flags he is certain he will perish. They are trying to convince him otherwise.

Sydney was unsure exactly who "they" were — perhaps other members of his sect, perhaps political friends — but he asked no questions. He was surprised that Claude had divulged as much as he had.

I am sure that in America —

Yes, Moscow also. And Paris.

He must be a very important monk.

He is to them, Claude said.

Because he is political?

Because he is troublesome, Claude said. And independent. He organizes strikes. He publishes declarations that the government doesn't like. They try to silence him and he disappears into his temple. And when he believes the time is right, he reappears with his followers or with one of his declarations. Hanoi does not know his intentions so they withhold support, at least they withhold it publicly.

So he's a puzzle, Sydney said.

He is. And they all want a piece of him, Moscow, Washington, and Paris. But he is too shrewd for them. He remains in Vietnam. He represents a third way so he remains in Saigon, because to go abroad would be to declare gratitude to whichever government takes him in. He is stubborn and very sure of himself, though perhaps less stubborn and sure of himself since the bombing. He was badly hurt and not only in his body. In that way he reminds me of my wife, who insists on going places she should not go, her stake in the forest for the birds and the market for her Coca-Cola. I spoke to her about it many times. But as you say, they breed confidence in Chicago. And in Vietnam also.

Claude had been glancing in the direction of the French doors and now he excused himself, he wanted to make a final check with the doctors to see that his wife was resting comfortably. When he returned in thirty minutes he was wearing a fresh shirt.

Sydney proposed a rendezvous at the Continental Palace, with the world-famous terrace where everyone gathered for drinks and intrigue, but Claude Armand said no, the Continental was too crowded. There was too much politics at the Continental, where the walls had ears; the tables and floors, too. The drink would be on him at the Cercle Sportif, where no one ever talked politics. People came to the Cercle Sportif to forget about politics. They could sit in the bar and talk undisturbed because everyone would be at the swimming pool, even your ambassador. They tell me he comes every day for a swim in the afternoon, up and down the pool, six laps, no more. He always drinks a lemonade. Monotonous, don't you think? The ambassador is in the pool and the commanding general is on the tennis courts. Some war, no?

In the event, neither the ambassador nor the general was present. The tennis courts were occupied by athletic Americans in white, gray-haired staff officers from American military headquarters and diplomats from the embassy, sweating hard in the heat. Of course there were Germans and Belgians and Poles and Indians and Australians; but, really, it had become an American club. Budweiser had replaced "33" Export. The high-spirited crowd around the swimming pool was younger, teenage girls in bikinis and their boyfriends in tight trunks, showing off on the high dive or oiling themselves with Coppertone. The air was heavy with chlorine and frangipani. Under the blue canopy near the giant palm at the far end of the pool, four thirtyish women in sundresses played serious bridge. Claude explained that they were the wives of diplomats and journalists; the teenagers were locals, sons and daughters of Saigon merchants, government officials, and army officers. The boys had arranged deferments from the army and spent their days at the Cercle Sportif, dreaming of a visa to America.

Waiters in white shirts and dark trousers moved here and there with trays of lemonade and beer. Watching a waiter approach four teenagers at poolside, offering his tray, bending slightly at the waist with one hand behind his back, Sydney was reminded of afternoons at Abenaki. The boys took their drinks without looking up or pausing in their conversations, and the waiter strolled off to the tinkle of ice cubes and laughter — and it was then that Sydney noticed his frayed shirt and worn shoes, and the soldier leaning against the palm tree, smoking a cigarette and looking at the girls, his rifle slung carelessly over his shoulder, barrel down.

Security, Claude explained.

God, it's nice at the Cercle Sportif, Sydney replied.

And just then a girl in a coal-black bathing suit rose, yawning like a cat, stretching, her arms and heels rising as if she were reaching for a gymnast's high bar. She was lithe and beautifully built and when she stepped to the edge of the pool and dove, she entered the water like a knife, leaving no splash or wake. She swam the length of the pool underwater, undulating like a seal, and rose at the other end with feline languor, mission accomplished.

Yes, it is, Claude said.

Inside the cavernous clubhouse, they were ushered to wicker chairs by a barman who greeted Claude with a surprised smile and a little ironic bow. Apparently they had not seen each other for some time. They chattered in Vietnamese and Sydney knew without being told that the Frenchman was asking about the barman's family, the old people, the wife, the children. The barman shrugged, clucking, a comment Sydney interpreted as "the usual." Then Claude put his hand on the barman's arm and spoke to him softly, and from the shock on his face it was obvious Claude was speaking of his wife and their two dead children. In the end the barman only shook his head.

They were seated in the farthest corner of the room under a ceiling fan that turned with the patience of the second hand on a wristwatch. The barman brought them both a gin and tonic and retreated into the silent interior. They were alone in the quiet and coolness of the huge room. In the distance they could hear the thwack of tennis balls and high-pitched cries from the pool.

Sydney tipped his glass and said, Your wife's health.

Claude said, Yes, thank you, and they clicked glasses. He sat back and stretched his legs, relaxed as if he were in his own living room. With his sunburned complexion, his canvas trousers and gumboots, he looked like any planter in from the fields for a sundowner at the club.

I'm sorry about the babies.

Claude nodded, his face clouded and withdrawn. If you had not stepped in, it might have been much worse.

I thought she was wounded, Sydney said.

No, they wouldn't harm her.

Sydney took that in and decided not to pursue it; but he remembered the boy with the carbine who had nudged Dede Armand with his foot as you might an animal. They sat in companionable silence for a moment, and then he smiled, gesturing around the vacant room, its wicker and dark wood, ceramic ashtrays on the tables. It was as comfortable as a ship's saloon and as private; no way of knowing the time of day or the shape of things over the horizon or whether they were in Saigon or Darien.

So civilized, Sydney said. This must have been the way things were in the forties.

There was a war on then, too.

But Saigon wasn't involved.

Not in the obvious ways, Claude said. The old-timers have some grand stories from the period. Sydney waited for a grand story but Claude was silent. At last he said, Smuggling and the like. And most everyone acquired a taste for opium and gambling, though not at the same time. The Cercle Sportif was at the center of things, everyone came here for drinks and a game of cards or backgammon.

But not anymore, Sydney said.

No, not anymore.

So it's a sort of no man's land.

You might say that.

A neutral zone, Sydney said.

Not a neutral zone.

Of course, Sydney said. The Americans.

Claude smiled blandly and said it had been years since he had been inside the Cercle Sportif, although his wife had been a regular when she worked for the embassy. She came with one particular friend for a swim at the end of the day but things became impossible so she quit coming. When she married him, a resident Frenchman, conversation became awkward. There were always questions, how they lived, how the plantation operated and whether it made a profit, and aren't you frightened out there in the — what did they call it, a strange word? — doonblocks —

Boondocks, Sydney said.

Yes, what are they?

The provinces, Sydney said.

— and she got tired of answering the questions and so did I because the answers were no one's business. They wanted to know her routine, day by day, and she resented it. They wanted her to spy for them. The last time I was here, I had business with the ministry and stopped for a drink on the way back, two Americans introduced themselves as rubber brokers. They wanted to make a deal for my rubber. The price they were offering, I told them I harvested rubber, not platinum, but they said they didn't care. They were interested in my operation and any information of a political nature that I might have. And if I happened to be aware of any military activity in my vicinity, why, the price would be increased. Of course they were people from your intelligence service, one of them my wife's friend. My God, so young. They couldn't have been more than a few years out of university. They wanted to give me ten thousand dollars as a down payment and I said no. And no again to twenty thousand. Then they said they could make things difficult for me and I said fine, go ahead. But I didn't like it. I walked out of the Cercle Sportif that day and haven't been back since. We have all had the same disagreeable experience with the Americans, who think this war is everyone's war and we owe it to you to collaborate, and when we decide not to, we're threatened with unspecified "difficulties," as if you owned the world and we had to pay rent to live in it. We're trying to get the rubber to market, that's all. We don't want anything to do with this other business. So we stay away from the Cercle Sportif. None of us come here anymore.

Sydney said, We?

Claude said, Planters.

How many are you?

Fewer every day. He rose stiffly and spoke to the barman. Then he used the telephone, leaning on the bar with his elbows, talking quietly into the receiver. The sun was lowering now, casting bright shafts of yellow light across the dark floor. There were no more sounds from the pool or the tennis courts but Sydney heard the growl of a jet overhead. Claude continued to talk on the telephone. The barman brought two fresh drinks and a bowl of nuts. On the margins of his vision, Sydney saw a figure in the doorway. He settled back in his chair, watching Rostok step into the sunlight and peer into the room. Rostok saw Claude Armand but paid no attention to him. Sydney, in the deep shadows at the far end of the room, sat motionless, his eyes cast down, willing himself invisibility. You have to remember that ordinary life goes on here, Rostok had said; and that was what this was, a routine drink at the end of the day. Rostok would be no help here, and Claude had had enough surprise for one day. Ros took a last exasperated look around, shading his eyes with the palm of one hand, and then he turned abruptly and left.

She's resting, Claude said when he returned.

Sydney nodded. He watched Rostok march down the path and disappear in the direction of the swimming pool.

They said they would call me if there was any change but you never know with them. They promised to keep a nurse in the room all night.

They know what they're doing, Sydney said.

Do you think so?

He shrugged. He had no idea what they knew or didn't know.

Claude smiled and pointed at the doorway. Who was that?

A friend. Rostok.

You didn't invite him in.

He'd ask for the rent money.

He works for you?

I work for him.

I know who he is, Claude admitted. He's around, here, there, and everywhere. Dede has seen him in the market. And I thank you again.

I like him, Sydney said loyally. But probably this isn't the time to make the introductions.

He's not CIA, is he?

No, he's not. And I'm not either.

Claude looked at his knuckles, nodding, suddenly distracted. When the telephone rang he rose to answer it, but the barman arrived first, spoke a few words, and shook his head. The Frenchman settled back into his chair.

She wasn't due for another six weeks, he said abruptly. Still, he had the nursery all arranged and an amah to help out. My mother sent us some baby things from Comminges. And Dede's friends in America sent books about babies. How to feed the baby. How to rock the cradle. These are strange things to learn from books, no? He paused expectantly, watching the telephone. She was so excited, arranging the nursery. It's a pretty room, the big window gives out onto the garden where Dede's bird feeders are. The deer come to graze and farther out you can see the rubber trees. It's a peaceful spot with southern light all day long, shaded in late afternoon. It's a wonderful place for children.

You were planning to stay on at the plantation, then?

Of course, Claude said. Where else would we go? This war can't last forever. It's impossible. It's not logical. What more can you do that you're not doing? And with everything you've done so far, you're still losing. The Vietnamese are laughing at you.

Sydney sipped his drink, taking his time about it. Claude had the common myopia. He had been in the Far East too long. He did not appreciate the immensity of America, its industry, its restlessness and sprawl, its impatience, its confidence, its anger and its desire. He was not aware that this was only the beginning of the war. All that had gone before was prelude. America was irresistible. This was the twentieth century eye to eye with the fifteenth, the arsenal of the modern world in joust with the bare knuckles of a rural peasantry led by an antique born in the Edwardian Age who had spent his youth making pastry swans for Chef Escoffier in the afternoon and wandering London's gray crabbed streets in the evening, dreaming his exile's dream of revolution. The coming battle would consume all South Vietnam. There would be no sanctuaries, no region immune from it. Claude's American wife would understand this if Claude didn't.

What do you mean, laughing at us?

Something absurd about it, something — and here Claude shrugged futilely.

Listen, Sydney said. He leaned forward and lowered his voice. He described what was on order, the inventory of the struggle to come, four reinforced infantry divisions before the end of next year, another aircraft carrier, as many as four more air wings — and as he recited the data he realized how colorless it was. You had to see the arsenal with your own eyes, the lethal beauty of the ships and the reptilian menace of the aircraft, all but invulnerable to enemies; and then he remembered the VC infantry on their bicycles, rice socks hanging from their shoulders. To witness was to believe. Sydney added that two billion dollars had been appropriated for reconstruction, roads and bridges, ports, airfields, clinics, schools. He told Claude nothing more than had been in the newspapers but Claude seemed surprised at the numbers. Judging from his expression, he suspected that Sydney was pulling them out of the air, American propaganda.

You and your wife don't want to be here, Sydney concluded.

They'll never give up, you know.

They won't have to. There won't be any of them left to go on. No army, no fighters.

You can't do it.

It has to be done, Sydney said with a vehemence that surprised him. We made commitments. We promised to do it. We said we would do it and we will.

It's hard to believe, Claude said.

Believe it. Go away for a few years, and when you come back South Vietnam will look like — California! Vietnamese only wanted what good Americans wanted — a full stomach and domestic tranquillity, an opportunity to go about their affairs unmolested. They were a subtle people whose politics shifted with the tides. They believed in magic and astrological signs. They were fatalistic. They were poised as acrobats, always moving in the direction of the net. But they could not fail to notice the progress made, it was everywhere to see. Indochina was the great test of American character. This had been true in all the other wars and it was true in this one. Anyone who sat on the sidelines would suffer a lifetime of regret, shame was not too strong a word —

Claude was listening intently, waiting for the voice of the Jacobin, the one who swept all reason before him. He waited for the fanatic but what he heard was an earnest imperialist who believed in California. This American was surely right to see the

Vietnamese as aerialists, not that he had ever met one. If he ever did, he would understand that there were no nets in South Vietnam. Yet this was also true. Americans were easy to underestimate. They almost asked for it, begged and pleaded to be underestimated in order that victory, when it came, would be sweeter.

Sydney said, In a few months the war will become general. You and your wife will have to choose sides.

You sound like one of those intelligence people.

It's not a threat. I'm afraid for your safety.

Well, Claude said, and smiled. Stop them bombing my rubber trees, then.

I can do that. I'll need something in return.

There's nothing I can give you.

Information, Sydney said.

Claude thought a moment. The information the Americans needed was in front of their own eyes; but probably they were the sort of people who did not trust what was in plain sight. He said, I can understand about pride, it's like an affair of the heart. But I don't understand why you care so much. What does Vietnam matter to you? Who wants it? Is it your capitalists? The munitions industries? Do you think there's oil here?

Sydney did not think the question worth a reply. He said, This is only the beginning.

We'll see, Claude said. I think you'll be out in a year.

At that, Sydney laughed. No chance.

Claude looked at his watch. You should leave now.

Why?

It's best for you to be in Tay Thanh before dark. The road is dangerous now.

The road is secure, Sydney said confidently. Rostok had seen to that.

Claude rolled his eyes. Some nights it is, and other nights it isn't. Tonight it isn't.

Do you know something I don't know?

Claude waited a moment before answering. I have no specific information, he said. The VC do not inform me of their battle plans. But I have lived here a very long time. After a while you have an instinct for things.

We prefer evidence to instinct, Sydney said.

Do you think you are in a court of law?

Those boys at the market, Sydney began.

Local cadre, Claude said.

You know them?

I see them around. I see policemen, too. I see your army. As I said, I've lived here a long time.

One of them was armed, Sydney said.

They did not harm my wife, did they? This was a statement, not a question. Claude rose and they shook hands. Nor you. They did not harm you. They had every opportunity. You were an unarmed American, yet they allowed you safe passage. Per- haps — and here he made a little gliding motion with his hand — Americans are not so important to the situation. Perhaps you are the tip of the iceberg, with nine-tenths invisible beneath the surface; and it is the nine-tenths that controls.

Sydney did not know what to say to that.

I thank you again for what you did, Claude said. I think you saved my wife's life. I am very grateful. I think you are making a terrible mistake in this war, but that is not my affair. In any case, my wife and I will remain here. We will have more children, and they will grow up on the plantation. I wish you good health, Sydney. And now I must go. I have no information to give you.

Every day now when Sydney woke, he thought of the Armands and heard Claude's voice. "They did not harm my wife . . ." He thought their conversation hallucinatory in its disharmony, the Frenchman refusing to believe what was in front of his eyes. It was the United States that was nine-tenths beneath the surface. But it was also true that in the Cercle Sportif reality took another form and color, that of seductive nostalgia. The reassuring bartender, the gin and tonic with its quartered lime, the sounds from the pool and the tennis courts. The war was far away. War's reminder was mechanical, the chug of helicopter gunships and the acrobatics of jet fighters, or the bicycle caravan on the Tay Thanh road.

A week later Sydney called the hospital to ask after Dede Armand, but whoever answered the phone claimed to speak no English and hung up. The day after that he asked Pablo Gutterman to inquire, using his private sources, and Pablo reported back that she had been discharged, healthy but weak. She had gone home to the plantation. Her husband had taken her home. Why do you want to know? I had a tip, Sydney said vaguely.

"I have no information to give you." Sydney took Rostok aside to explain the encounter and its unsatisfactory conclusion; he said nothing about the Cercle Sportif. He described Claude Armand, muscular, rangy, dressed in a khaki shirt, canvas trousers, and gumboots. He was often bemused. He had the looks and bearing of a colonial planter, meaning he walked into rooms as if he owned them, friendly with the help. An attractive man, Sydney said. I was drawn to him and tried to give him what advice I could, none of which he accepted; and he did not accept an offer to collaborate, either. He was well spoken with excellent English and fluent Vietnamese, droll when he wanted to be.

No question he knows things, Sydney said.

But whatever they are, he's not telling.

He evidently loves his wife very much and is not too shy to say so; not too shy to describe the nursery they had furnished and the life he envisioned with his children. He believed he could live between the lines as he always had, and if his twins had lived, they would be between the lines also. The war was a nuisance that would go away sooner rather than later.

I give you Americans a year, he'd said.

But he lives in a different Vietnam than we do, Sydney went on. His Vietnam is governed by his trees and by the seasons, weeding and plowing in April and May, planting in June and July, tapping the latex during the dry season. I have no idea how many trees he has, nor how many laborers. I was told that it takes one laborer to tend one hundred and fifty trees, so if we discover the number of trees we'll know his workforce. Sydney watched Rostok write a few words in the notebook he always had with him.

I don't know what good that will do us, Sydney said. And I have no idea of the precise location of the plantation.

We probably ought to leave them alone, he added.

Unless we can persuade his wife to see the plain light of day.

Really, I doubt if they can help us. They don't know much. They know less than they think they do, Ros.

So why not stop bombing his rubber trees?

But Rostok did not think that would be practical.

Finally, and with reluctance, Sydney described the scene in the market, Dede Armand in pain, the young VC with his carbine, the boys arguing — and when he looked up they were already across the field and disappearing into the forest. Armand's wife did not seem frightened, only in pain and nervous about the American clinic. She insisted on the hospital in Saigon. She issued her instructions and took it for granted that she would be obeyed. She behaved like a colonial, too.

But Claude knew the VC. He said they were local boys, harmless. He spoke of them as if they were friends, or anyway not enemies. I confess I don't know what to make of the Armands.

They are mediocre people, Rostok said.

Big Dumb Blond

*A*T TEN they gathered around the oval mahogany table in the former dining room of the whitewashed villa in the near suburbs of Saigon, an hour's drive from Sydney's house in Tay Thanh. A patchy lawn surrounded the house and a low wall surrounded the lawn. Bougainvillea grew at the base of the wall. Gardeners tended the bougainvillea when they weren't leaning on the wall, gossiping and looking into Nguyen Phan Street at the traffic, or feeding mice to Tom J., the indolent python in the wire cage on the rear lawn. At lunchtime the gardeners collected under the giant plane tree next to the front gate, the tree a souvenir of one of the gallant French admirals who had arrived with the fleet in the 1850s, and stayed on for a time as proconsul. He had caused the tree to be brought from a grove at his country house in Normandy. He wanted something to remind him of home.

The men around the table rarely looked out the windows, thrown open to the air and protected by curvy wrought-iron bars. They were absorbed in the documents in front of them, statistics concerning rice deliveries, vaccinations, dikes, schools, roads and bridges, along with after-action reports from the military, intelligence summaries from CAS, embassy appraisals of political conditions in the countryside and, naturally, the press scrapbook from USIA. They had been instructed to read the dispatches carefully, though in practice they rarely did; enough difficulty trying to construct a narrative from the statistics in front of them.

From Washington material arrived by pouch or by cable, important personnel changes in the government and additional rules and regulations owing to congressional action, and always a thick stack of classified requests — "action this day" — from the Pentagon and the White House, inquiries into the most minute business, the status of the market at some forgotten hamlet in Hau Nghia province or the condition of the road network in the Camau mangrove swamp or the children's brass band at Ban Me Thuot, the instruments donated by the Junior League of Cleveland. Did they get their saxophones? Many of these requests came to Llewellyn Group because Rostok was known to have a quick reaction time; request today, answer tomorrow. Added together, all these statistics were intended to give a reliable estimate of the situation. How went yesterday's struggle for the hearts and minds of the population? Are we better off today than we were yesterday? Fresh proposals, please.

Always among the cables were the itineraries of the many visitors, assistant secretaries of this and that, congressional delegations, think-tank bigwigs, industry supremos, and the academic specialists, linguists, economists, sociologists, military historians, agronomists, nutritionists, and newspaper publishers eager to see things themselves, firsthand. They all had to be cared for, fed and watered, billeted comfortably in a room with air conditioning. They had to be shown the world-famous terrace of the Continental Palace Hotel and ferried to a hamlet and briefed aboard the colonel's personal helicopter. They had to be given lunch at Cheap Charlie's and dinner at the Arc en Ciel; and there were other entertainments as well, but those had to be requested specifically.

Had one of the team thought to look up, daydreaming in the drowsy Saigon heat, he would see only an ordinary street beyond the low wall that surrounded the villa, and the life on the street. Of course they were laughed at, condescended to, and derided by those on the frontier of the war, the soldiers, intelligence agents, and journalists. Llewellyns were the boys in the green eyeshades, bean counters, master bureaucrats and movers of paper from IN box to OUT box or the reverse, depending on the seriousness of the document, meaning its weight. The more musclebound it was, the less likely to languish in the IN box. If asked, the members of the Group would have said they believed in the principles of the Enlightenment, a thirst for knowledge, a reverence for science, and a conviction in the perfectability of societies, even primitive societies with scant experience of democratic government. With knowledge came mastery. The salient question was simple: Was there time enough to gain an accurate estimate of the situation, and then to bring it into line, and then to *act*. And finally to convince the newspapers and the networks that they had turned the corner at last. So it was inevitable that the indolent python in the wire cage on the rear lawn was named Tom J.

They were often irreverent.

Fuck the hearts and minds of the people, Pablo Gutterman said. We require the hearts and minds of the *New York Times*.

They were eight, sometimes ten around the heavy table, everyone dressed monotonously in short-sleeved white shirts and white cotton trousers and loafers except for Sydney Parade, who wore worn blue jeans and a Lacoste tennis shirt. Rostok presided, and in his absence his deputy Blind Pablo Gutterman, whose eyes were so weak he often used a magnifying glass to inspect the small type of the cable traffic; and on bad mornings he had someone read them to him. With his slouch, his bad eyes, and his Panama hat, Pablo looked like a dissipated academic exile, someone who had unaccountably washed up in Southeast Asia after some low campus scandal.

The former dining room was enormous, a rectangle with a high ceiling and powder-blue walls, wainscotting where the walls met the floor. Rostok insisted on retaining the admiral's etchings of French provincial life — a Romanesque church at dusk, vaches grazing in a symmetrical field — that decorated the walls; to remind everyone of those who had gone before, he said. Between the etchings were photographs of the President, the ambassador, and the commanding general of American forces, these men supervising the room with severe expressions. Magenta tiles on the floor sweated in the heat and at some point each morning someone stepped wearily to the window and closed the blinds against the sun's desiccating rays. Everyone smoked cigarettes except Pablo Gutterman, who smoked a pipe. Two electric fans moved the air about but by midmorning the atmosphere was torpid, the men frustrated and thinking of lunch.

The room had a history. The admiral passed the villa down to the colonial administrator, and then it was occupied by a succession of civil servants, the last a functionary who attempted to hold things together during the tumultuous postwar era. What his precise function had been, no one knew or would say; something to do with the economy, perhaps tax collection. He was fondly remembered by his many Vietnamese protégés, Monsieur Gosse, strict but fair, always dressed in a white linen suit and a floppy hat, a heavy onyx pen at attention in the breast pocket of his jacket. A little blue stain announced the Mont Blanc's leak. All his jackets had the stain. Monsieur Gosse never arrived at the office before ten and left it promptly at twelve-thirty, to lunch on the terrace of the Continental Palace Hotel. If there was a race meeting at the track in Cholon, he attended it, always returning at six P.M. after the heat had begun to dissipate. He was always fresh, having taken a slow swim at the Cercle Sportif following the races and a citron pressé following the swim. Monsieur Gosse was careful to pace himself to the wretched climate, even at the racetrack.

The Vietnamese had bought the villa from the French authorities after the colonial administration collapsed following the debacle at Dien Bien Phu. And after a suitable interval the Americans had leased it from the Vietnamese, the contract negotiated by the wife of a general in the Ministry of Defense, a formidable personality whose many commercial activities nicely paralleled the government's. The villa came fully furnished, even to the bistro glasses and cutlery in the pantry, the fluffy blue towels in the bathrooms, and the wooden filing cabinets in the study. Madame Vinh prudently removed the extraordinary scroll painting in the foyer, Fan K'uan's *Scholar's Pavilion in the Cloudy Mountains,* the mountains and the clouds above and beyond the mountains ominous and discouraging. The peaks seemed to rise to the heavens, the gorges to the depths of hell. The pavilion could be swept away at any moment, and the tiny figure under the crooked tree beside the cloud-filled gorge as vulnerable as a pebble in an avalanche. Madame Vinh made her decision the minute she met the American negotiator, Boyd Lllewellyn. She did not find Monsieur Llewellyn agreeable, and her astrologer told her Llewellyn had entered a particularly susceptible phase of his life. The scroll painting was not valuable; the eleventh-century original was somewhere in Taiwan. This one was a clumsy copy. But Monsieur Llewellyn was certain to be an American influenced by allegory, the sort of American who found omens everywhere underfoot. The artist had meant a celebration of humility, but an Anglo-Saxon would find much to ponder, and to fear.

Still, the villa was suitable in most respects. The dimensions of

the former dining room were somehow French and the chandelier in the ceiling, that was French, too. When the lads from CAS
came to sweep the place they found a tiny microphone in the
crystal, the cord winding back through the walls to a recorder in
one of the wooden filing cabinets in the study; but a mouse had
eaten through the cord so the device was inoperable, and the
tapes were missing in any case. This caused much amused speculation. Was it the Vietnamese bugging the French? The Reds
bugging the Vietnamese? The Vietnamese bugging the Americans? Madame Gosse bugging Monsieur? No one knew.

The wooden filing cabinets were a mighty nuisance because
the drawers stuck in the humid weather. The locks were insecure.
Rostok had cabled personally to Administration to send metal
cabinets soonest but nothing came of the request, not that Ros
was prepared to let it go. He had turned the problem over to
Pablo Gutterman, who had slid it to Sydney, who had passed it
on to George Whyte, who supposedly had a friend at Highest
Levels in Washington. Each week George sent a fresh cable but
there was never any response from Administration. Meanwhile,
the team used screwdrivers to pry open the swollen drawers.

And it wasn't only filing cabinets. They were short of manila
envelopes and stationery, legal pads and memo pads. They were
short of ballpoint pens and paper clips. If anyone needed a dic-
tionary or a thesaurus he had to borrow one from Rostok's surly
secretary. They had scores of typewriters but the typewriters
were useless because they were French, unaccountably left behind in the general confusion, with the French keyboard, AZERTY
instead of QWERTY, only four transposed keys but those four
could ruin a report. Of course the Vietnamese secretaries could
use them; that was the keyboard they had been taught. But many
reports were too sensitive for the secretarial staff, loyal as they
might be and no doubt were. Sensitive reports had to be typed
personally, and with the perverse French keyboard the ordinary

thirty-minute typing chore turned into an hour or more with dozens of errors; and if the document was classified Secret or Confidential the encoding was a nightmare. Administration had sent a hundred new IBM electric typewriters but those had been rerouted at once to the embassy under heavy marine guard; and a hearty laugh all around because Administration had neglected to send converters, AC current to DC. A CAS lad helpfully offered to pick up a hundred dozen on his monthly visit to Hong Kong but those had gotten tied up in Vietnamese customs because he had foolishly sent them through the mails from Hong Kong — through the ordinary god damned mail, can you believe it? And no one knew whom to bribe to get them out of customs in a timely manner, so there the converters sat, in their boxes, useless.

Finally Sydney surrendered and walked over to MACV headquarters where he knew a colonel in Procurement. Groveled, did his dance, wheedled, promised — but what could he offer an army colonel? The military was up to its eyeballs in creature comforts, whiskey, Kansas City steaks, percale sheets, stereo equipment, tennis racquets, wristwatches, and Leica cameras. Of course they did not have Western women but Sydney didn't either. So — did the colonel have children? The colonel did. Was one of those children perhaps a son? He was, age ten. Well then, two tickets behind the dugout for Opening Day, 1966, by which time the colonel would be rotated home to Bethesda. The Senators and whomever the Senators were playing, with luck the outfit that featured Mickey Mantle. The colonel smiled and cocked his head, thinking. With some spending money, Sydney said, enough for beer and hotdogs and Coke and popcorn for the boy, and a hat and a Louisville Slugger. The colonel put his hands behind his head and leaned back in his swivel chair, thinking some more. And an autograph, Sydney said, playing his last card. Mantle's, Berra's, on an official American League baseball, something for the boy to treasure his entire lifetime. In the silence that followed, the colonel yawned and said at last, Deal. And before the close of business that day six Royal typewriters, manuals, arrived by truck along with fifty reams of paper and ribbons enough to wrap a tank. That night Sydney wrote a letter in longhand to a man he barely knew, a member of the board of his old foundation who happened also to be a minority stockholder in the New York Yankees. Would you do a favor for a brave soldier far from home?

So at ten hundred hours they assembled around the mahogany table with cups of coffee or tea. Rostok and Blind Pablo took pho, the aromatic vegetable broth favored by peasant Vietnamese. Almost at once Sydney's attention began to wander, to the listless world beyond the barred windows, the bougainvillea at the base of the low wall, and the admiral's plane tree at the entrance to the drive. Occasionally when he was looking at it a great leaf fell, feathering patiently to the lawn, where a gardener retrieved it and placed it in a burlap sack. In the thick heat of midday everything moved in slow motion, even the gardeners staring blankly into space, leaning on their rakes, waiting for a leaf to fall.

Inside the conference room, the men around the table yawned and attempted to concentrate on the business at hand. Rostok rapped for order. Everyone was aware of the coming visit of the undersecretary, his first visit in-country. It was imperative that he be given the facts with the bark off. The embassy will try to keep him under wraps, Rostok said, so that their agenda will be the controlling agenda. But he is a friend of mine so I have arranged for a long afternoon in Tay Thanh, an afternoon off-*piste* as it were, an afternoon of enlightenment for an official visiting for the very first time. Sydney and I will brief him on the progress we're making. And then we will deliver him to MACV, who will brief him on the progress they are making; and they will be two different kinds of progress. But Syd and I will get there first, in order to establish the context of things.

Question is, how to put a human face on nation-building.

They have the body count, we only have hearts and minds.

They can talk about the battalion they annihilated. We can talk about the school we built and the vaccinations we administered. But we can't show the happy face of the farmer whose field we irrigated. Because maybe we didn't win his heart, only his mind. To indicate he was making a joke, Rostok smiled unpleasantly.

You are all invited to contribute, Rostok went on, if you think there is some special point that Syd and I should make. Something vivid. Something convincing. One side of one piece of paper only, please.

Next, Rostok said, there were indications — nothing firm, nothing set in concrete — that budget would increase. He smiled at the sudden show of enthusiasm around the table. To that end, it was necessary for each man to draw up a wish list *with supporting documentation*. Rostok spoke at length of the various possibilities, along with the appropriate, meaning effective, descriptive language required to satisfy the accountants . . .

About the safe, George Whyte said.

We'll get to the safe later, Rostok said.

Around noon, someone complained about the frequency of the meetings, so many meetings that no work got done. Statistics were going uncompiled; they floated free, aimless as insects. Unorganized, they were invisible. There was also a certain injustice. None of the group members in distant regions were commanded to attend weekly meeting. The one in Camau had not been seen for months. His evening radio message was the only evidence that he was alive. There was another, somewhere along the mountainous border in II Corps, whose numbers were entirely unreliable yet he was untouchable because a reporter had written an admiring article about him in a newspaper; and one of the TV networks followed up. This Llewellyn had emerged as such an intelligent and sympathetic character that one of the National Security Council assistants in the White House wrote him a pat-on-the-back letter for LBJ's signature. "We need more fine young Americans like you . . ." This one spent his days in his office and his evenings in a squalid Montagnard village taping the songs they sang to each other and to their children, strange hypnotic songs that brought tears to his eyes as he listened to them. He was in his second year in the province and would surely reenlist. The experience of my life, he told the reporter, describing his encounters with "my Montagnards." In his spare time he was writing a book about the Montagnards and their music.

At about one, the business discussion wound down. Each man had his assignment and his instructions as to methodology and deadline. Lunch was served and everyone relaxed, waiting for whoever had the latest gossip to speak. The men around the table were attracted to misfortune, the more lurid the better, the freak airplane accident, the sergeant major cashiered for theft, the alcohol problems of this official or that. Dicey Dacy's adventures once consumed a whole afternoon. It was as if they were saying to outsiders, You think it's bad? You don't know half. The gossip sounded malicious but wasn't really. It was only that nation-building was at the bottom of the food chain. Supplies were short for everyone but the military, so naturally when the military erred — as it did frequently — schadenfreude resulted. A simple fact of life: the military got the good ink and the civilians the bad, except for eccentrics like the character who had fallen so deeply in love with the Montagnard tribesmen and their dreary two-toned music. Wasn't it natural that in these circumstances there would be rivalries? There were only so many columns in a newspaper that could be devoted to good news, the vaccinations of schoolchildren or the installation of water treatment plants. Of course they believed the press was malevolent, brainwashed as it was by the army's public relations supremos. Every newspaper reporter secretly coveted commissioned-officer status, and looked with loathing at civilians like — themselves.

Pablo Gutterman usually spoke first.

Our fine airborne brigade got its ass kicked last night.

Rostok said, I heard. Out near Parrot's Beak.

No, Pablo said. Closer in. Sydney's territory, somewhere in Tay Thanh district. A faulty intelligence report, according to my source. Maybe they were set up, maybe not. They thought they had gold, some hoi chanh who's been semi-reliable in the past. Claims to have been a VC political officer in Xuan Loc. It was his tip. But you never know, what with all the smoke and the mirrors. Maybe they screwed up in other ways, technical errors. Maybe they misread the map in the darkness, confused the co-ordinates, got themselves dropped into the wrong rice field, the usual snafu. Maybe the translators got one word wrong. It's happened before.

Mucho KIA, Ros said.

And wounded, Pablo said, lifting his eyebrows, aware that the table had fallen silent, everyone looking at him. His information was rarely wrong. Pablo Gutterman had lived in Indochina since the mid-1950s, had married a Vietnamese, and even now owned his own villa in Bien Hoa. He had worked for one of the trading companies until the assassination of Ngo Dinh Diem. When the trading company liquidated assets and relocated to Hong Kong, Pablo was hired by the aid administrator as liaison to the intelligence community. He spoke adequate Vietnamese and was said to know everyone worth knowing, and his wife was no less au courant. In due course he was appointed deputy director of the various aid programs, and then Boyd Llewellyn drafted him for the Group.

Vietnam was his home, he said, and he had no intention of leaving it, ever. He had not been back to the United States in many years and that was a problem for him. He was not in the picture. The government had changed unimaginably since Eisenhower was in charge, and the country had changed along with the government. Kennedy's businessmen who had taken charge at the Pentagon were different than Ike's. They placed their confidence in computers and systems analysis and information on demand. Action this day meant action this day, not tomorrow or next week. Pablo had trouble understanding the new men, and trouble also explaining the subtlety of Vietnamese institutions, not that these new men cared much about Vietnamese institutions, opaque Asian affairs of scant relevance.

Of course Pablo had lived in Vietnam for too long and had lost perspective. He no longer understood his own government and the society that it represented, so when the assistant secretaries and the lads from the inspector general's office arrived in-country for briefings, he was kept out of sight. Pablo? Pablo's on the early flight to Can Tho, helping out with an interrogation. If he had an observation to make, Rostok made it for him in language the visitors could understand and relate to. Blind Pablo was said to be in his late fifties, though he looked much older with his stoop and his thinning hair and mottled complexion, watery eyes blinking hard behind flesh-colored spectacles. Looking at him, anyone would think he had a terrible hangover; and no one would ever guess that he loved Vietnam and would never leave, ever. More than any of the others, Pablo had a stake in success.

A night lift, Pablo went on. Round about first light. The works, an hour's artillery preparation and the usual bombing runs.

Did you say Xuan Loc? Sydney asked.

On the perimeter of your district, Pablo said.

Sydney looked at him. Aren't we supposed to be informed when they're mounting an operation in our sector?

Depending on the sensitivity of the intelligence, we are. That's the way it's set up, the procedure. But they don't trust us. They think we'll blab.

I thought it was a hard-and-fast rule, Sydney said. No exceptions.

There are no hard-and-fast rules here, Sydney. You know that.

Because no one informed me.

Get on with it, Rostok said irritably.

Pablo sighed. They were a company of airborne in choppers —

A hot LZ, Rostok said, indicating that he, too, was aware of the facts of the disaster. He did not like it when Gutterman upstaged him with classified information from his private sources.

VC waited until the flight was about ten feet off the ground and then hit them with rockets. Six choppers down, two more damaged.

Seven dead, a couple of dozen wounded, Rostok said.

Gutterman shook his head. No, Ros. The latest figures are ten dead and twenty wounded. He paused to allow this information to sink in before he delivered his coup de grâce. And four missing.

Missing? They wouldn't've left their wounded. Airborne wouldn't leave the wounded behind.

Did, Pablo said. Four missing, including the company commander. He was in the lead chopper.

Jesus Christ, George Whyte said.

I knew him, Pablo said. Capable fellow.

Christ, George Whyte said again.

Rostok was drumming his fingers on the table, staring at Pablo Gutterman.

They had no choice, Pablo said. They dropped into an inferno. And communications went haywire. Our close air support was useless because our people were all mixed in with the VC. Pablo paused to trace some lines on the surface of the table, then erased them with his fingers. He was thinking of the stench and the appalling confusion, and the noise. He said, Hit them with napalm or a bomb and you waste your own people, too. And it was dark because they hadn't waited for first light, believing they could achieve surprise just as they always had at Bragg. Our troopers were strung out and scattered but managed to set up a defensive perimeter along the soft dikes of the rice field. They were returning fire but they couldn't see the VC so it was ineffective. The action didn't consume more than about twenty minutes but I think the minutes were long for them. When our reaction force went in at first light they didn't find a single enemy casualty, not one. They found our survivors, including the twenty wounded. And they found our ten dead, stripped of weapons and anything else of value. Wallets, wristwatches, boots, packs. A couple of the bodies were pretty badly mutilated. And the missing are still missing.

Another cock-up, Rostok announced.

A stir at the table, George Whyte and one of the others trading sympathetic glances. Rostok was always severe, brutally unkind when he discovered recklessness or stupidity, always products of excess and overconfidence.

Sydney was looking out the window, watching the gardener retrieve a leaf, examining it closely before placing it in the burlap sack and moving back to the shade of the admiral's tree, where he leaned on his rake and stared into the street, still as a bronze statue. He said, What was the mission, Pablo? What did they hope to find? According to the information of the turncoat.

A base camp, Pablo said. Certainly a headquarters of some kind and lightly defended. That was the turncoat's promise. That part was emphasized, which was why they went in lean, with a company instead of a battalion, and at night instead of first light. They expected the advantage of surprise. But why would a head-quarters be lightly defended? Answer is, it wouldn't be. And it wasn't.

Night assaults, always dangerous, George Whyte said.

Not if the intelligence is accurate, Pablo said. And everyone was quick to say that morale was high. They wanted it so badly.

The headquarters, Sydney said.

Yes, the headquarters, Pablo said. A highly rated objective. Gain the objective and you shorten the war. I suppose they thought it would be a headline-making success, and perhaps that was why they selected Company B.

Rostok shook his head. They think they can throw a thousand artillery shells on a landing zone and that cleanses it. They're crazy. They don't learn from experience . . . Rostok went on to describe the VC's doctrine of defense, spider holes and tunnels, and the weapons, specifically the 40-millimeter RPG2 antitank free-flight rocket, effective range about the distance of a well-struck nine iron, adapted by the Soviets and the Chinese from the German Panzerfaust system, extremely reliable, deadly, and cheap, about the price of a good bottle of schnapps. Sydney listened to Rostok talk on and on, his monologue littered with homely similes as he described the successors to the RPG2, the RPG7, the RPG7D, and the RPG7V, all longer ranged, more powerful, more accurate, favorites of the IRA as well as the VC but not as yet fully deployed in Vietnam. The table listened with respect because it was Rostok talking and everyone was fasci-nated with the enemy's arsenal, except Sydney, whose attention had begun to wander again; he was thinking about the four missing troopers, surely captives or dead somewhere in the vicin-ity, and unlikely to be rescued because while the army's maps were accurate to a meter, they did not disclose the deep structure of the terrain, the life under the skin; on these maps the countryside was as featureless as a suburban lawn. He watched the gardener move from the shade into the sunlight, squint, and retreat back to shade.

They wait until the last second before they fire, Rostok concluded. Exemplary fire discipline. And with rockets the choppers are fat targets, hanging in the air like a big city street light.

There seemed nothing to add to Rostok's kriegspiel.

Why Company B? Sydney asked.

The captain was connected, Pablo said after a moment's silence. He was someone's nephew.

So there'll be an inquiry, Rostok said. To find the responsible party.

Yes, Pablo said mildly. I expect there will be.

The poor bastard, Rostok said.

Yes, Pablo said. He was a nice boy. Perhaps somewhat rowdy. But he was avid. He was gung-ho. He volunteered for the mission.

I don't mean him, Rostok said. I mean the battalion commander or whoever they'll hang out to dry, the VC commander being unavailable for questioning. I doubt they'll go as high as brigade or division. Depends on who signed off on the hoi chanh, who guaranteed his bona fides. Who proposed the mission. Who decided on the night drop. Who calculated the risk-benefit. There'll be pieces of paper somewhere, and all the papers will have signatures attached to them. Just a very simple cock-up but I smell court-martial.

You've always had a good nose, Ros, Pablo said.

That's why I'm where I am and you're where you are, Rostok said.

How well connected was he? Sydney asked.

Congressman's sister's boy, Pablo said.

That's a four-alarm blaze, Rostok said.

It surely is, Ros. And there'll be urgent efforts to get him back.

Search-and-rescue-type efforts. Above-and-beyond-the-call ef-forts. In fact, they have recon teams ready to go tonight, not that they have the slightest idea where to begin the search, other than the drop zone itself. When I left they were bickering about whether to call in the Special Forces.

Airborne doesn't like to admit they need help.

They don't like the green beanies.

They'll need CAS, too.

They like CAS even less.

In the silence that followed, the men around the table could hear telephones ringing in the outer office. A secretary put her head in, motioning at Rostok, but Rostok waved her away. He never allowed the telephone to interfere with the ten o'clock meeting. The secretaries were instructed to say he was out of the office and unavailable. When the secretary mouthed, The White House, Rostok waved her away again.

He said, Let them wait.

Then, to Pablo, What else?

They're not having good luck generally, Pablo said. Seems the boy wrote some letters home. There were one or two aspects of army life that he didn't care for and there was a promotion he was looking forward to that he didn't get.

Congressman's nephew, Sydney said. That means an inquiry, hearings with testimony from all concerned.

Maybe, maybe not, Pablo said softly. He was staring into the middle distance, thinking out loud. My guess is, they'll argue that hearings will do more harm than good, call attention to the missing captain. Identifying him as someone who's connected. No telling how the Reds will react to that, we haven't much experience with POWs in the South. VC may have a different view of things from their brothers up north. Our Reds aren't very worldly, are they? Probably they don't have a firm fix on our federal system. Probably they don't know what a congressman does or his place in the scheme of things. So our people are worried about that. For the moment they're keeping everything quiet. They're keeping the lid on. So let's us keep it quiet, too. Give them some elbow room.

No press, Rostok said, looking sternly around the table.

They've classified the operation Top Secret as of this morning.

You seem to know a hell of a lot about it, Pablo, Sydney said.

I do, Syd. I surely do. He paused again to trace his lines on the surface of the table, then erased them with his fingers. I got the full briefing this morning, where the troopers went and why, and with what results. There's still some confusion about the map coordinates. But they were pretty clear about everything else. There's a panic situation, no question. They're worried and they have cause to worry. It was a botched operation. If the VC have him and decide to march him to Hanoi and he appears on Red television reading a typed statement, it's a hell of an embarrassment.

For everyone, Rostok said.

A propaganda victory.

And these affairs have a way of getting into the newspapers. People talk, it's natural. Troopers talk when they've been mauled and they think it isn't their fault. And before you know it, there're reporters nosing around and asking if there've been any intelligence failures lately and if it's true that a captain's missing and presumed captured. So I'd guess they have a week's grace, max.

And then Rostok had a fresh thought. Why did they brief you?

Pablo said, They want our help.

Do they now? Rostok said with a sharp laugh. Come to us for help? When they never give us squat? When they never give us the time of day? I don't believe it. What do they want?

They don't know what they want, Pablo said. They want us

to keep our eyes open. Report suspicious activity. Ask around. Maybe we'll hear something that'll help them. Pablo smiled bleakly and placed his hands flat on the table. They were a little sheepish about it because they know they've been pricks in the past. He looked directly at Rostok, his eyes huge behind the lenses of his spectacles. I promised full cooperation. I said you would be around to talk to them personally. Listen to what they have, make your own assessment.

They have my number. They can call me.

As you wish, Ros.

They want a favor, they can come to me.

I'm sure you'll hear from them.

They're looking for someone to share the blame.

It wouldn't be the first time, Pablo said. Still. Bit far-fetched, don't you think, Ros?

No, Rostok said.

What did he look like? Sydney asked, realizing he had used the past tense as if the man were already dead. What else do we know about him?

Nice-looking boy, Syd. Big kid, off a farm somewhere in the Midwest. Built like a truck.

That's good, Sydney said.

I suppose it is, Pablo replied.

Sydney heard the false note, the hesitation and the little sigh at the end, and wondered about the thing unsaid. Pablo removed his glasses and pinched the bridge of his nose. He turned to stare myopically out the window at the motionless gardeners. Sydney wondered what sort of life Pablo Gutterman led with his wife in the bungalow in the suburbs, what he did in the evenings and on weekends. He was rarely seen at the Brinks for the movies or at the various restaurants in Saigon or Cholon. He and his wife did not entertain, at least they did not entertain Americans. There was mention once of summer holidays in the mountains around

Dalat but that was before the war moved south. Someone said he played golf at the course north of the city, that he had a Saturday foursome and bet dollar-dollar Nassau as if he were still living in Miami. His partners were Vietnamese businessmen, one of them his brother-in-law. Hard to imagine Pablo in a golf shirt and slacks, squinting through his spectacles, lining up a putt. Most of the Llewellyns had no private lives away from the job. Day and night were identical. Their conversations always had to do with the situation in all its forms, metaphors and scenarios, as Rostok liked to say. Pablo Gutterman continued to stare out the window at the gardeners. Evidently he had said all he intended to say about the missing soldier. And then Sydney realized they did not know his name.

George Whyte filled the sudden silence with a windy digression on the limits of the military mind, unimaginative yet reckless, avid for success while avoiding responsibility for failure, addicted to heuristic slogans and the hard lessons learned in the previous war. The Pentagon had entirely too much money, it made them careless . . . But by then the others had drifted off to a worried discussion of personnel changes at headquarters in Washington, memos arriving every day with mysterious signatures, realignments in the office of the Comptroller and the office of Management Planning as well as Procurement and International Training. The godly hand of that bastard Boyd Llewellyn was present but not visible; no one knew what he was after beyond his habitual obsession to control the paper, the IN boxes and the OUT boxes. Something sinister was transpiring in the office of Inspections and Investigations, perhaps a new deputy director or counsel. The place was a revolving door. They were bearing down with unnatural zeal and promising a visit in-country before the end of the year, and in the meantime were demanding fresh statistics that could more accurately measure progress —

Forget them, Rostok said.

You can't *forget* them, Ros.

The reports of the Group go directly to the White House. Some of you still don't understand. Our lad with the Montagnards? White House was delighted with the coverage. Our lad isn't burning villages or wasting civilians. Vice President himself has taken an interest, you see.

But the Pentagon signs the paychecks, George Whyte said.

And writes the efficiency reports, someone else threw in.

Do the minimum, Rostok said wearily. He looked at his watch. So, George, what happened to the safe? I assume it's installed and running.

Little problem there, Ros, George Whyte said. It was too heavy for the damned floor.

What do you mean? Rostok demanded.

We got it upstairs all right. He waved at the ceiling. Last night, it took five men to do it with ropes and pulleys. It's a big Mosler, you know. Weighs a damn ton. It's just as awkward as can be. He smiled sadly, another hope dashed, and said no more.

Where is it now?

George pointed at the ceiling. Up there, he said. Third floor. Half in and half out of the floor. The beam cracked. We can't budge it.

Can we open the door to the safe?

George shook his head. It's stuck. We can't get to the combination lock. Thank God the second beam held or it would've fallen into the basement, maybe killed someone on the way down.

And no one thought to check the floor?

That's Procurement's job. It's their responsibility. Obviously we needed a structural engineer and we didn't have one. I'm afraid we need a smaller safe, Ros.

Rostok sighed, one more worry in a busy day. Where are the reports?

Where they've always been, Ros. Locked in the filing cabinets in the big closet. Secure enough for the time being.

See to it, Rostok said.

And the Mosler?

Get the smaller safe, George.

I mean the one that's there. That's stuck. That's betwixt and between.

Tell Supply to reinforce the ceiling.

Yes, Ros.

And keep it quiet.

Will do, Ros.

The meeting began to break up. George mentioned that *Doctor Zhivago* was playing at the Brinks and wondered if anyone wanted to join him for the film and a steak later at the roof restaurant, a nightcap or two and early to bed.

Rostok had a dinner with the deputy at JUSPAO.

I have a mahjongg game, Pablo said.

Sydney had two sociologists. He fished in his pocket for the memo. I'm supposed to brief them on the role of women in Vietnamese society. And what they think of the war. Anyone know any anecdotes?

They don't like it, Rostok said. A woman told me that only the other day.

Can you flesh that out a little, Ros? Her name and age. Economic status. Education. And how many of her children have been killed?

Pablo Gutterman gathered up his papers and prepared to leave.

What was his name? Rostok asked.

Who?

The congressman's nephew.

Smalley, Pablo said. Captain Harry Smalley.

What else do you know about him?

Not much, Pablo said. West Point, class of 'sixty-three or

'sixty-four, somewhere in there. This was his first command, he'd only been in-country a few months. When I met him, he was playing poker and listening to loud music. Drinking beer. Complaining. They were in stand-down. I remember his hands were so big the cards disappeared into them.

His CO say anything?

His CO said he was a big dumb blond.

Anything else?

Smalley said this one thing to me. He was restless, eager to get back to the field, into action. He said, "I hate stand-down. I hate bivouac. Bivouac's no good. Equipment rots, men get into trouble."

Did he say what kind of trouble?

No, he didn't, Ros, Pablo said. I think he meant trouble generally. Trouble of the spirit, undefined trouble, trouble that comes when discipline breaks down. Because of the idleness.

Rostok looked at him strangely. Makes no sense, he said. When you're in stand-down, you're safe. No one's shooting at you. You play poker, drink beer, sleep late in the morning. Stand-down's every soldier's dream.

Not Smalley's, Pablo said.

Big dumb blond, Rostok said.

He was a soldier, Pablo said.

Make me a memo, Pablo. Everything you know about him. Everything that you can remember. Memo on my desk tomorrow? Make a call or two if you have to. I'd like a full description, too. So if we find him sitting in a cathouse in Bien Hoa we'll know that's him, the missing Captain Smalley. Can you do that, Pablo? Confidential, personal to me. And anything you can dig up on the hoi chanh, his name and age, his bill of particulars. When he defected and where and to whom and what he got for his trouble and who gave it to him. Who controls him? CAS? The army? And any speculation you might have from your private sources, a likely place they might take our captain for safe-keeping. Any speculation at all, no matter how out of the way or off the wall.

That may take a while.

Close of business tomorrow, Rostok said, and turned to leave the room.

Why do you want this, Ros?

That's my business, Rostok said, and walked through the door.

They listened to the click of his heels in the corridor, then watched him hurry across the lawn to his Scout, the one with the long aerial and the yellow light on the roof. He jerked his arm in the direction of his driver, who was talking to one of the garden-ers. Rostok was already in the car and reading from some docu-ment when the driver leapt into the driver's seat, backed up, and hurtled away in a flurry of gravel.

What was that about? Pablo asked.

I imagine he'll want to brief his good friend the undersecre-tary, Sydney said. He will want to do that personally so Highest Levels know that everything possible is being done to rescue the young man and that Rostok himself personally is on the case with his own information, information supplied to him by private sources unavailable to the embassy or the military —

Me, Pablo said.

You, Sydney agreed.

But I don't know anything more, Pablo said.

Then tell him that.

You try telling him that, Pablo said.

Probably he'll forget about it tomorrow.

Rostok never forgets anything, Pablo said.

Sydney began to laugh. He forgot to return the call to the White House.

No, Pablo said. He wants privacy.

*

Back in his office at Tay Thanh that afternoon, Sydney found a letter in his IN box, creamy stationery with initials on the back flap, an invitation to lunch a week hence, twelve noon, tenue de ville, regrets only, Dede and Claude Armand. Accompanying the invitation was a hand-drawn map, most detailed, handsomely decorated, directions to Plantation Louvet.

The next day he called Pablo Gutterman for advice as to a tailor. He needed slacks and a shirt, the things he had brought with him were not suited to the climate. After listening to Pablo's complaints about Rostok, Sydney was rewarded with a tailor's name. And the day after that he drove to Monsieur Tan's in rue Catinat, a few doors away from the Continental Palace. Monsieur Tan suggested a white linen suit, an ice cream suit for the tropics, a suit that breathed and kept its shape. A suit that would not be out of place in California or Texas or even Paris in France. Delivery in three days, twenty dollars U.S.

Be careful, Pablo had said when Sydney asked him for the name of a tailor.

Plantation Louvet

*T*HE WEATHER TURNED. Heavy clouds motored down from
the North and the temperature fell ten degrees. The milky sun
disappeared as if it had never existed and the rain forest appeared as a damp monochrome. There was an urban shape to the
gray light, the sort of pall that wraps New York or Chicago on a
foul autumn day. Sydney was late rising and stood quietly for a
long time looking out the window of his bedroom at the street.
The smell of the forest was as rank as compost; and then the
wind came up and the drizzle began. He watched schoolchildren
troop up the street in the drizzle, their books in bright plastic
satchels. They walked two by two, holding hands, as orderly as a
column of infantry.

He heard Mai moving about in the office below. She was
singing softly to herself. He dressed slowly in the shadowless
gray light, thinking that the room had improved since it belonged to Dacy. There was a picture of his daughter on the
bureau and a poster of the *Normandie* that he'd bought at Orly.
He owned a clock, a transistor radio, and a bright red bedspread

he'd found at the market. Of course the room was clean, tidy as a monk's cell, and he wondered when he would begin writing on the walls and hiding whiskey bottles in the closet. The Malraux lay on the bedside table unopened. On the floor was a foot-high stack of press clippings thoughtfully sent over from USIA, and a month-old copy of *Time*. He wondered whether the World Series had begun and who was in it. He looked at the picture of his daughter and realized he had heard nothing from her in weeks; when he first arrived he had a card from her every few days, a picture of an animal or a New York landmark with her scrawled upside-down signature and "love." When he wrote her next he would tell her about the farmer who had surrendered his mind but was withholding his heart, a sentiment that would appeal to Karla; and then he remembered he had two unmailed letters to Rosa in the glove compartment of his car. The front door opened and closed and he watched Mai hurry away to the café, her ritual morning tea with her friend Thuy.

It was still raining an hour later when he spread the map on his bureau, tracing the route to Plantation Louvet with his finger. It resembled a labyrinth, Tay Thanh to Xuan Loc, then north from Xuan Loc. He had never been north of Xuan Loc, a region the government had abandoned because there was nothing important to protect, only a few peasant villages and the rubber plantations. The roads were unfamiliar and some of them seemed little more than cart paths or trails. The odometer would be essential — 11.6 km north of Xuan Loc, past the ruins of the fort and the Buddhist shrines nearby, turn right; 2.5 km and then left; 1.3 km another left; .5 km and left again; 2.6 km a sharp right at the fork; and 7.2 km straight ahead to Plantation Louvet. On the map the plantation was marked with a little French tricolor. *Pay close attention to the distance,* Dede Armand had written in her rolling schoolgirl script, *there are no road mark-*

*ings. Drive slowly. You should not meet anyone, but if you do,
don't stop. Drive on. Good luck.*

He felt like a colonial himself in his ice cream suit and pale
blue shirt, foulard tie neatly knotted, shoes polished. The suit fit
beautifully, as the tailor promised it would. All he lacked was a
pith helmet and a walking stick. When Sydney looked at himself
in the mirror, he began to laugh. All Americans in South Vietnam
would be better off if they dressed like planters, supervising their
domain with colonial hauteur. He lit a cigarette and stood at the
window watching the drizzle turn to mist; and then, giving another glance into the mirror, he went downstairs.

He moved to straighten the papers on his desk. He aligned the
pencils next to the IN box, and then he saw the letter, bone white
with the address typewritten, the sender's identity top left in
raised letters, Greener, Leman & Kis, Attorneys at Law, 612
Broadway, New York. His feeling of well-being vanished at once
at this intrusion from Manhattan, so distant and irrelevant. Letters from New York lawyers had no business in his IN box.
Sydney did not open the letter but stared coldly at it, as if it might
speak of its own accord. The postmark was three weeks old.
Certainly it had passed through many hands, yet the envelope
was pristine. The law firm was familiar but he could not place it.
Then he remembered that Otto Kis was a lawyer who specialized
in left-wing causes, the noisier the better. He had bad teeth, a
high-pitched voice, and a manner of high martyrdom. And he
was a friend of Karla's.

Otto Kis announced that he represented Karla Parkes. He
intended to file a decree for divorce promptly. The grounds were
desertion — and here the letter wandered into legal thickets
too dense to penetrate, and Sydney had no desire to try. He
looked away out the window to the street. A convoy was passing; the mist had turned to drizzle. He let the letter fall, like any

beachcomber who had found an unwelcome message in a bottle washed ashore. Greetings, Sydney Parade. You're due in court! And the beachcomber wondering, How did they find me? What do they want? He thought he had been living in a parallel world beyond the reach of Earth's daily light, a black hole of sorts with its own special atmosphere and rules of engagement, and wartime code of conduct. Of course she wanted the marriage over and done with so she could get on with things. She wanted him out of her life. Their marriage was old news. It belonged to the past, which seemed to him changed utterly in the light of the present. He lived in Vietnam. Vietnam was the conjugal bed. The marriage was hers and she could do with it as she wished. The days when they had loved each other had vanished, and even the memory of them had faded. In some sense they could be said not to have existed at all. They were the notes on the score after musicians had packed up their instruments and left the stage.

He picked up the letter and weighed it in his palm; heavy official paper, the sort of stationery Stalin would use for his own decrees. The words roamed the page. Sydney noticed a snide reference to "your war" and "the inconvenience" if this and that did not come to pass. He scanned the first page and was into the second, understanding little. Then, near the end, a sentence that seemed to state plainly that his client was prepared to grant joint custody of their daughter and had no objection to visiting rights that were flexible and in the best interests of the child, et cetera . . . Rosa would remain in her mother's care. That was not negotiable. In fact, none of it was negotiable, including alimony and child support. The numbers that followed seemed to Sydney quite large, but surely that was only the opening bid, a bluff. Please let me know the name and address of your attorney . . .

He looked at his watch. It was late. It was time to leave for Plantation Louvet.

He slipped the letter back into the envelope and put it in his desk drawer. There was no reason why Karla could not have what she wanted. Money was of no use to him in Tay Thanh, and his daughter was on the other side of the world. Then he remembered an incident with his father many years ago. Sydney was at the tiller. They were sailing in calm waters in Long Island Sound under a cloudless sky when he felt a tap on his shoulder; and when he turned he saw the thunderheads boiling in from the west. His father laughed and laughed when Sydney hastily came about and made for port. You have a tendency to ignore things that aren't in your immediate vicinity, Syd. You've got to look over your shoulder *all the time,* because bad luck's always there. So he would ask his father to speak to old Jim, his golfing partner, an avuncular sort who specialized in wills and trusts. Jim was especially good with fine print and women, and would prove more than a match for Otto Kis. He would write his father as soon as he found time; and there would be much to describe of lunch chez Armand.

Then Mai was in the room looking at him wide-eyed. She had pulled on a sweater against the chill and stood hugging herself. She had never seen him in a suit and did not know what it portended. She watched him hastily fold a map and put it in his pocket. Sydney explained that he was off to lunch with important visitors from the United States. He took a last look around, then gathered up the bottles of Beefeater and Martell, gifts for his hosts. He fetched the carbine and a black umbrella that had stood unused in the coat closet these many months and told Mai to take the day off.

The plantation house stood at the end of a long tunnel of evergreens, fat at the bottom and slender at the top. They were widely spaced. Back of the evergreens stood the bulbous palms of the plantation laid out in rows that produced a kind of optical illusion. The rows went every which way and then merged in the distance to become a dense and formless green. In the dull light of this wilderness it was impossible to know the direction he was headed. He might as well have been underwater. Yet the bungalow was in sight, exactly as she had promised it would be.

Stone turrets flanked the long drive. Atop each turret was a life-size cat in bronze, green with age and the weather, blank-faced. In the heart of the great forest the turrets and the cats seemed a fragment of the imagination of another age on another continent, or an apparition from a child's illustrated fairy tale. The mist eddied, swirling across the road so that the bungalow vanished and reappeared and vanished again. He had a sense of abandonment, of a dwelling empty of life or of purpose, a place that came and went according to the weather or the season or the time of day — or whether a guest was expected for lunch, tenue de ville, regrets only. Sydney wondered if he had misunderstood the day or the hour, but Dede Armand's invitation was clear and specific. He rolled down the window and listened hard but could hear nothing but the damp rustle of leaves in the forest.

He was filled with the sudden excitement of discovery. He had no idea what he would find at the end of the tunnel. He felt privileged, for now he would see for himself the sort of life the Armands lived in their location between the lines. As he drove slowly up the driveway he noticed beds of flowers placed here and there among the evergreens, and around the beds wooden benches. Probably that was where she watched her birds, though there was no sign of bird life or any other life. The driveway gave into a square parking area framed by a foot-high privet hedge. He saw now that there were dim lights inside the bungalow. The front door was open so he could see through a long hallway to what he supposed was the verandah; and then he remembered the photograph of Dede and Claude at the coffee table, the table laden with magazines and books, a Matisse drawing on the wall behind them, a sense of happy domesticity. The space at the end of the corridor was flooded with light, as if Plantation Louvet was provided with its own personal sun that could be switched on at will like a lamp. There were soft white curtains in the front windows and a brass-rimmed chandelier in the hallway. The bungalow was smaller than it appeared from the end of the driveway, the outside walls of stucco and wood and topheavy with a corrugated iron roof. The place had the easy, regular dimensions of a modest country house in New England. The whole was pleasant to look at and composed the way an artist composes a picture. The Land Rover was parked under a lean-to.

Sydney slid the carbine under the seat and collected the bottles. He was dismayed at the trash in his car, crumpled cigarette packs, opened and unopened C rations, an army-issue knapsack, a bag full of nails, weeks-old copies of the *Saigon Post,* all the personal effects of a working man who had no private life, unless you counted the unmailed letters in the glove compartment. In any case, they were out of sight. Out of mind, too, because they had been there for a week, neglected in the press of business; and the days had been cloudless. Such a simple matter to forget those who lived in the world an ocean away, and the reward for it was a letter from a lawyer and a bad conscience. The bad conscience arrived at predictable times and places. No one would imagine that a man in an ice cream suit and a blue shirt, a tenue de ville as specified by his hostess, his arms full of liquor bottles, would have a bad conscience because he had failed to notice thunderheads on the horizon — but such was life in Llewellyn Group.

A shadow moved in the hallway and then Dede Armand was standing on the front steps of her bungalow, frowning because the mist had turned again to drizzle, motioning for him to hurry inside. But he took his time straightening the creases in his trousers and checking the knot in his tie. He alighted from the Scout, pulling the umbrella behind him and thumbing it open. He walked slowly across the gravel to the stoop, the drizzle tapping gently on the cloth. At that moment he seemed to have lost his bad conscience. He stood a moment in the wet, looking at the American woman who stood impatiently with her arms folded, an amused expression on her face. Perhaps it was his tenue de ville, perhaps his deliberate manner. He dipped his head, offered her the package, and said sincerely, So happy to be here, Mrs. Armand.

They sat in the sunroom. Claude Armand offered a variety of gin drinks or wine, the usual Algerian plonk but drinkable when chilled. They all took gin from Sydney's quart of Beefeater. The room was as comfortable as he had imagined it, the furnishings bright and well used. Of course he recognized the poster and even the magazine covers seemed identical to those he had seen in the photograph. The room looked out on a vast gray lawn, water puddling; apparently their personal sun had withdrawn. Beyond the lawn were the rubber trees with their every-which-way symmetry. Visible two hundred yards down were the sheds where the rubber was processed. Wisps of smoke escaped from roof vents. Claude described what they did and how they did it but Sydney did not pay close attention, observing instead the workers who came and went, machetes in their belts. When he asked how many workers he employed, Claude smiled and said it varied depending on the season; more at harvest time, less during the planting. They were dependable men, Claude said. Some of them had been working on the plantation for three decades, since before the war. The wages are pitiful, he said. But they get along.

Dede disappeared into the kitchen and returned with a plate of crackers and cheese and cracked crab with savory salt. Sydney complimented them on the cheese, and Claude said his brother sent it from Comminges once every month. Asian cheese was terrible. Asians didn't eat much cheese and therefore didn't know how to process it properly. Their cows were the wrong breed. Their cheese tasted like whey and wouldn't spread. They can't make cheese and they can't make wine.

Isn't that right, darling?

Or crackers, she said. These are English crackers.

My brother sends crackers, too.

When he'd walked into the sunroom, Sydney had had a sense of a conversation just ended. The Armands were cordial enough but something remained suspended in the room. He remembered an actor's remark that grief was the other face of grace, and when Dede Armand made a hesitant motion with her hand, touching the cocktail glass on the table, her manner was laden with dolor. Then he knew that they had been talking of their twins, dead now a month or more. Claude was solicitous of her, touching her arm when he spoke, always keeping her in focus. She was present but not present also, her body here but her thoughts in some private realm.

When Claude spoke of some problem with production — a vat had broken and they were attempting to jury-rig a part — Sydney watched one of the workers trot up the lawn, slowing when he reached the bungalow. He was reluctant to intrude but finally tapped on the window with his fingernails. Claude went to the door and spoke a few words, then returned with an apologetic expression. Another problem with the vat. He would have to see to it.

Will you be all right here? he said to his wife. It shouldn't take long.

Lunch, she said.

I'll be back for lunch, Claude said.

Can I help? Sydney asked.

No, Claude said. Stay with my wife.

He kissed her on the cheek and told Sydney where the ice was. Sydney and Dede Armand watched him move off down the lawn with the worker, who was explaining something, waving his machete in disgust. Claude put his arm around the other's shoulders and for a moment they looked like father and son, the Frenchman dwarfing the Vietnamese; and suddenly Claude laughed loudly, the sound carrying up the lawn to the sunroom where Sydney and Dede Armand sat in uncomfortable silence.

Make a drink for yourself, she said. And one for me, too, light on the gin.

Lime? he asked.

I thought I would die, she said in a voice so low that he thought he had misunderstood her. She sat on the couch with her head on the back cushion, her hands crossed on her belly. It was so unexpected, she said. I never believed anything could go wrong, and then from one moment to the next I could feel them dying inside me. It felt like a stampede, some awful bucking and charging inside me. And everything had gone so well. The doctors were so pleased. I made a stupid trip to the market and one minute I was a mother and the next minute I wasn't. It took no time at all. Something had gone wrong and they still don't know what it was. Was it only that the stars were out of alignment? Not likely. We live a simple life here, Sydney. She touched her upper lip and moved her head on the back cushion as if to deny what she had said. Perhaps it wasn't so simple but we do try to live with the bare essentials. We have what we need. You were kind to me, Sydney.

I apologize for being cross with you in the car that day, she went on. I was afraid you weren't listening. And I was not myself.

He sat across from her now. She had left her drink untouched on the table and continued to stare at the ceiling as she talked.

We are not frivolous people, she said. And then, fiercely, *We are not frivolous people*. We respect the land. We work hard. We feel we belong here as much as anyone, even the Vietnamese. The French are proud of Vietnam, you know, the Napoleonic code and their language, French culture. It's true they exploited people, as colonial regimes will. The system is — unwholesome. It's disgusting. The French did not understand the changing times and instead of bending to the wind they fought it and lost everything at Dien Bien Phu. Claude believes that there are debts still to be discharged, and perhaps he is right. But it's in the past. It has nothing to do with the here and now. The Vietnamese understand that we love the plantation and that we pay what we can afford to pay. The plantation is productive, even with the bombs and the labor troubles. The disruption of production. Don't you feel that when you have lived in a place and loved it that you belong to it? And it to you? I do. Claude does. He has had many offers in Malaysia and Cambodia. Thailand, too. But he has refused them all. I insisted on it. And if it comes to pass that we are no longer welcome here, then we will leave. But not before. They will have to deport us as undesirables, as you would a criminal or a subversive.

She said, In America you can make another life, find yourself a new personality, put another face to the world and an alias to fit the face. Bored in one place, go to another. Change jobs, change cities, change wives or husbands, change beliefs. But in the end you are the same person with the same troubles. You grew up in Winnetka, danced the tango at Abenaki, necked in the back of a Chevrolet convertible, liked boys with curly hair, took a major in art history, learned to distinguish the Northern Sung from the Southern Sung, the one offering consolation and the other asymmetry. The great scrolls of the five dynasties are fifty feet long and you view them five feet at a time. Did you know that, Sydney? Probably not. Probably you're more in the line of Edward Hopper or Degas. I went abroad because I wanted to know something of the world, and perhaps the boys with the curly hair were responsible, along with the Northern Sung. Now I have my house and my husband. I have my birds. I am cataloging the birds of Vietnam. Nothing has changed for me except that I have become devout.

She paused to take a small sip from the glass before her.

I hated the Abenaki Club. Do you know why? Todd told me this. Each spring they planted tulips along the fringes of the circular drive at the entrance to the club. Probably there were five hundred tulips, all colors. Red and white predominated but there were purple and pink also. When the tulips died in June they ripped them up and replaced them with — I believe pansies. They tore them from the ground and threw them away because a tulip bulb, uprooted before its time, dies. The members did not want to see dead tulips in their loop. The tulips had fulfilled their function, you see. So they were discarded in favor of pansies. Marigolds, too.

He was paying the closest attention to her and was dismayed now to hear the sound of explosions, not far off as usual but nearby. The house shook. When he turned his head he saw the windows streaked with rain, so the sound was not bombs or mortars but the drumming of rain on the corrugated iron roof. He saw that smoke was no longer visible from the vents on the roofs of the sheds at the end of the long gray lawn. The racket grew as the rain fell, a downpour that lasted for many minutes before it began to ease. Dede Armand continued to stare at the ceiling, her hands flat on her belly. She was evidently still pondering the flowers, because her lips were moving.

Rain turned to drizzle and drizzle to mist and far away over the clouds Sydney saw a splash of pale blue sky which vanished as he looked at it. He was trying to remember Karla's contemptuous snarl concerning art history majors at the Seven Sisters. Cashmere connoisseurs, she called them.

That's what the Americans want to do with Vietnam, Dede said.

He looked at her and realized she had been talking while the rain fell and he had not heard a word.

She said, I've been away for so many years. I never thought much about patriotism or nationalism. When Kennedy was killed, Claude and I were on the beach in Thailand. Marilyn Monroe dies, the Berlin Wall goes up, the Beatles, Sputnik, books published, movies made. I hear about these things weeks, months later. They have nothing to do with me. And I looked up one morning and a company of American soldiers was in my back yard, they'd lost their way. I didn't like the way they looked at me, so I pretended to be French. Vat ees eet you vant? And I showed them the way out, and I was happy to see them go. What are they doing here? No one wants them except the wretched clique in Saigon who lust for the old way of life, the hunting lodges in Dalat with plenty of servants to keep things going, and vacations in Singapore and the Philippines. And they think the Americans can get it for them. All they have to supply is bodies for the South Vietnamese army. It's disgusting. And what about us?

What are you thinking, Sydney?

He was looking out the window at the sheds. Smoke had begun to feather from the vents. No doubt Claude would be back soon. He said, I'm thinking we live in different countries. I've invented one and you've invented another, and somewhere there's a third that's undiscovered.

Reinvention is the opiate of Americans, she said.

It's what we do best, he agreed.

She raised her head slightly and smiled winningly. You look dapper in your tenue de ville, Sydney.

He said, Tailored for the occasion by a venerable gentleman in rue Catinat.

Monsieur Tan, she said.

Yes, him. Does everyone go to Monsieur Tan?

Not everyone, she said. Hong Kong is the city of choice for the bespoke tenue de ville. Almost as stylish as Savile Row and much, much cheaper. We used to go once every few months but now it's been — almost one year.

He watched Claude emerge from the shed to stand quietly in the mist talking to the Vietnamese with the machete. They seemed to be arguing about something, Claude vehemently and the Vietnamese with patience; and then he saw Claude shake his head and look back inside the shed.

She said, We dress up now and again. When we have friends in to lunch or dinner we always make an effort. We refuse to give in. Of course in the past year it's become more difficult to arrange evenings, the countryside's more insecure every day. It's unpredictable. Before, we had — ways and means to plan ahead. Now we never know from one day to the next the nature of the military operations, who's moving and where. But still, we manage. We have a fine community of friends, French and Vietnamese both. Two Corsicans run the plantation next door and one of them has a Swiss wife, Marta. You're the first outsider we've ever had in this house, and you're not a true outsider because you were so kind to me. I suppose also we are Americans together in an environment that is not entirely suitable. It is unwholesome, wouldn't you say? I am trying to make you see why Plantation Louvet is so important to us.

I know it is, he said.

The family is important to the Vietnamese.

It is to everyone, he said.

But she rushed on as if she had not heard him. She said, Plantation Louvet is more important than ever now because *they* are here. Yes. That's what things come down to, you see. We had the priest come here for the service, only our close friends invited. You have met him. He's the one you spoke to in the church. It's often difficult for him because Catholics support the Saigon clique. Father Nguyen told me you had offered to repair his roof for him. Are you going to do it?

I haven't heard from him, Sydney said.

You will, she said.

Then I'll do it, he said.

So we had the service here with the priest. We buried them — and here she waved her hand in the direction of the forest beyond the sheds, a wilderness that seemed to stretch to the margins of the known world — out there, two simple markers. They will be impossible for anyone to find. But we know where they are. Our children are now part of the plantation, so we will never give it up. To Claude and me it's sacred ground, the place where the priest said his few words and we said goodbye. We hate what is going on around us but that's not our responsibility. We can do nothing about it except endure it for however long we have to, until it goes away. We will live here forever because our son and daughter are here. Do you have children, Sydney?

A daughter, he said.

You should be with her, Dede Armand said. Her voice rose and she moved her head from side to side, her face pale as ashes. You should be taking her to riding lessons at Abenaki and to the Metropolitan Museum. You should see that she has her music lessons. You should help her with her math homework and take her to a matinee. My father left my mother when I was seven. I've never forgiven him. I didn't see him for weeks and weeks and then he showed up at school one afternoon and I burst into tears, I was so angry. He had no right to do it. He told me he had bad conscience but that he would get over it. Do you have bad conscience, Sydney?

He did not reply to that, though she was leaning urgently forward, expecting him to answer. He made a little motion of assent with his hand, clearing his throat, waiting for her to finish her inquisition or whatever it was. He wondered what was keeping Claude.

It's hard to live with, she said.

Yes, he said.

It's a cobweb on your spirit, she added. The cobweb is made of iron.

He said, We are not perfect —

No kidding, she said, mustering a half-smile that promised more than it delivered. She took a small sip of her drink.

She said, Once you have it, it's yours forever.

Bad conscience, he said.

"That which I should have done I did not do," she recited, and then Claude Armand stepped through the door, apologizing for the long delay. The problem was more complicated than he had anticipated. However, it seemed to be fixed for the moment. Apparently.

Dede walked slowly into the kitchen.

Lunch at last, Claude said.

The table was nicely laid, heavy long-handled flatware and white porcelain bowls with pale blue flowers on the sides. A spray of wildflowers in a glass vase formed the centerpiece, the ambiance reminiscent of Winnetka, if Winnetka were tropical. Sydney and Claude stood awkwardly behind their chairs listening to Dede move about in the kitchen. Claude poured red wine from a stone pitcher and murmured that his wife had had a bad night, more bombing and the rattle of helicopters close to the house, closer than they had ever been, all of it well after midnight. They were dropping phosphorus flares that lit the sky, the light so fierce you could see it with closed eyelids. She was upset and unable to sleep with the noise and the light so they both got up and put a record on the phonograph and played chess. No sleep until first light.

Was she all right with you? Claude asked.

Fine, Sydney replied. She seems to think I have a bad conscience.

Do you?

Yes, Sydney said.

It's very hard on her, Claude said. She doesn't sleep and she doesn't eat properly. She thinks there is something she could have done. She wonders why she went to the market that morning. You can see that she is not herself. I'm sure she told you about the service for the babies and that fool of a priest who's unreliable. He's one of Diem's henchmen although he claims to have reformed. His church does not serve the people and he's opposed to those who do serve the people. But he said a good prayer even though he was nervous, so nervous his hands shook.

Sydney said, Why was he nervous?

He couldn't turn the pages of the Bible because my people were looking at him. That was why he was nervous, because he knows what they think of him. Of course my plantation workers were there. It would have been insulting to exclude them.

Of course, Sydney said.

My wife wanted them there.

Do they resent your wife because she is an American?

They have come to know her and now they like her. In the beginning it was difficult, you can imagine. And now they have sympathy for her. They have no sympathy for the priest. And if I can give you unsolicited advice. If you fix his church you'll be doing the people no favors. It's a big favor to him and his archbishop, but that's all it is. No one goes to his church except Dede, who goes sometimes in the afternoons to pray alone. She will not go to his mass.

After a little silence, Claude said that he had proposed a long weekend in Hong Kong but his wife did not want to go with the memory of the funeral so fresh. A weekend in Hong Kong would not be agreeable, even a suite at the Mandarin, with the shopping and a meal on the terrace of the Repulse Bay Hotel. She has a good friend who works for one of the American trading companies, but the friend was in America on leave, so that was another reason not to go. There were so many reasons he had a hard time keeping them straight. Then he had an idea they would go to the mountains near Dalat. He had a friend with a house there, it was beautiful terrain with many species of birds unique to Indochina. Dalat was where Bao Dai had his summer palace. The French built it for him so that they could go there to shoot tigers. It was great tiger country. But that idea was no good because there was fighting again in Dalat.

I didn't know that, Sydney said.

The government's keeping it quiet. They lost another battalion.

Where did you hear that?

It's well known, Claude said.

Sydney smiled. Whenever you heard a surprising fact and asked for the source of the fact, the answer always was "It's well known." He said, Dalat sector is quiet. Was quiet. Was supposed to be quiet.

It is now, Claude said. But the government is not in charge.

So Dalat's out, Sydney said.

There aren't any tigers, either. They killed all the tigers.

Not so, Sydney said. A Special Forces team got one near Dak To. Big one, male.

I don't believe it, Claude said.

It's well known, Sydney replied.

My wife hates the idea of killing tigers.

From a helicopter. With a machine gun.

How sporting, Claude said.

The female got away. And the cubs got away, too.

They could have used rockets on the female and the cubs. That way, they would have killed them all.

Probably it didn't occur to them. The rockets.

There are still a few elephants around Dalat. Bao Dai used to ride one.

If I were an elephant, I'd watch out. I think I'd go to Laos or Thailand or even China. If I were an elephant, I'd emigrate.

Marxist elephants in particular, Claude said.

Sydney said, Since Dalat isn't going to work out maybe you should take her to France, take her shopping in Paris, visit the Louvre, visit your family in Comminges. It would be a change for her, someplace new and different, not so many memories and the violence is under control. Wait a month and then encourage her to go to America where she could see her family.

My wife doesn't want to go to America, Claude said glumly. We have spoken about it often. She has no use for America. She says she is ashamed of her country. I don't approve. Countries have a way of behaving idiotically and never making amends. But one must never place one's faith in nations, one's own or any other nation. Don't you agree? At any event, my wife prefers Vietnam and the life we have here. And I must manage the plantation. It doesn't run itself. Someone has to be in charge night and day, especially now. The helicopters were very, very close to the house last night, and the flares were annoying. Why were they so close?

Night operations, Sydney said.

Then Dede Armand was in the room with a tureen of steaming pho and a platter of whitefish smothered in water chestnuts and slices of pineapple. Claude held her chair, and as they sat down to eat the sun broke through the billowing clouds and flooded the room with golden light.

The Life of the Mind

*T*HEY ASKED Sydney about his daily life in Tay Thanh, how he went about things, what he did with his evenings and weekends. How do you *live* here, Sydney? What do you do for amusement? Do you have a girlfriend? As he began to relate his comings and goings, his evenings in and his evenings out, he realized how paltry his existence was. Across the table, Claude and Dede Armand listened with a polite show of interest. Anecdote followed anecdote, none of them especially illuminating. He was describing the life of a bank clerk.

His father had told him romantic stories of life in France in the Second World War, General Gavin occupying a medieval château near Sedan — a film star installed in one wing, a beautiful American war correspondent in the other — and Field Marshal Rommel at Château Roche-Guyon on the banks of the Eure, gazing every day from his high terrace west to the hills on the margins of Normandy and imagining the half million Allied troops on the march just over the horizon. On soft nights Rommel could hear the rumble of bombs and artillery and knew that however many panzer divisions he could summon, they would not be enough; so he went in to dinner with his senior officers, bottles of claret from the château's cellar warming the discussions.

I have never been to the Eure, Sydney said.

A sluggish river, Claude said. Wide in some places, narrow in others.

Picturesque, Sydney said.

I suppose so.

Sydney remembered the night on the Tay Thanh road with Rostok, his first night in Asia, and told them about the stealthy figures on bicycles, the tick-tick-tick of the wheels and the brush of cloth, the VC whose spectacles had slid to the end of his nose so that when he looked into Sydney's face, he saw nothing but vegetation. And how they had so completely vanished into the night, leaving no trace but some marks in the road. When Rostok asked to spend the night, he brought his revolver into Group House with him.

So Sydney was neither a general nor a field marshal, only an anonymous member of a group whose objectives were dubious; or perhaps there were so many that he had trouble keeping them straight. Nation-building was a demanding business, especially in Asia. He described the weekly meetings at Group House, the bureaucratic miseries and the impossible requests from Washington.

He told them the story of the Mosler safe and the listening device in the chandelier, and the visit of the undersecretary; it had been announced and was therefore not classified information but he was able to add details that caused the Armands to smile between bites of whitefish. He told them about Blind Pablo Gutterman and the difficulties of trying to work with the American military. God, they were voracious —

And then, without quite understanding how it happened, the

transitional thought or sentence, he was talking of Karla, how they had met at the concert in the church downtown, Karla in black with her white scarf leaning into the cello, drained at the conclusion of the German Requiem. God, she was wonderful looking but unpredictable, savage one moment and serene the next. He was looking at the five fist-sized Buddhas arrayed in a bookcase, imagining them as the five inscrutable faces of Karla. Her mother had given her the middle name of Engels, Marx's collaborator, who in his meticulous search for new categories of the downtrodden and the victimized had managed to discover the entire female sex, an insight that so appealed to Magda Parkes that she saddled her daughter with his name. But the effect was not all her mother had hoped for.

Let me tell you the sort of thing she got up to, Sydney said.

This is how strange they were.

When she was a teenager living in the Bay Area, she and her friends assembled a scrapbook, they called it The Ugly Brides Book. They'd cut photographs from the *San Francisco Chronicle* of the week's homeliest brides, sullen, rat-eyed, misshapen girls who would never draw an admiring glance but had managed somehow to attract a fiancé. Karla and her friends had more than a hundred photographs by their senior year in high school, girlish hilarity on Sunday afternoons in the Bay Area, the paper spread on the living room floor, arguing over the candidates and then selecting the unlucky few for inclusion in the scrapbook. She still has it. She brings it out from time to time and makes up stories about what happened to the homely brides and their loutish grooms. Naturally Karla and her two girlfriends were fair-faced and doe-eyed and slender as starlets, popular with boys. To Magda's delight, her daughter became a cheerleader in her junior year, the year before she discovered the cello and in-justice generally.

Magda was Czech. Picture her now, built like a stevedore, beset with a racking cough from the sixty Balkan Sobranie hand-rolled cigarettes she smoked daily. Her hair was short and looked as if it had been trimmed with garden shears, her eyes a wintry blue; she had the most delicious laugh, ruined only slightly by the hacking cough and the lumbar wheeze that went with it.

Sydney, darling, could you fetch me a pilsener?

I disliked her on sight, and then suddenly we were the best of friends. She had an exile's view of the world. She believed her country's history disappeared in 1938 when the West allowed the Nazis in. That was when she became a Red, more in protest against the bourgeois values of London and Paris than out of any sympathy with Stalin. She thought that with the Reds in charge, the Czechs could begin to write their history once again. In 1939 she and Karla left Prague for California, her husband remaining behind to work with the partisans; they never heard from him again and do not know even now whether he is dead or alive. Very possibly he is alive, since the marriage had not been happy and he was unsuited to life in America. Everyone knows that exiles make bad witnesses, and when Czech history remained mute, dead on the page, Magda blamed Stalin for destroying the promise of communism and blamed the West for corrupting democracy with capitalism. She said that the only virtue left for the Czechs was irony. It was a way of surviving, getting along from one day to the next, even if the days were identically dreary. She said that in 1938 the Czechs surrendered their history to outsiders and that was the one thing you must never do. It was unforgivable. You had an obligation to be one of the authors of your time, an obligation she herself had failed by leaving her country at its hour of maximum danger. She had done this for the sake of her young daughter, a sound enough explanation though not a serious excuse. She could not forgive herself.

And I took her point. I sympathized with her. She thought about Czechoslovakia all the time, loving it, disappointed in it, grieving for it, angry with it, always frustrated — and laden with guilt. Magda was no fool. I agreed with her about writing your own history and being present at the end of one era and the beginning of another. Meaning, not to allow history to unfold in your absence or as a consequence of your indifference. That was the reason I came to South Vietnam.

Sydney saw Claude and Dede look at each other in — perhaps alarm, perhaps amusement.

He said, Magda worked as a seamstress in her apartment in the Bay Area. She had many rich clients who invariably called her "a treasure" or "that marvelous Czech woman with the beautiful daughter." She rarely went outside and never mastered English beyond the phrases necessary to talk politics. Karla brought her the news, described the social and economic conditions of the United States, described the life of the American mind; she reported the events of the day, the Bomb, Hiss, the Rosenbergs, Joe McCarthy, Sputnik, the march on Selma, Kennedy's election and Nixon's final ignominious defeat. Magda knew what Karla told her, and Karla was not always a meticulous reporter. She was mischievous. She created a fanciful America of incipient race warfare and a restless, militant peasantry that looked to Europe for its socialist blueprint. Beyond the windows of the apartment on Buena Vista was an appalling smog of resentment and arrested expectations; and the war in Indochina was scheduled as a diversion from these unresolved conflicts. How much of this Magda believed was hard to say. She had her own inner compass. Her own, as Karla liked to say, context. But she had a good heart. She never ceased to care. She never gave up.

The glass is in the fridge, darling. And have one yourself.

Politics drove me and Karla apart, Sydney said sourly. We disagreed on the shape of the modern world. He continued to stare at the five Buddhas, now in full sunlight. The shadows of the Buddhas were sharp against the planes of the bookshelf and now he saw that each Buddha had a different aspect, slender through obese, and their expressions ranged from contentment through indifference to fury. He took a swallow of wine, and Claude refilled the glass at once. He knew this was one glass too many, his words were beginning to drool around the edges and he had the familiar scratch behind his eyeballs. Both Armands were listening carefully now, their faces betraying some bewilderment at the turn to the conversation — monologue, really, because in his heat and desire Sydney was not pausing for questions, indeed appeared unaware that anyone was listening to him. He spoke as if reading from some memorized text, including the non sequiturs.

Karla's political *conceits,* he amended, now that Magda's voice was gone from his memory. It would be too flattering to call them beliefs since they rested on a quicksand of prejudice and hysteria, meaning ignorance of the facts and the lack of a sense of proportion as to what was possible in a dangerous world. She never understood that coincidence was not conspiracy, and in that way she was not truly her mother's daughter; and she did not have Magda's apocalyptic vision of things, the express train of history running headlong into the wretched cul-de-sac of the Soviet empire. Magda insisted that history ended with the disappearance of Czechoslovakia in 1938 because she believed that Czechoslovakia was the soul of Europe and Europe was the soul of the West. Absent Czechoslovakia, Europe was flyblown Dealey Plaza without the grassy knoll. Europe would not be Europe until Czechoslovakia was restored to it. She believed this as passionately as Freud believed in the subconscious. She wanted a Czechoslovakia free of Russians and irony, as Freud wanted a subconscious without the dogma of free will. A simple leap of faith from that precipice to the next: the West did not exist in any recognizable form, certainly not a moral form, because it was deprived of its compass, ego or superego, depending on how you parsed Freud.

Sydney considered the matter and then he said, Perhaps you could say roughly the same thing about the United States today and its relation to South Vietnam. Many do. For isn't South Vietnam poised between East and West, a prize as great as Czechoslovakia.

Hysteria, Dede muttered, but Sydney did not hear.

Karla was not interested in the West, Sydney said. And she believed irony only a bourgeois word for false testimony, the escape hatch that let you out of the locked room, a refusal to accept responsibility for crimes against humanity. Karla measured things on a Marxist yardstick, even the music of Gustav Mahler, Mahler whose greatness was circumscribed by suburban romanticism and a decadent admiration for military themes, adagios in the first instance and marches in the second; and in the mighty Second Symphony he had inserted a tango, as if at any moment Fred and Ginger would float in from the Wienerwald.

Anyone could understand about hating the war, there wasn't much about it to admire, but since troops had been committed and were dying every day it was not practical for America to simply disappear one dewy morning, leaving South Vietnam to the barbarians who were trying to destroy it. Yes, destroy its history. The regime in Hanoi was a dictatorship on the Stalinist model. It didn't have genius enough to create its own politics so it borrowed the politics of a discredited Slavic state with all the usual totalitarian circus acts, secret police, politburos, prison camps, propaganda, and cult of personality. It did not care about the suffering of its own people.

He saw another look pass between Claude and Dede and added, I wanted it so badly.

In the silence that followed, Dede said cautiously, Wanted what?

Wanted what Magda wanted, Sydney said. To be part of the life of my time, and it did not matter where that life was led. I believed history did not stop for Americans, and vice versa. That afternoon at the Foundation, Rostok was persuasive. He had a variation on Magda's theme: when America was involved, the matter was important, and when America wasn't involved, the matter was ephemeral. The stakes were high all around. Walking home that night, I thought about the war and wondered if I had been hasty, allowing myself to be swept along by Rostok's words. I looked in the window of a bookstore, a display commemorating the fiftieth anniversary of Second Ypres and Gallipoli. There were photographs of the carnage surrounded by newly published books. I stood alone at the window while people moved around me, men and women hurrying home to dinner or the theater, indifferent to Second Ypres and Gallipoli. One of the photographs showed a group of young men, jaunty in forage hats and puttees, leaning on the hood of an ambulance. At that moment I saw myself as one of the ambulance drivers. Not a combatant, a witness — and somehow, however the war came out, someone who could be said to have done more good than harm.

I thought — he looked up with a disarming smile and took another swallow of wine — that I might learn something in Indochina. I thought I might learn whether an abstract principle was worth fighting a war. Whatever I gained would be worth much more than whatever I lost.

Also, he said, I was bored.

Never discount boredom as motivation.

I was bored to death with the Foundation. Bored to death in New York, and my discontent was infecting the family, Karla and my daughter both.

But I have to tell you this also, he said. Standing in front of the bookstore window looking at the ambulance drivers, I heard a roaring as if I had held a seashell to my ear. Surely this was a sign, though of what I was not certain. Later, Karla said that anyone who had anything to do with this war in any capacity was as guilty as if he had put the barrel of a gun in a child's face and pulled the trigger. Resistance meant resistance, according to Karla.

And what have you learned? Claude said.

That Karla was wrong, he replied. That there are people like you who live between the lines, neither one thing nor another. You live in the shadows, without allegiances except to the life that you have made. And that you won't give up. It's a mystery to me how you manage. Also, I have learned that South Vietnam is not Czechoslovakia, exactly, but is not entirely removed from it, either.

Strange lessons, Claude said.

I hope you are not offended, Sydney said.

We are not offended, Dede said.

I admire the way you live, Sydney said.

It isn't admirable, Claude said. It's what we have.

So she never knew her father, Dede said. Karla never went back and he never came out.

Sydney nodded.

I don't know mine, either, she added.

They think he's alive, probably a commissar in Prague.

Mine's alive, Dede said. He used to take me out to lunch on my birthday but he stopped when I went away to school. He's a bond salesman living somewhere up the Hudson, Rip Van Winkle country. New wife, new baby. Wife number three, baby number four.

Karla rarely mentions him, Sydney said. I don't think she thinks about him. Karla's always been self-sufficient. She's a law unto herself. When Karla left Europe, Paul Parkes was a dead letter.

She thinks about him, Dede said.

Maybe she does, Sydney said. I don't know.

Trust me, Dede said.

And Magda? Claude asked.

I don't know where Paul Parkes fits into Magda's theory of history. Probably he's inconvenient to it.

I'll get the cognac, Claude said.

I'll make coffee, Dede said, rising to collect the plates. She seemed to sway as she moved around the table stacking plates and flatware. When Sydney offered to help, she shook her head. Claude followed her into the kitchen.

Sydney lit a cigarette, feeling sheepish. He had not intended a tour d'horizon of his wretched marriage and careful life in New York. He had difficulty convincing them and in the end probably he had failed; that was usually the case, you could never see into another life. Probably they would not think his wretched and careful but normal, the sort of safe middle-class life that people everywhere wanted for themselves. Democratic systems promised that life, monotonous days, a steady job, Sundays in the countryside, a baseball game on a soft summer night, a concert under the stars. He did not know what had made him go on and on about Magda. He was surprised he remembered as much as he had. He had not spoken to her in a year because she and Karla were on the outs and Karla did not want him involved, meaning choosing sides.

Sydney finished his cigarette and still the Armands had not appeared. He could hear them in the kitchen talking, the confidential murmur reserved for married people who were fully attached to each other and dependent equally. He knew it well and missed it now. He missed the early mornings in Manhattan, Karla still asleep in their bed, the sky-blue duvet pulled to her throat, her soft hair spilling onto the pillow. Her eyes were shut but she was smiling. She appeared to blush in the light of early morning and then she moved, stretching herself. Her hand appeared, her fingers slender and supple as a cat's tail, flopping on the sheet. He knew she was dreaming. He thought he had never seen anyone so beautiful. He sat on the edge of the bed and willed her to wake but she rarely did; and then she would shudder voluptuously, smile again, and say something in her downy just-awake voice and he would kiss her on the neck. She moved farther under the covers and then she had part of him under the covers, too, a leg and an arm, and she would begin to laugh softly, her arms around the small of his back. She had something she wanted to tell him, what she remembered of her dream and his place in it. But the memory always feathered away before she could get it out. So he would invent a dream for her, a gaudy, complicated affair, ribald, full of promise. Tell me again, she murmured.

At that moment Dede came through the door with a tray, Claude following close behind with the bottle of Martell and three glasses.

The sun began to fail, casting long shadows through the living room. Dede poured coffee and Claude set ponies of cognac before them. They sat in companionable silence, listening to the songs of birds. Dede had thrown open the window and the room was filled with the thick scent of the forest and something else, acrid fumes from the factory shed at the bottom of the lawn. She stood at the window sipping coffee, dressed in a white shift, the crucifix at her throat, bangles on her wrists, looking like any settled suburban matron at the end of the day. She was evidently fatigued, her shoulders slumping as Karla's did at the end of a long rehearsal. Sydney looked at his watch and reckoned it was about time to say goodbye. He wondered how he could tell them gracefully that he wanted to come to them again for lunch or dinner. He liked their company. He liked the way they were with each other, communicating with a glance or a raised eyebrow. Together they seemed the essence of conjugal life and he wondered whether that was because of or in spite of their isolation from the war around them. He wondered how they had found each other and whether they knew right away, as he had with Karla; probably they were people attracted to extreme situations, such as those who lived on the slopes of a volcano, rising apprehensively each day to glance at the boiling cone. He suspected that between the Armands much was concealed, a specific zone of privacy that no outsider could break or would wish to break. They lived by their own lights.

Sydney looked up to see Claude staring at him with an expression that suggested he was reading minds, and not liking the text.

Claude said, Can your Rostok be trusted?

The remark was so unexpected that Sydney was startled. He answered truthfully, I suppose so. It would depend.

Depend on what? Claude said.

On what was at stake, Sydney replied. He thought a moment and attached an amendment, At stake for him.

You mean, him personally?

From the window Dede murmured, *Claude,* in a voice somewhere between apprehension and resignation.

It's all right, Claude said.

Be careful, she said as if she were speaking privately, tête-à-tête.

Claude said, Do you mean personal risk?

Not risk in a physical sense, Sydney said quickly. Rostok doesn't care about that because he thinks he's invincible. He does not want to be cornered, to be put in a position where he might be — outflanked. He likes to be able to see ahead, around the next corner. He likes to see from today to tomorrow. Meaning, to identify the contingencies. He watches his back. Your wife has worked in the government. She knows what it's like, the rivalries and the knives in the back.

Claude grunted doubtfully, reaching for his cognac and sipping, staring into the middle distance. Dede did not move from the window, where she stood listlessly watching her birds through a pair of binoculars.

Rostok likes to be in control of things, Sydney went on. He likes to be in charge and be certain everyone knows he's in charge. If he sensed a situation where he could be at the mercy of other people or unpredictable events, he would worry. Rostok worried is Rostok unreliable. He knows he has enemies, people who want him to fail and aren't above pushing things along. But in his own way he's very able. He's shrewd and he knows what he wants and will bend rules to get it.

That's what you need to know, Claude, Dede said from the window.

What are you seeing? Claude said.

I thought I saw a Bonaparte but it was only an ordinary parrot, Dede said.

Keep looking, Claude said.

Usually at dusk it's the best time. They're always moving around at dusk. You should find yourself a pair of binoculars, Sydney. Vietnam has the most extraordinary array of avian life. But I guess I've mentioned that before. She opened the door and stepped onto the verandah where she stood with the glasses lowered. In the distance they heard the beat of a helicopter.

Is his word good? Claude asked.

He very seldom gives it, Sydney said. Almost never. But when he does give it, his word's as good as anybody's.

That's not encouraging, Claude said.

It wasn't meant to be, Sydney said.

And you, Claude said. What about your word?

My word's good, Sydney said. I don't give it often, either, but that's because I can't deliver the way Rostok delivers. I can get a roof on a church but I can't stop them bombing your rubber trees. I thought I could, but I can't.

Claude said, Where do you fit in, then?

Sydney went through it again, Rostok and Pablo Gutterman and the others, Rostok in charge and Gutterman doing what Rostok gave him to do. He, Sydney, was third in line. But Rostok was the principal, he said, knowing that was what Claude was asking. But when the Frenchman did not reply, only continued to stare into the middle distance, Sydney said, What's this all about?

I understand you've lost someone, Claude said.

Sydney shook his head. He thought that the Frenchman meant Karla but the expression on his face showed otherwise.

What do you mean?

Your young army officer, Claude said. Captain Smalley.

Yes, Sydney said. He's missing. He and three comrades from an action a week or so ago. They were ambushed, hit hard, a very bad scene. They went in at night without sufficient force and were overwhelmed. Many dead and wounded and four missing. We'd like to get them back, all four. It's important to us.

Claude nodded soberly.

Very important, Sydney said.

That will not be possible, Dede said from the doorway. She gestured with the binoculars in the direction of the forest.

There are ways and means, Sydney said. He hesitated and

added, Some kind of exchange or other reward. There are people working on it now, in the embassy and at MACV. And Rostok's working on it, too. I'm certain something can be worked out, something beneficial all around. Naturally we would have to verify. We'd have to know the situation. Where they are and in what condition. We'd have to communicate with them. And we'd have to approve the terms, of course.

Three of the four are dead, Claude said.

Rest in peace, Dede said.

The big one's still alive. Smalley.

Badly injured?

I don't know the nature of his wounds. I don't have that information. The information that I have is that he's alive and being held. I know he's been on the march, here and there over the past few days.

Where is he? Sydney asked.

Claude moved his head vaguely. Why, he's out there —

Sydney followed the Frenchman's line of sight, to the forest and the hinterland of the forest. Smalley could be anywhere, aboveground or below. He could be in a village or on a boat. He could be in the hills to the west or over the border in Cambodia or Laos. He could be in Saigon or one of the coastal cities, Qui Nhon or Nha Trang, though that was less likely. He would never be found unless his captors wanted him to be found. He had effectively disappeared from the known world, a ghost soldier.

Sydney said, Is he being well cared for? Are they looking after him?

I suppose they are, Claude said. It's not a suite at the Continental.

You know what I mean, Sydney said.

My information is limited. I doubt if there's torture. Is that what you mean?

They like torture, Sydney said.

Not always, Claude said.

Are they locals?

Claude shrugged and did not reply.

They are local, Dede said.

Claude glanced sharply at his wife, then turned again to Sydney. Is Captain Smalley important in some way? More important than an ordinary infantry captain on assignment?

They say so, Sydney said.

Who is he, then?

This must be between us, as friends. Are we friends?

Yes, Claude said.

He's related to a congressman, Sydney said.

I thought it was something like that, Claude said. There are rumors, more rumors than usual. We have them all the time but these are different. There's activity in the district, night patrols and so forth. Interrogation of villagers, offers of money or threats, depending on who's doing the interrogating. Helicopters checkerboarding. It's more activity than we've ever seen. So the people here had an idea that this captain might be out of the ordinary, a special sort of captain. They thought he must be a spy despite the uniform.

He's not a spy, Sydney said.

If they knew he was a spy, they'd shoot him.

He's not, my word.

I'll let them know, Claude said.

You've spoken to the people who have him?

Not directly, Claude said.

Indirectly, then.

I get word, Claude said vaguely.

Sydney hesitated, then asked, Is it good for him? Is it better for him to be somebody or nobody? Does he have a better chance if he's somebody or if they think he's somebody? Do they know what a congressman is?

Maybe, Claude said.

And if they don't, someone could tell them.

Claude was toying with a rubber band, wrapping it around one finger and then another, drawing it tight like a bowstring, and holding. I don't know what they think, he said finally. I don't know how they think. It's one of the things I like about the Vietnamese, because they don't know me, either.

The poor bastard, Sydney said. He had a sudden image of Smalley curled in a bamboo cage, disarmed, exhausted, thirsty, feverish, frightened, near tears. He had always been the biggest boy in his class. His size protected him. Probably he had heard a lecture at Bragg, What to Do If You Are Captured. Lesson one: don't be. And when the laughter died down in the darkened auditorium, he gratefully fell asleep. They said he was a nice boy, just a big dumb blond. It wasn't likely that he would talk his way out of it, or make a marvelous escape.

Claude raised his eyebrows, continuing to toy with the rubber band, pulling it until his fingers stung; and then it snapped. He said, It isn't pleasant for him. And it'll only get worse. They have no facilities. They're — very young. They're inexperienced. They're nervous. They don't want to make a mistake because they know they're responsible if something goes wrong. Something goes wrong, and they're in as much trouble as Captain Smalley.

Sydney said, So they might execute him to have done with it.

Claude said, Might.

Sydney said, Why are you telling me this?

Claude did not reply for a moment. He was looking at his fingers, white where the rubber had made its noose. Dede had moved off the verandah and onto the lawn, out of earshot. He said, Perhaps there's something to be done. I don't know what it is but your Rostok might. If he's as clever as you say he is.

I'll tell you something, he said.

What you do with it is your business, so long as you leave us out of it.

Claude leaned close and confided that one of his workers had brought him a message. Captain Smalley was in the district. Local cadre were holding him until one of the headquarters commissars could take charge. Their radio was broken so they had sent a runner to Central Office in Tay Ninh. The local cadre were waiting for instructions and until then were keeping their American in one of the caves. But they're nervous and worried that they've done the wrong thing. And the American — and here Claude allowed himself a sympathetic smile — is not responding well to captivity.

Do you know where he is exactly?

No. They would never tell me that.

Can you find out?

I would never ask, Claude said.

Why did they tell you anything at all? What was the purpose of their message?

Claude sighed. They're out of their depth.

I'd say they are.

They're just local boys, Claude said. They don't want much. They want to be let alone, mostly. And for the Saigon administration to resign and the Americans to resign with them so they can set about building their socialist paradise. They think that once Uncle Ho is in charge everything will be fine and they can go back to their villages, their farms, and their girlfriends. Meanwhile, they have an American officer they don't know what to do with.

And they want your advice?

Not in so many words, Claude said.

But they sent you a message?

One of my workers brought me a message, Claude said.

So they trust you, Sydney said.

They don't think I'm their enemy. I have nothing against them. What is an enemy, anyway? Someone who has what you want or has taken what you think is rightfully yours. Or you see something in a man that reminds you of your worst self. I want nothing from them except their labor in return for wages. I suppose in the socialist paradise they will confiscate this plantation. But they'll still need someone to run it, and it makes no difference to me who I report to. That will be an affair between Hanoi and Paris. The work itself will not change. We are governed by the seasons, by temperature and rainfall. It's the same for farmers everywhere.

Sydney listened impatiently to this strange recital.

A few nights ago one of your bombs almost got them. It missed by a hundred meters. So they decided to move their bivouac. And they wanted me to know.

Sydney ignored the obvious question and said instead, You could tell them the Americans would make an arrangement. Ransom, if you like.

They don't take instructions from me, Claude said.

Still, Sydney said. Obviously you have some influence with them.

I have no influence. That I am not their enemy does not make me their friend.

They sent you a message, Sydney said. That counts for something.

That is what I think, Claude said abruptly. Take it for what it's worth. I believe that if it was up to them, they'd keep Captain Smalley for themselves. They'd like to make their own arrangements for Captain Smalley. But it isn't up to them. Once the commissar arrives from Tay Ninh, the captain is out of their supervision, probably on the trail north under escort. Either that or the commissar orders an execution. Captain Smalley disappears, fate unknown. Perhaps the commissar is angry that the captain was not killed on the spot because, believe me, at Central Office they know about the congressman, who he is and what he does, and his specific gravity in his own milieu. They would be calculating his propaganda value alive and his propaganda value dead; and that would depend on who is being propagandized. So it's logical that there's important radio traffic between Tay Ninh and the North. What do we do with this captain? It's probably a decision made at the top, maybe Giap personally, or even Ho.

Sydney nodded, wondering what the captain knew of this. Most likely nothing, but hoping all the same.

The commissars don't like our locals, Claude went on. Peasant boys always in need of reeducation, often too independent for their own good, and generally naïve. Often politically unreliable. Our locals know who's in charge and don't like it. They're loyal southern boys and don't like being dictated to by the hard-faced northerners. They're proud of what they did a week ago. They took an infantry company out of action and they captured a captain, and not just any captain. And now they're waiting for instructions. Unless they already have their instructions and are carrying them out right now.

It's been ten days, Sydney said.

It takes them time, Claude said.

Will you talk to Rostok?

Out of the question, Claude said. He looked over Sydney's shoulder, out the window to the lawn and the plantation beyond.

What should I tell him, then?

Not much. As little as possible, since these events are unpredictable and he won't be in charge. When I know more, I'll get a message to you.

Claude, Sydney said patiently. That isn't helpful. Smalley may have only a day or two to live, maybe less. Whatever we can do, we must do. He opened his mouth to continue, then held back. He looked at the bright cover of *Paris-Match*, a radiant Princess Grace rising to mock him. He took a sip of cognac, the taste sweet and smoky, a man's drink for the end of the day. The coffee had gone cold and he was out of cigarettes. He wondered what Smalley would make of this afternoon, so controlled and civilized; a fine lunch, a rambling, intimate conversation, and binoculars for the birds. So you want me to keep this information to myself, Sydney said dully.

For the moment, Claude said.

We don't have a moment, Sydney objected.

You feel sorry for your big dumb blond, Claude said. You want to help him. But as it happens, so do I. *So do I,* he said again, fiercely, scowling suddenly. Then he was out of his chair and looking wildly out the window, tapping on it, muttering Oh merde. In a moment he was out the door and striding down the long green slope, Sydney in pursuit. Dede was nowhere in sight. Claude called loudly but she did not answer. They entered the plantation and at once were inside a watery green world. The light seemed to stop at the great overarching branches above them, the air almost viscous, redolent of raw latex and rotting vegetation. Claude hurried along the narrow path between the bare trunks of the rubber trees, leaping now and then to avoid fallen branches, and in minutes they were deep in the wilderness of the plantation, the house invisible behind them. Here and there were signs of occupation, footprints, a scrap of paper, empty tins, animal bones, a plastic sandal, a cold campfire. The sour odor of human sweat hung in the vast silence, along with the intimation of urgent conversations just ended. Sydney's shoes slipped on the slick path and when he steadied himself against the trunk of a tree he noticed the long diagonal cut, a vessel at the base to collect the creamy latex. He fell behind and when he halted, listening for Claude, all he could hear was his own breathing and the rustle of his clothes when he waved his arms to brush the mosquitoes away. The light was an unnerving milky gray, shadowless and without definition. He knew he was hopelessly lost in a place without landmarks. Sydney followed Claude's tracks farther into the symmetry of the plantation.

He was almost upon the Frenchman before he saw him standing at the edge of a clearing. His wife was kneeling before two gravestones. There were other gravestones round and about. The ones at Claude's feet were from the previous century, the names both French and Vietnamese. At the far end of the clearing were prayer flags, black lettering on white cloth, the cloth frayed and so thin you could see through it. Buddhists believe that the winds carry the prayers over the surface of the earth, consoling the dead and the living. In the flat light the graveyard had the aspect of a surreal painting, things out of place, the flags jittery, the latex vessels overflowing, Dede in white against the green earth, the gravestones standing straight as soldiers and overhead a late afternoon moon, pale as ashes.

When she rose, Sydney could see the dirt on the hem of her dress. She turned and looked directly at him but gave no sign of recognition; and then she bowed her head to say a final prayer to her children. Claude came up behind her and put his arm around her waist, saying a few words. She took his hand and gripped it, her head moving this way and that, as if she were not in control of her movements. She began to keen in a voice so thin it could not be heard twenty feet away. When a breath of air caught the prayer flags, she fell silent, watching them shudder, their skirts flaring, sighing some kind of fantastic language of the dead.

Sydney turned away, leaving them alone. He picked his way slowly back down the path. The sound of a helicopter in the distance brought him back to the task at hand. He thought about Smalley all the way to the Armands' house, in deep shadows when he arrived; and by the time he reached the main road, night had fallen and the moon was bright. His heart was cold and he wondered now if that was the cause of his bad conscience or the result of it.

Pablo's Hat

*P*ABLO GUTTERMAN sat staring glumly at his Panama hat.
The hat rested on the metal table next to the tall glass of lemonade that was sweating in the heat. It was nine in the morning on
the all but empty terrace of the Continental Palace. The city
struggled to life, the street filled with the racket of engines and
exhaust fumes. From the river came the hollow-sounding horns
of freighters maneuvering in the narrow channel. Cigarette girls
were in place on the sidewalk across the street. Pablo's brother-
in-law had complained that they were selling dope along with
Chesterfields, and any day now they would be selling themselves.
There were so many GIs in town spreading wickedness. Pablo
nodded at something Sydney Parade said, then resumed his contemplation of the hat.

Sydney continued to explain. Even his explanations had explanations.

Perhaps it was time for a new hat, not that anyone sold genuine Panamas in Saigon; this model, bleached the color of clotted
cream, was the one favored by Miami gangsters, and Orson
Welles in the sunny summer scenes of *Citizen Kane*. Pablo raised

his eyes to survey the street, damp from last evening's rain. You would think that rain would freshen the atmosphere, bring the tang of the sea inland where it would do some good, serve to remind the population of distant Asian horizons, meaning a sense of possibility. But it never did. The rain was a monotonous peninsular rain that did not even clear the dust from the city's sultry climate, blue with exhaustion. Pablo watched Mrs. Han, the pharmacist, open the door to her shop, step outside, and stare disapprovingly at the cigarette girls on the corner. Then she glared at the ashen sky. A low sheet of cloud moved west to east but at street level there was no breeze. More rain was on the way.

So that's the broad picture, Sydney said, pausing but briefly before he moved into another digression, a detail he'd forgotten, something about Claude Armand's loyal Vietnamese workforce and trouble with production quotas.

Mrs. Han disappeared into the interior of her shop, not before glancing at the terrace, raising her eyes fractionally at the sight of Pablo in conversation with the young American in blue jeans. Pablo gave a little nod of his head but she did not acknowledge it. Only the night before, his brother-in-law informed him that a shipment of pharmaceuticals had arrived in Cholon and was being sold on the black market. Penicillin was the most sought-after but it was also the most likely to be adulterated, fabricated in unsanitary conditions or simply bogus, sugar tablets in a counterfeit vial. People were likely to die unless the shipment was seized, and that was highly unlikely because — and here his brother-in-law named the wife of a general in the Ministry of Defense, owner of a successful trading company. Can you find out about it, Pablo? And let us know what you discover? We can give you the location of the warehouse, but the Americans will have to be responsible for the confiscation of the goods. Our own police can't be trusted. This is all the fault of the Americans. If they were not in our country, there would be no black market.

So tell them they must do what is right. Pablo said what he always said, that he would do what he could. In this case, everything depended on how much the Americans valued the general's good will. Pablo looked at his watch, waiting for Sydney to finish.

So I don't know what to do, Sydney said.

I have a thought, Pablo said.

Claude thinks there's a possibility they might consider an exchange or some quid pro quo. That's assuming our captain is alive. Claude wasn't specific. Maybe he was only guessing.

They don't do business that way, Pablo said. They never have. They're back-of-the-head people. You think you see through them and then you understand that you're looking at a mirror, reading your own thoughts. They're patient. They're stubborn. I think you could offer them an atomic bomb and an airplane to deliver it and they'd think about it for a month and say, No, not until you evacuate. Not until every last infantryman is back in California. Then we'll think about your offer.

Risk-benefit, Sydney said.

Pablo tried again. He liked Sydney Parade, a man eager to learn but often attracted to the wrong lessons. He said, Listen to me, Sydney. They don't think in terms of benefit. They're concerned with winning, only that. We like to think of them as the inscrutable face of Buddha. We believe that if we discover what animates them, we can outsmart them. But it's all beside the point. They don't care if they outsmart us or not. Outsmarting is not what they do. Fighting is what they do, and they do it well. They've been doing it for a very long time with only the back of their heads to guide them. It's the life they've chosen. They respect it. It's the reason they exist, I suspect. They believe they are in harmony with the universe. They hear its heartbeat. As good Communists they are never plagued by doubt; and in that way they remind me of Dicky Rostok. Marxism is a kind of natural law. When they die, they will die as honored men, welcomed by their ancestors. They have a plan and they will adhere to the plan no matter what we do or don't do. We're irrelevant to them.

You're a pessimist, Pablo.

Pablo shook his head sadly and shooed away a fly that had lit upon the brim of his Panama hat, no doubt one of the ancestors visiting, a signal of approval. To believe the revolution would be defeated by Western arms was to believe in the modern world, the superiority of Western virtue and Western spirits, and he knew no Vietnamese who did. They all had their bags packed but they had nowhere to go. He watched Mrs. Han sweep the sidewalk in front of her shop; then he had a sudden image of Captain Smalley underground, wet, wounded, insects feeding on his wounds. He was hurting. He was cold. Captain Smalley did not appear to be a resourceful soldier, and the longer he was in the bush, the worse it would get. If Smalley was still alive, it was a miracle from heaven.

There's a way, Sydney said. We just have to find it.

Pablo decided to speak more slowly. He said, They don't like negotiating, Sydney. They tried it twice in Switzerland and it didn't get them what they wanted. Switzerland was very far from Vietnam. They were outmaneuvered by white men in double-breasted suits. In 1945 they tried to enlist the friendship of the United States. That didn't work, either. So they believe they are alone in the world except for alliances of convenience like the one they have with the Soviet Union. They looked at their circumstances and decided on a strategy of unconditional victory, no matter how long it took them or how many died. Any other strategy was unworthy. And the American government decided to oblige them. Am I being clear?

You still haven't answered my question, Sydney said.

What have you told Rostok?

Nothing yet, Sydney said.

Will Claude talk to me?

I doubt it, Sydney said.

You have to be careful with Rostok, what you say to him. He isn't careful with information. Pablo opened his mouth to say more, how you never knew Rostok's angle-of-the-day, how he always had a subtext that was more important than the text, how he let his love of intrigue get the better of him. But he had made these observations before, so he did not make them now.

Probably I should take what I know to the military and let them handle it. They're entitled to the information.

He's their man, Pablo said.

Their responsibility, Sydney agreed.

They have the ways and means, Pablo said, and did not add that the means were too much and the ways too limited.

And I have to protect Claude.

That you do, Pablo said. He's taken risks.

And meantime, that poor son of a bitch Smalley is somewhere in the rain forest —

Dead or alive, Pablo said.

Claude thinks there's a chance he's alive.

Pablo thought a moment, remembering something his wife had said a few nights before. He was suddenly uneasy. At last he said, We would need evidence. In the absence of evidence, take it to the military. Tell Rostok later. He's tied up anyway with that friend of his, the Washington character, the assistant secretary.

Undersecretary, Sydney said, smiling because Pablo had no sense of rank or precedence.

There's nothing you or I can do, Pablo said. Nothing Rostok can do. Nothing Claude Armand can do. Give it to the military.

All right, Sydney said.

I know the man to go to. He's discreet. He's not a fool.

Let's go, then.

Pablo threw some bills on the table and picked up his hat. The sun was peeking through the sheet of cloud, a kind of fluorescent glow. The city did have its own animal charm, the swish and slither of some creature of the underworld, lawless, unpredictable. He watched the cigarette girls approach two Americans who had emerged from the Caravelle Hotel across the square, journalists from the look of them. They were blinking in the light and reaching for their wallets. Their shirt pockets bristled with pens.

Then Sydney's hand was on his arm. My God, he said, that's Dede Armand right there. He pointed at a Western woman disappearing into a taxi. Before he could say anything more, the taxi was gliding away in heavy traffic toward the river. Sydney could see her silhouette in the rear window.

The lady asked me to give you this, the waiter said, and handed Sydney a thin manila envelope.

How did she know where to find me? Sydney said.

The waiter shrugged and drifted off. The cab disappeared.

Well, Pablo said. Someone did.

Sydney opened the envelope and looked at its contents, a single sheet of paper.

This changes everything, he said.

Sydney and Pablo were drinking coffee at the oval mahogany table at Group House when Rostok arrived, his Scout spinning into the driveway, scattering gravel. He had been given bodyguards, four slender Nungs in camouflage gear who carried Swedish K submachine guns. The Nungs spilled from the car, brandishing their weapons at the startled gardeners. Rostok watched the show, then growled some cryptic order that caused the Nungs to retreat to the shade of the plane tree. One stood at attention while the others began to break down their weapons. Rostok hurried inside the villa. Sydney and Pablo heard him loudly issuing instructions to the secretaries. Then he was in the conference room, rubbing his hands and chuckling.

Had him for an hour, one on one. He wanted it that way, Syd, tête-à-tête with no third parties. He's a good man, knows how to listen, knows what he doesn't know, always plays the hand he's dealt. Now he's with the general in the general's jet, heading to some godforsaken firebase in Three Corps, more briefings with the charts and the bar graphs . . .

Rostok poured coffee.

. . . one major for each chart, one lieutenant colonel per bar graph.

But I got him first, Rostok said.

One on one, sixty uninterrupted minutes. Sorry again, Syd. But it was his call.

He went to the door and called for George Whyte, but George wasn't there, an urgent errand in Cholon. Rostok cursed. Whyte was never around when you needed him. Whyte was always off on some always-urgent mission and wasn't it odd that these missions never failed to occur when he, Rostok, needed something done without delay, in this important instance an exact accounting of the annual budget, how much spent, how much on hand, how much in the pipeline — and the Top Secret wish list because the wish list was about to come true, thanks to the progress made this morning one on one with the undersecretary, who understood the situation at once. Rostok stopped then and took his usual place at the head of the table, smiling sardonically.

And I'm being promoted to brigadier general.

How can you be a brigadier general? You're not in the army.

That so, Pablo?

That's so, Ros.

Equivalent rank, Pab. I'm counselor of embassy as of eighteen hundred hours today. So that I can talk to those bastards at MACV eye to eye on a level playing field.

Congratulations, Pablo said.

General, Sydney added.

Sarcasm does not become you, Syd, Rostok said.

Ros, we have some information, Sydney began.

But Rostok wasn't listening. He was staring out the window, watching his Nungs fieldstrip the Scandinavian furniture.

And I have some other news, he said, this news not to leave this room. It looks like sometime next year the President of the United States will pay us a visit. Talk to the troops, it'll be a morale booster. Maybe for him, too, right around the time of the midterm elections. It'll be a snap visit, no advance warning, and I can promise you that Llewellyn Group will be significantly involved. In the planning.

And the last thing, Rostok continued. The undersecretary was briefed this morning on the efforts to find Captain Smalley. He didn't hear anything positive and he was triple pissed because the boy's uncle is a friend of his and asked him personally to find out what he could and put the heat on, highest priority, et cetera et cetera. Simple truth. They don't know where he is. Captain Smalley has vanished. Hard for them to explain to the undersecretary that while South Vietnam looks small on a map, it's a big country when you're on the ground. Everything looks alike. And the suspicion is they live underground. They're underground men.

What's their plan? Pablo asked.

They don't have one. They're running patrols.

They have no intelligence at all?

They have plenty of information, because they're paying for it. I don't know that I'd call it intelligence. They have numerous reports, Smalley sighted here, Smalley sighted there. Smalley bound and blindfolded, led away in the direction of the Parrot's Beak. Smalley seen in village A en route to village B. Smalley in a whorehouse in Danang. Smalley in an opium palace in Cholon. Smalley dead, Smalley alive. They don't believe any of it and they're right not to, but they check each report, try to verify what they can; and they come up empty.

CAS involved?

Unofficially, Rostok said.

I think I know where he is, Sydney said.

Rostok looked up. Where is he?

Tay Thanh district.

Alive?

I don't know that.

Where'd the information come from?

I have a map, Sydney said. Delivered this morning on the terrace of the Continental Palace Hotel.

Who delivered it?

A waiter, Ros. In a plain manila envelope.

Let me see it. Give it to me now.

Sydney slid the envelope across the desk. Rostok took the paper from the envelope and peered at it, turning it first one way and then another. He was silent, obviously making no sense of it. At last he said, It doesn't look like a map to me. It looks like one of those x-marks-the-spot things you got when you were a kid, find the buried treasure. A box of Fig Newtons.

You have to know the district, Pablo said. He walked around the table and laid the map on its surface so they could all see it. That's in the vicinity of a string of hamlets called Song Nu. A river connects them. And trails about wide enough for an ox cart. It's not territory we consider secure. In fact, we consider it under the control of the VC. You approach it by this road — and here Pablo jabbed a fat thumb at the map — and go in by the river or the trails. No one knows very much about Song Nu. There's no reason to know anything about it. Some Cao Dai in there.

Who are the Cao Dai? Ros asked.

Religious sect, Pablo said. They have four saints, Christ, Buddha, Marx, and Victor Hugo. Peaceful people for the most part. Serious, mysterious people.

Rostok raised his eyebrows. Victor Hugo?

Victor Hugo. He's one of the minor saints, along with Jeanne d'Arc.

Rostok pointed at a scribbled sentence on the map. What does this mean.

Roughly, "Come and get him."

A challenge?

I don't think so, Pablo said. I think it's a straightforward invitation. Smalley is here. Come and get him.

Rostok was still staring at the map that made no sense to him. Do you think it's genuine? You have no idea how many characters have come tumbling over the transom at MACV, claiming to know where Smalley is or where he was or who has him and what they intend to do with him.

No one's asked for any money, Pablo said.

Where did the waiter get it?

He didn't say, Sydney said.

Rostok looked out the window at his Nungs. They had finished fieldstripping their weapons and were now dozing in the shade of the plane tree. The gardeners worked around them, collecting leaves when they weren't leaning on their rakes. Lazy bastards, he said to no one in particular. Then, to Sydney: Do you know where he got it?

No, Sydney said.

Why did he give it to you?

No idea, Sydney said.

We're on the same team here, Syd, Rostok said.

So let's see, Rostok went on. You and Pablo are sitting on the terrace of the Continental Palace and a waiter walks up and hands you a map disclosing the location of the most wanted infantry captain in Indochina and walks away without a word, not even waiting for a tip. And why does he choose you? Why not the ambassador? Why not the commanding general? Why not me? Why was it you, Syd?

They know I'm the representative in Tay Thanh. Why not?

What does Claude Armand have to do with this?

Nothing, Sydney said.

I think it's his map, Rostok said.

It isn't, Sydney said evenly.

Pablo said, I think it's genuine. And it isn't Armand's. Isn't the question, What are we going to do with this information?

Take it to MACV, Rostok said.

That's one solution, Pablo said.

Tell me another one, Rostok said.

Pablo returned to the map and began to describe the terrain in detail. The hamlets covered an area fifteen kilometers long by five kilometers wide. Inside the boundaries were rice fields and the river, and a heavily forested hill. Inside that perimeter you could hide a battalion of infantry and no one would know. You could send a regiment of American troopers and they could not cover it all; and it was likely that the VC had at least one underground complex, absolutely undetectable unless you knew it was there. The infantry comes in with its gunships and artillery and the people vanish. You'd never find them. And I suspect Smalley would vanish with them. You'd never find him, either. I think this is a different sort of invitation. I think they're saying, Come in alone. We'll take you to him. Pablo thought a moment, recalling the remoteness of Song Nu, its unapproachability and the tremendous reserve of the inhabitants. They spoke to you with their faces averted, reciting ordinary small talk as if it were Shakespeare. They reminded him of true believers reading from the Bible, or Reds from Marx. He was there visiting his wife's cousin. They stayed only a few hours and walked out by the same route as they had walked in; that was seven or eight years ago and he had not been back since. The children stared at him as if he were a djinn come to display his appalling supernatural powers; and then he realized they were fascinated by his hat.

Rostok said, You're saying that the army will muck it up, kill a lot of people and not find Smalley.

My guess, Pablo said.

You seem to know a lot about this place, Pab.

I was there once visiting, many years ago. Strange place. I didn't like it. But I remember it.

If the army doesn't go in for Smalley, who does?

I do, Pablo said.

Rostok smiled and then he laughed, a huge, cold guffaw.

Pablo remembered they parked off the district road and at once three men emerged from the forest to guide them to the hamlets. They walked for a while along the river, then struck off on a trail. He remembered the swish of his wife's ao dai as they moved through the brush. After an hour they were joined by two more guides, and then a third and a fourth, and by the time they reached Song Nu One they were a formidable procession. When he asked his wife what it was all about, she smiled and replied that was the way villagers did things and not to be alarmed, they were hospitable people. Simple but hospitable, she amended. Not accustomed to strangers. At the end of the visit she giggled and said, They will always remember you because of your hat.

Impossible, Rostok said.

Fine, get someone else, Pablo replied.

The army, Rostok said.

Then Smalley's dead, Sydney said.

You seem damned sure of yourself, Syd.

I'm thinking of Smalley underground, and what's written on the map. What Pablo says is logical. I agree with it.

It's fanciful, Rostok said. Intuition isn't good out here, and if you screw up we're all in the soup. Besides, it's dangerous.

Depends on who's in charge, Pablo said. I don't think it's the VC. VC would've killed him by now or taken him north.

How do you know he's not dead?

I don't, Pablo conceded.

Well then, you're flying blind.

Trouble is, Sydney said, this is our information. It came to us, for whatever reason. We give it to the army and the army fucks up, it's on our heads, too. And Smalley, he's on our conscience.

Point taken, Rostok said. And the reverse is also true, that if we developed the intelligence *and* spring the lad, we're the heroes of the day. Llewellyn Group's on the map. He paused to consider the thought.

Llewellyn Group isn't the point, Pablo said, an unpleasant edge to his voice.

Rostok ignored the remark. He said, Do you think you can get in and get out safely? With Smalley? Smalley injured. Smalley dead weight. Who knows what sort of shape he's in or even if he's alive.

Fair chance, Pablo said.

It has to be better than fair, Rostok said.

All right, then. Better than fair.

I'll go with you, Rostok said. At the magnitude of this offer, a wide smile crossed Rostok's face. Just then he might have been appearing before television cameras at the news conference at Group House, a shaken but elated Captain Smalley at his side, Rostok unsmiling as he denounced the savagery of the enemy. The White House is on the line, Mr. Rostok.

Not necessary, Pablo said. He was tempted to add, Suicidal, but did not.

Under a white flag of truce, Rostok said.

Pablo saw them walking through the forest waving hand-kerchiefs, the villagers applauding before the shooting started. I've already turned Sydney down, Pablo said. I know the people in these hamlets and I think they'll remember me, and I'll come to no harm. If I didn't believe that, I wouldn't do it. He nodded stiffly, believing every word he had spoken. The people of Song Nu lived according to their own lights. For whatever reason, they had decided to surrender Smalley, an alien in their midst; when he was gone, they would return to contemplation of their minor saints, forgetting utterly the inconvenience in their midst.

Rostok was thinking hard. Anyone could see he had the beginnings of a plan, and that alarmed Sydney. Rostok said, I'll give you my Nungs.

For what? Pablo said.

Protection, Rostok said.

Forget the Nungs, Pablo said.

They're good boys, Rostok went on. Loyal boys. Well trained and well paid. They're just lazier'n hell. Good fighters, though. Ruthless.

Pablo watched them dozing under the admiral's tree. The gardeners were moving in slow circles, collecting leaves. There was no traffic in the street. Pablo blinked perspiration from his eyes and put on his hat, trimming it just so. He thought he would go home for a siesta, lie quietly under the mosquito netting and think about tomorrow. He stepped to the door, then turned for a final word to Rostok. He said that the map was meant for him, not Sydney. Claude Armand had nothing to do with it in any case.

He said, What's needed here is absolute secrecy and discretion on your part because people have put their heads in a noose and you hold the noose. So we'd need your word on this, Ros.

Aye aye, Pab, Rostok said with a distant grin.

We can't deviate from these plans, Pablo said.

Of course not, Rostok agreed.

*

The next morning Pablo Gutterman said a tender goodbye to his wife. He said he was going to Song Nu on business and if he did not return by evening to call Sydney Parade in Tay Thanh. She accepted this information without comment, not even to ask what the business was. She had her own intuition and had received what she called an "ingling." Naturally Pablo trusted her without reservation and had told her about Smalley's disappearance and presumed capture. She had said then that she did not believe the boy was dead. That was not the way things appeared to her. He always listened carefully to her and was startled when she added that death was never to be feared. There were many things that could be taken from you that were more precious than life.

He had said, I don't understand.

She had looked at him fondly and said, My Pablo.

Now she patted his cheek and told him she had been to the astrologer Tri the day before and he had assured her these were auspicious times for them. Mr. Tri was confident, and Mr. Tri was never mistaken.

She said, Since my cousin died, I know no one in Song Nu. But it is not a dangerous place so long as one stays within bounds and proceeds with modesty. She said he presented an imposing figure in his white suit and Panama hat, and then she giggled; it was not at all the costume that he wore on weekdays. It was not a suit for business, was it? She kissed him and mussed his hair, and then she straightened his tie. Pablo went a little weak in the knees when he pushed open the door to his house and waved. He never liked leaving her, even for an ordinary day at the office; and this was not an ordinary day.

You are protected, she told him as he walked to the little Fiat parked in the street.

Trying to be light, he said, Is that a promise?

A promise, she said.

Goodbye, darling.

By nightfall, then, she said.

He drove to the place just off the district road, parked, and began to walk. Soon his white suit was spotted from the damp and dirt on the leaves. He was sweating under his hat but he dared not remove it. He was aware what a comical figure he looked, some character from a fifties French farce. He should have asked his wife to take a photograph but she did not as a rule believe in photographs, thinking them bad luck and needlessly provocative to whatever spirits hovered round him.

The path was muddy but there were no tracks, neither animal nor human, and no sign he was being watched, though someone would be watching to make sure he did not stray from the path or take a wrong turn. Probably they knew how defective his eyesight was and how hard for him to distinguish among shadows. They were clever people and would leave no trace of their presence. So long as he proceeded correctly they would not show themselves. The forest was featureless yet alive, the leaves dripping water and small creatures rustling nearby. The odor of the forest was bitter in his nostrils. He did not remember the path from his trek years before, but he was reminded of the tropical forests of his boyhood home in Florida. They were featureless, too, and dangerous in different ways. He had been a decent woodsman as a youngster but that lore had left him long ago. He had no need for it here; he was a city man. He had a scoutmaster who had taught him how to blaze a trail and make a fire without matches and how to move slowly while watching for snakes. He was not moving slowly now and there was no need for stealth. They knew where he was and when they felt the time was right, they would make themselves known. He tried and failed to remember the scoutmaster's various warnings about poisonous snakes. He had a terrible fear of snakes and knew to keep to the middle of the path.

He was beginning to tire, losing his concentration. He paused to take off his hat and wipe his forehead with the back of his hand, breathing hard. He noticed then that there were no birds, either audible or visible. The middle-of-the-forest silence was unnerving and then he heard the faint swish of river water. He remembered the river and the wooden bridge over it, and rice fields on the other side. The sky cleared and the sun began to shine, casting sharp shadows on the path. He put on sunglasses against the glare and picked up his pace. The absence of birds and the sudden sun gave him a second wind. Now the path narrowed and he had to walk sideways to clear the bushes on either side; he knew that they were only a few yards from him, moving parallel to him. He removed his hat again so that they could see him clearly, harmless Pablo Gutterman here to take away their inconvenient infantry captain.

There was no bridge across the stream and for a moment he thought he had lost his way. Then he saw the footings and bits and pieces of wood and a crater on the other side. One unlucky H-and-I meant that he would have to wade across. He took off his shoes and socks and rolled up his trousers, watching all the while for snakes and hoping someone would appear with a boat. He did remember that the first of the Song Nu hamlets was no more than a kilometer distant, if that. He put his socks inside his shoes, tied his shoelaces together, and slung the shoes around his neck and started across, slipping on the stones, holding his hands out for balance as if he were on a high wire. He wondered what they thought as they watched him, an overweight middle-aged civil servant fording a stream in the middle of the forest. Un-armed, not dangerous. And frightened, he said aloud, alarmed then by the sound of his own voice, deeper than usual. On dry land once more, he put his shoes and socks back on and began to hurry.

He was upon the first hamlet before he knew it. The houses

were built into clearings, their lines so clean they seemed to merge with the trees beyond. The hamlet was an extension of the forest and governed by it. A faint odor of woodsmoke hung in the air but the place was empty, not even a dog or a chicken. Pablo cautiously looked into one of the houses, not crossing the threshold but leaning in to look and finding nothing except an overturned cooking pot, its contents congealing in the dirt. A gray smock hung on a hook and a pair of black sandals was visible under a stool. In all his years in Vietnam he had never seen an empty hamlet. There were always old people and children looking after one another; it was hard sometimes to tell who was in charge. The last time he had been here, his party looking like fashionable Parisians come to visit the poor relations in the provinces, the place had been filled with life, the women admiring his wife's silk ao dai and the children fascinated by his Panama hat.

The sun moved behind a thick bank of cloud and he took off his sunglasses. The color of the forest changed from dark green to light. The path was well worn. Behind the wall of green he felt the wilderness, wilderness spread farther than any man could hike, wilderness so thick you could lose your way in five minutes. Whole civilizations could flourish in it and never be detected. When he last traveled this path he found the atmosphere alien but cordial; it had the monotony of the grave or of outer space. He thought that all he could do now was continue, walking as quickly as he was able and turning his eyes from the evidence of civilian unrest.

Ahead of him a figure emerged from the forest and he knew without looking that another was behind him. They appeared to be unarmed and moved with a lightness of foot. They did not look at him or make any sign they were aware of his presence. Another ten minutes on, they approached the second village, a cluster of wooden buildings open to the air. The quiet was absolute. The one leading the way — he was slight and stepped on the balls of his feet, hands parallel to the ground like a dancer — pointed to the biggest of the houses, built like the others, on stilts with a long staircase leading to the first floor. And then the guide took a step sideways and glided into the forest, leaving Pablo alone in the clearing. Somewhere far away a dog began to bark and was quickly silenced. Then he heard the thump of an approaching helicopter and froze until that sound, too, faded. He began to walk slowly toward the long staircase, mounting it with difficulty and peering at last into the interior, so dark he had to wait a moment to allow his eyes to adjust. The air was close and carried the sour smell of the sickroom.

Smalley was sitting on a pallet, his back resting against the wall, his arms folded awkwardly in his lap. He was wearing his army fatigues but the insignia of rank was gone. He was blindfolded, and then Pablo saw that one arm was in a sling and that the blindfold was a crude bandage. Smalley appeared to be unconscious. He spoke softly but Smalley did not reply except to move his foot. Pablo bent to look at the bandage. Smalley's face was unshaven and blood was on his shirt. His wrists were crisscrossed with tiny cuts. He groaned then, a sound that seemed to come from somewhere inside his chest, rising to the height of the ceiling, the voice of the deepest self in terrible agony; and not only physical. Pablo spoke into Smalley's ear, explaining who he was and where they were, and that no harm would come to them. He said they were going to walk out of the hamlet together. They had been given safe passage. But it was necessary to hurry. Do you understand what I am saying to you? He looked at Smalley's feet and saw he was wearing sandals, two sizes too small from the look of them; everything about Smalley was disproportionate to the surroundings. He was the giant in the doll's house. Pablo remembered his complaint about stand-down: equipment rots, men get into trouble.

Pablo explained once again that they would leave immediately. The matter was urgent. The worst was over. Each needed the other, and if they cooperated they would be home by nightfall. A meal, medical attention, rest. He gave Smalley a reassuring pat on the back. When he tried to lift Smalley by his arms he met no resistance; they were soft as putty, without tone or sinew, or will. The captain appeared quite content to remain where he was, in a senseless, numb place not entirely of this world. When Pablo pulled hard, Smalley's body came away from the wall. He tumbled on his side and lay there stricken, groaning horribly, his breath coming in short strokes. Tears trickled from beneath the bandage, and they were not tears of pain or of humiliation but the tears of one who believed himself damned with no chance of redemption.

What did they do to you? Pablo said. My God, what did they do?

But Smalley gave no sign of having heard.

Pablo believed that to go forward he had to take Smalley back in his memory, to the moments before capture, when he was a professional soldier responsible for his men and the success of the mission.

Forgive me, Pablo said. Then he stepped back and with a sudden violent motion slapped Smalley full in the face.

Captain Harry Smalley was a full head taller than Pablo Gutterman but his head seemed to have shrunk, collapsed into his neck so that as they stumbled down the trail they seemed about the same size. Smalley's good arm was draped over Pablo's shoulder and he leaned heavily, trying to find balance as they walked. Smalley continued to groan, though more softly now. He seemed eager to please. From time to time he spoke, a word or string of words that made no sense, but the tone was apologetic. Somehow the sling that held his right arm had fallen away, revealing a long, ragged wound. With his right hand he kept smoothing his blond hair, stroking it the way you would a cat's fur. And that seemed to bring him some comfort.

The trail did not look the same going in the opposite direction; the sun was now behind them. When they came to the stream, Pablo was startled. He thought it was farther on. Then he saw his own footprints and remembered the place where he sat to put on his shoes. He was thinking about snakes and the absence of birds, and what lay ahead. They forded the stream staggering like drunkards, Pablo careful to keep hold of his hat. The hat had become a talisman. It had gotten him into Song Nu and it would get him out. His wife had promised that he was protected and the protection was the hat, though her astrologer was owed thanks as well, along with the guides, if that was what they were. He knew there was only a certain amount of luck in the universe. It was finite. Chance was finite, too, and they were not the same thing. He hoped to God he had not used up what luck he had been given or had earned.

I'm as crazy as you are, he said to Smalley.

Pablo stopped to clean his eyeglasses, streaked with sweat and fogged from the midafternoon heat. Smalley stood quietly at his side, turning his head like someone waiting for a traffic light to change. After he had replaced his glasses, Pablo thought to look behind him — and there, not twenty yards away, was a little gathering of villagers, an old man and two old women flanked by younger men and women. Some of the women carried infants. They looked at him incuriously. When Pablo raised his hand in a gesture of farewell they averted their eyes, turning to walk back up the trail; and then they seemed to vanish, becoming one with the forest. His eyesight was so poor, he could not be certain. Maybe they were shadows. But it was logical that they would see him out as they had seen him in. The milky sun was lowering behind them, and birds returned in flocks. Smalley replaced his arm on Pablo's shoulder, and it was then that Pablo noticed Smalley's bare feet. Somewhere en route the captain had lost his sandals. His ankles and toes were lacerated. Behind them on the path were bright drops of blood clinging to the razorgrass and the sharp rocks, a spoor such as an animal makes. Smalley seemed unaware of any of this. His face was impassive, his breathing shallow.

At the top of a rise, Pablo halted. He waited for a breeze but the air was still. He motioned for Smalley to sit but Smalley remained standing, his arm on Pablo's shoulder, staring into the monotonous distance. Pablo saw no sign of human habitation, only the forest stretching to the horizon. There was no smoke from cooking fires and if there were villages, they were concealed beneath the canopy of trees. The leaves were heavy and limp in the still air, veined like a human hand. He listened hard but heard no sound beyond the call of the birds. He moved close to Smalley, measuring his left foot against Smalley's right. But Pablo had small feet, and his shoes would not fit. He reached with his fingers to peel a leech from Smalley's instep, and when the leech came away Pablo saw bone, as white and soft to the touch as soap. And still Smalley did not move or make any sound at all beyond the sigh of his breathing.

Help me now, Pablo said.

But his wife did not answer.

He took off his hat and waved it at the forest.

And at that, Smalley looked at him curiously, the way a child does when an adult makes a strange or unexpected gesture.

My wife, Pablo explained. I depend on her. She knows things about the country that I don't and never will. And I forgot until a moment ago that she said my mission would be successful. And so it shall.

His white suit was filthy and streaked with Smalley's blood. He put his arm around the soldier's waist and pushed gently. They advanced a step at a time, keeping to the middle of the trail. All the way back, Pablo told Smalley about his wife, how they met and where they courted, her disappointment when she discovered they would have no children. Foreigners thought Vietnamese women were difficult, humorless and fierce, hardhearted, materialistic. But foreigners were wrong because they looked at things through the Western prism, and were frequently disconsolate. They were beside themselves with anxiety at the refusal of Vietnamese to conform, and to desire what Westerners desired. Desire was ranked differently on the scale of things; and virtue was a function of the spirit. They never saw a Vietnamese woman with her family, or paying homage to her ancestors. His wife was a lovable woman with the gift of prophecy. They lived in a plain stucco bungalow in the suburbs with a lawn in front and a garden in the rear. In a tropical climate, anything grew. Vietnam will never be without flowers.

Pablo did not know if Smalley was listening and it did not matter. He wanted to talk about his daily life with his wife, their evenings together in the bungalow and vacations by the sea or in the mountains, the presents they gave each other at birthdays and anniversaries, the private names they had for each other. He told Smalley things he had never told a living soul. In that way the two Americans stumbled on for an hour or more until the Fiat was in sight.

Pablo helped Smalley into the small rear seat, stuffing him through the door as you would a bundle of laundry. He sagged sideways until he was half on and half off the seat, finally sliding the rest of the way to the floor. Pablo avoided looking at the captain's feet. He threw himself behind the wheel, put the car in gear, and raced away. For the first mile he drove recklessly, then throttled back. He did not want to attract attention even though traffic was light and Smalley could not be seen. He passed trucks and motocyclos and once pulled to the side of the road to allow an American convoy to pass. He had promised Sydney he would drive directly to Group House in Tay Thanh. Rostok was supposed to arrange for an ambulance.

Approaching Tay Thanh, Pablo was not surprised to see Rostok's Scout parked at the side of the road, his Nungs drawn up around it. This was not part of the arrangement, but it wasn't Rostok's nature to follow arrangements. Rostok made his own arrangements. So Pablo parked behind the Scout and waited for Rostok to say what he had to say.

Pablo took off his hat and laid it on the seat. Rostok began talking at once, a catalog of regret, another wasted effort, a wild goose chase to the back of beyond, a wild throw of the dice doomed to failure. No Vietnamese was to be trusted, ever, no exceptions. Now we look like idiots, he said. Naïve idiots who chose to go around the chain of command, with the usual catastrophic results. If the army ever finds out about this, I'm on my way home and it's your fault, you and Parade —

He stepped back when he noticed the blood on Pablo's jacket.

He's in the rear, Pablo said.

He is?

On the floor, Pablo said.

Rostok peered through the window to the rear seat and said, Jesus. Is he alive? Rostok pressed his forehead against the glass to get a better look, shuddering at the sight of Smalley motionless.

He's in terrible shape, Pablo said. He's injured. He's delirious and doesn't know where he is.

Jesus, Rostok said again. Well, let's take him in. Let's get going now. You've got quite a story to tell, Pab. And this lad, he does, too. You drive him and I'll tag along behind. I'll give you my Nungs. Unless you want it some other way.

Pablo stared at Rostok. Then he said, Who's there? Who's at the House?

The ambulance, Rostok said. Sydney, too. And I asked one or two friends from the press, just in case we got lucky. I didn't tell them what it was about. I didn't let them know who we were bringing in. Better not to raise hopes.

You didn't give them my name, Pablo said.

No, I didn't, Rostok said. But we'll have a little press conference, you can tell them the bare bones of what went on out there, your valiant efforts, how you did it, and so forth and so on. Smalley, too, if he's capable of it.

He isn't, Pablo said.

Well, then, it'll be just us two and Syd. You can change that jacket if you want. Personally, I wouldn't.

It's your show, Ros. You do it. And if you mention my name I swear to God you'll regret it as long as you draw breath.

Pablo, Pablo. You've had a long day. You've done heroic work. But that's uncharitable. That's the farthest thing from my mind!

With surprising gentleness, the Nungs transferred Smalley to Rostok's Scout. Pablo pulled away first. In the rear-view mirror he saw Rostok talking urgently into the radio, pounding his fist on the hood of the Scout as he spoke. When Pablo passed Llewellyn House in Tay Thanh he saw half a dozen men in tailored khaki suits gathered on the front lawn. Television cameras recorded Sydney Parade standing in the doorway reading from a sheet of paper; and then Rostok arrived, beating a tattoo on the Scout's horn. So he had wasted no time; and if an ambulance was in the vicinity, Pablo could not see it.

He was stalled on the outskirts of Tay Thanh. All traffic was halted to make way for a long convoy of Vietnamese troops returning from some action in the field. Wounded men were packed into open trucks, closed trucks following shortly. Those were the trucks filled with dead. Flies were crawling over the canvas. The people by the side of the road averted their eyes, handkerchiefs over their mouths and noses. The stench remained after the trucks had gone on. Pablo got out of his Fiat and stood in the shade of a rubber tree preparing his briar pipe, tapping the bowl, packing the tobacco just so, taking his time with the match, taking more time achieving an even draw.

He stood with his arms crossed, smoking while he watched the convoy with its appalling cargo. Overhead he dimly saw a flight of American jets, Phantoms from the sound of them. They came over low, flying in V formation like geese. They hurtled across the sky and were gone before he knew it. The roar of the engines remained, intensifying before it receded. The Phantoms were followed by a long string of helicopter gunships; he counted ten and then another flight of twenty or more. His pipe had gone out so he lit another match, the flame steady in the windless air. The Vietnamese convoy came on and on and finally ended. Civilian traffic began to move but Pablo stayed under the rubber tree, smoking his pipe and thinking about Smalley. He guessed his wife's prophecy was correct. What they had taken from him was more vital than life.

The explosions, when they came, were faint but grew louder. They sounded like the stutter of a distant thunderstorm. He felt the ground move underfoot and still the stutter continued. He looked at his watch and five minutes later it had not ended. Five minutes beyond that the explosions went on until at last they faded, echoing, and then ceased altogether except for the residue in Pablo's head. The silence was welcome. Surely there would be an ambulance for Smalley by now. Pablo listened to the birds; and high above he heard the Phantoms returning to base. His pipe was dead and he tapped the bowl against the heel of his hand. He knew his wife was waiting for him but he could not move from the shade of the rubber tree. He decided to stop for some coconuts, and mangoes if he could find them; and later on, at dusk when the air cooled, he would mow the lawn as he had promised. He put the pipe in his pocket. He was drained of all emotion and could think only of his ritual tasks, buying fruit and mowing the lawn. Pablo watched the last of the Phantoms flying south and knew then that Rostok's first call was not to Sydney Parade but to military headquarters, and that Song Nu had ceased to exist.

The Arsenal of Democracy

*T*HE PHOTOGRAPH that appeared on the front pages of the world's newspapers that Sunday became a morbid emblem of the early days of the war. Reading from left to right, Sydney Parade, Captain Smalley, and Dicky Rostok — Smalley towering over them both, his hands crossed abjectly in front of him, his head listing at a strange angle, his hollow eyes staring downward as if something there had caught his attention. Rostok had removed his bandages for the picture. Parade and Rostok were suitably solemn in the presence of one who had survived such an ordeal — and while the picture captions were tactful, even uplifting, most readers turned from the page in pity at the sight of the helpless giant between the two healthy nondescript civilians. He looked as if he were their prisoner.

The full story of the rescue of Captain Smalley was one of the small secrets of the war. On that, Rostok kept his word. Military headquarters disclosed no details, citing confidentiality of methods and sources. CAS similarly was silent. The bombing of Song Nu disappeared from all after-action reports. For a while there were tantalizing newspaper accounts purporting to describe the activities of the little-known Llewellyn Group, since it was assumed that Rostok and Parade had something to do with Smalley's liberation, a premise that Rostok did nothing to discourage but would not confirm, either. These stories were of the working-quietly-in-the-shadows-of-the-war-without-fanfare variety, and earned Rostok favorable notices where it counted at Highest Levels. Of course, without fresh details to animate his story, the hero captain vanished — only to be reborn some months later when the photographer won a prize. Where was he now? He was at Walter Reed Army Hospital, doing splendidly and improving each day. No, he was unavailable for interviews. He had been promoted to major. He had been awarded the Silver Star for gallantry. No, Major Smalley was not expected to return to active duty. His uncle, the congressman, said in a statement that his family still hoped for a full recovery.

One more related secret remained.

When Pablo Gutterman arrived home that night, his wife was not there. He was alarmed and waited nervously in their garden, listening for her footsteps, eating one mango after another. When she appeared at last she was distraught, her eyes damp with grieving. She said that the hamlets of Song Nu had been destroyed, with terrible loss of life. And the people there were blameless! VC had tortured the American and left him in the hamlet for the people to dispose of as they saw fit. They notified Monsieur Armand, who seems to have notified the American authorities. How could he do such a thing? What business was it of his? This was not his affair, but he should have left it alone. And now there was nothing left but rubble and a hill of dead. And now you are involved, Pablo. You share responsibility. They do not blame you alone. But they are very angry. There must be something you can do to settle your own account.

Armand was not involved, Pablo said, lying to his wife for the first time in their life together.

He *was,* she said. And this Parade —

Sydney wasn't involved, Pablo said, and then thought, Second time.

Who then? Who was responsible?

Rostok took charge of Smalley when I brought him out. The arrangement was that he would return Smalley to the authorities and that there would be no reprisals. But he called the military, and the military decided to bomb. Revenge for what was done to Smalley and the others who had been captured. Rostok broke his word.

You must have nothing more to do with Rostok, she said.

I know, he said.

You must promise me that.

You should have seen Smalley, Pablo said. He was pathetic.

I saw the hill of dead, she said. That was pathetic also.

Pablo left early the next morning in the Fiat. The sky was lowering again and rain was in the air. He thought of the many seasons he had lived in Saigon, the governments that had come and gone and the revolution that went on forever. He and his wife lived in a state of ambiguity, always knowing more than they could tell and never knowing quite enough. There were always mysteries, and boxes within boxes, all surrounded by rumor and innuendo. The level of violence was predictable and logical in its own way, and then VC practiced their black arts on Smalley and as a consequence a village disappeared. He found nothing to admire in this war, no principle worth a single human life. For years he had lived on the war's margins and knew now that an avalanche would sweep them all away. He only wanted to live normally with his wife in their bungalow in the suburbs. He had arranged a kind of disappearance for himself. On the weekends of the hottest months they traveled to her family's cottage in the mountains of Dalat. They fished. They played golf. They loved each other. Then the revolution came to Dalat; or perhaps it was always there and he hadn't noticed. After many seasons he found himself accepted, more or less; in any family there were seven circles of intimacy and he reckoned he was at the third or fourth circle. He and his brother-in-law were fast friends. Now there was a chance they would cast him out, and if that ever happened his marriage was ended. He did not know what he would do then. He could not imagine himself living in Vietnam without his wife and he could not imagine himself living in Florida under any circumstances; or anywhere in the vast and unencumbered United States. He was an expatriate, but that did not make him a colonial. He was an American who worked for Americans, but that did not make him an imperialist. He only wished to get on from day to day living normally.

Song Nu was important to his wife's family for reasons he only dimly understood. It would have something to do with his wife's cousin; perhaps there were other ancestors buried there. He would never know the full truth of it, because the deepest part would be inexplicable even to his wife. But he could see in her eyes that part of her own soul was lost when Song Nu vanished. Then he remembered poor Smalley; part of his soul had disappeared also. Pablo wondered if in some region of his mind Smalley thought he was going home to a fine Main Street parade. But no, the captain's mind was occupied by appalling shadows; there was no room in it for marching bands and a welcome by his uncle and a speech by the mayor, his mother so proud.

Pablo showed his pass at the gate and was escorted to the office on the third floor, the one where they double-checked ID at the locked and guarded door. His old friend the colonel was waiting for him with coffee.

Pablo related the events of the day before, omitting no names when he gave the source of the information. The colonel did not take notes, nor did he interrupt. Pablo described the walk in and the discovery of Smalley and the walk out. He described the guides and the empty hamlets. He said he saw no VC, which did not mean that they were not there, only that he had not seen them. He believed in his heart that they had evacuated Song Nu altogether, leaving Smalley as the object lesson. If this analysis was correct it meant that the bombing killed only civilians, the very civilians who had been trying to help. They were the ones who had sent the map to Claude Armand.

The colonel nodded, sighing. He looked out the window, then back at Pablo.

He said, We had to do something.

Why is that? You had Smalley.

You saw what they did to him. We couldn't let it pass unnoticed. Song Nu was what we had. Song Nu was a target of opportunity and we took it. And no one here suggested we refuse it.

And the mission was to destroy it.

Totally, the colonel said.

Once you had the information from Rostok —

The colonel gave a little wag of his head, affirmative.

He should have kept his mouth shut, Pablo said.

Well, he didn't. The colonel offered a little wintry smile and said there was an aftermath, amusing if the entire matter wasn't so grisly. Rostok wanted the undersecretary to be leading the reception committee but something — some sixth sense perhaps related to conscience — told him that was a bad idea and he told Rostok he'd pass. He'd stay where he was, at the ambassador's residence. Godspeed, he said.

Rostok can't be trusted.

You were outstanding, Pablo. Just outstanding. If you hadn't volunteered to go in, that boy would be there now, most likely dead.

Do you agree you owe me a favor?

I agree I owe you a favor, Pablo. The army does, too.

Pablo walked the colonel through the conversation he had had with his brother-in-law. He gave the precise location of the warehouse and the contraband inside. Then he identified the owner, the enterprising Madame Vinh, whose husband was so prominent in the Ministry of Defense. Pablo suggested that a platoon of sappers could do to the warehouse what a wing of Phantoms had done to Song Nu.

The colonel said, Shit.

Too tough for you?

Tough enough. The general is an untouchable. That makes his wife an untouchable. Two untouchables and you want me to blow up her warehouse.

Good luck to you then, Pablo said, rising.

Pablo Gutterman resigned from Llewellyn Group the next week and went to work for one of the Texas construction companies surveying the port at Cam Ranh Bay. They needed translators and someone who knew the region and could talk convincingly to the Vietnamese military. Soon, however, everyone understood that Pablo was persona non grata at the Ministry of Defense, and in certain sections of the American command as well. He was let go after a month and went to work for one of the charter airlines, but that ended badly, too.

Six months after the bombing of Song Nu he found something with a Swiss agency involved with refugees. The Swiss complained constantly of the heat and the food, the corruption and bloody-mindedness of the Vietnamese, and the indifference and arrogance of the Americans. But they were serious about their work and allowed Pablo free rein in the countryside, where he spent most of his time. Eventually he dropped from sight.

Rostok hated to see him go.

Pablo got things done, Ros said. He was an asset. I don't mind admitting that I was hurt that he never even said goodbye. I wanted to give him a party, he and the frau. I know he held me responsible for the bombing. He never understood that things get complicated in wartime. Logic doesn't rule. It's a sort of whirl, Syd.

Sydney did not reply. He was watching a Taiwanese vessel motor slowly upriver in the direction of the main wharf, mindful of the German hospital ship tied up at the long quay in front of the Majestic Hotel. The river was not wide and on its far side the shacks amid the plain of reeds that went to the water's edge were clearly visible. A few months before a sniper had wounded a water-skier who had ventured too close to the reeds. Nurses leaned over the rail of the hospital ship, laughing and drinking Coca-Cola in the brutal heat of midday. The nurses were blonde and looked as if they belonged in dirndls. One of them waved at an officer on the deck of the Taiwanese freighter. He nodded and turned his back before he made the obscene gesture.

I walked in to work that Monday and he was gone, Rostok went on. His desk was cleaned out. He never said goodbye, never left a note. After that mess with the charter airline I heard he went to work for the Swiss, and that's just as well. He can't get into trouble with the Swiss. Pablo never had the heart for dirty work.

They were standing under the awning of the Majestic, having finished lunch at the rooftop restaurant. Sydney said, Let's walk to the wharf.

Now you, Rostok said. Just when you're learning the ropes, you're leaving. That's the trouble with the effort; the minute a man learns what's what, his tour's up and he heads home. And the joke is, what you learn here isn't transferable. It's specific to this time and this place. Our hard-won knowledge ain't fungible, Syd.

Sydney waved at one of the nurses and she waved back.

So now I'll be holding down the fort with George Whyte.

That's not much firepower. Still, he's a pretty good man with the accounts. Not as good as Dicey Dacy but good enough. Wonder what the hell ever happened to Dacy, don't you?

I'm sorry about your dad, Rostok said after a moment. They were walking along the crowded street that bordered the river, a warren of warehouses and rundown cafés, and here and there a tailor's. Rostok's Nungs followed at a respectful distance. Prostitutes in miniskirts loitered in the doorways but paid no attention to the American civilians, so obviously officials of one command or another out for an after-lunch stroll. The Taiwanese freighter moving upriver was searching for an anchorage out of sniper range of the shacks on the opposite shore. There were two other boats maneuvering in the channel and another tied up at the main wharf, the offloading about to begin.

You were close, Rostok said.

Yes, we were. We tried to stay in touch, but.

Isn't it awful, the way the time flies?

He was no better on his end. Difference was, I knew what he was up to and he had no idea what I was up to because I never explained. Too difficult. I'd write him a letter and the sentences fell apart. I was happier writing fairy tales to my daughter.

I'm sorry about the screw-up with the cable. They sent it to the consulate by mistake and it took them a while to locate you.

By the time I got word he was already in the ground. His wife didn't want to wait, and I can't say I blame her but I wish to hell she'd held off for a few days so I could have been with him. He didn't even know he was sick. They gave him a death warrant one day and he was dead three days later. Sydney opened his mouth to continue, then didn't. This was not Rostok's business. When he called his stepmother the next day she told him what she had omitted in the cable. Fred killed himself, she said in a voice filled with contempt. He went to his workshop, took one of his Brownings from the closet, and placed the barrels on his heart. He leaned into the barrels and just managed to trip the trigger with his thumb. That was his answer to the doctor's death sentence. I found the body, she went on, as he expected I would. I believe he wanted me to. He had a record on the phonograph and a square of walnut in his vise, and there was no note, so I have no idea what was going through his mind, except that he was determined that I find the body, which I did minutes after the explosion. Not a pretty sight, as you might imagine. Missy came for the funeral. Karla couldn't make it. I didn't know where you were. So we went ahead with our plans because there seemed no reason for delay. I will be selling the house, by the way, and moving to Florida. If there's anything of your father's that you want, you better make a list. The police have the shotgun.

I think he gave up, Sydney said suddenly. I think he didn't see the point to massive resistance. He just said the hell with it and — passed away. That was the difference between him and us. He said the hell with it and we haven't.

We're not terminal, Syd.

Yes, we are. We just can't believe it. Sydney had a vision of a handsome corpse, The Effort rouged and barbered, well tailored, lifelike in its repose. Why, he looks just like he's asleep!

Rostok stared across the eddying surface of the river. A sampan was making its way upriver, hugging the opposite shore. He said, Mine died when I was a kid. Damn fool stepped in front of a train.

Sydney nodded, not trusting himself to speak.

We're taking casualties, Syd. Pablo off in the boondocks with the Swiss, your dad dead, our wives God knows where. And now you're leaving. Give my regards to Broadway. Sydney did not reply, remembering the letter from Otto Kis that had arrived on Monday. He had not opened it owing to the press of business, a file that had been lost or stolen. He had slipped the letter into his desk drawer intending to read it later. And he had forgotten it entirely. It was a certified letter, heavier than usual, four pages at least. The envelope was marked Urgent and bristled with importance. The hell with you, Kis.

I'll miss you, Syd, Rostok went on, filling the awkward silence. We've had good times along with the bad. God, you were green. Remember that first dinner in the café at Tay Thanh? I thought, Jesus, I've got one who's younger than springtime. But I knew you well enough to know you'd catch on. You're a quick study. You'd learn about Cao and the advantages of a bum leg. You'd get used to it. You'd learn the ropes because you've got ambition same as I do, only not quite so obvious. You've made a mistake leaving now because things are going to get interesting. We're in it for keeps. We're in it the way the French were in it, but we're not French so we have an advantage. We have no territorial ambitions, none whatever. So it's not anywhere near terminal, Syd. I'd call the odds even-up.

Rostok continued to handicap the odds. One of the prostitutes raised her leg to inspect something on her calf. She was smooth as suede, small-boned, probably no more than fifteen years old though it was hard to assess the ages of Vietnamese women. They all wanted to look fifteen; anyway, the ones on the street did. Sydney had wanted to go with a prostitute but never did and now never would. He had slept with one of the network reporters and one of the academics on tour, the academic on a government grant administered by Sydney's old foundation; the director had told her to look him up. He and the academic had gone to Guillaume Tell for dinner and drank Scotch after Scotch, disclosing their life stories, then trading anecdotes of the war, leaning across the table, their fingers just touching. We're into it now, she said as they were leaving the restaurant. The director feels we must do what we can for the effort, and you wouldn't believe the money that's available.

He had taken the reporter to one of the private upstairs rooms at Les Affreux. He had worn his ice cream suit and he remembered the hush in the restaurant as he and the reporter mounted the stairs to the second floor, closing the door of the private cabinet behind them. They found a bottle of wine on ice and hors d'oeuvres on red plates. No sound reached them. They sat side by side and toasted each other under an impressionist landscape, Ajaccio at dusk.

Where did you find this place? she asked. She was blushing.

Do you know Pablo Gutterman? he said in reply.

It was too dangerous to drive back to Tay Thanh, so he had returned with them to their rooms, the academic in the Caravelle and the journalist in the Continental Palace. Sydney had an idea that neither woman was accustomed to alcohol and that he was in the category of a reckless adventure, something that was expected of them in the war zone and could be forgotten for that reason; forgiven, too. Each was married and had children. They had paid for dinner, since they were on expense accounts and he wasn't. And you're a bona fide source, Sydney. Tell me again about nation-building, where it goes from here. He believed they wanted a souvenir for their scrapbooks, something to remember beyond the briefings. Still, they were pleasant enough evenings with no harm done and no regrets, at least on his part. He wasn't sure about them.

Pretty girls, he said absently.

Remember that night? You said they carried fifty-seven varieties of clap.

They didn't then. Probably they do now.

More propaganda, Rostok said.

Is this the voice of experience I'm hearing?

God damn right, Rostok said. Young girls and their flutter. Young girls and their happy smiles. They know tricks you wouldn't believe, they're naturals at bedtime. I think their mamas were French taught.

Sydney watched the stevedores scramble up the gangway to begin the offloading. They were carrying cartons by hand and he moved closer now to see what the cargo was. The ship was too small to carry heavy munitions. The first consignment was whiskey, the Cutty Sark label unmistakable. The stevedores brought the whiskey cartons down the gangway and laid them neatly on the dock where other stevedores transferred them to the quayside warehouse. He noted that the two prostitutes had disappeared, and he guessed they were inside with the whiskey.

Reminds me, Rostok said. What's happened to Armand?

No idea, Sydney said.

You haven't seen him?

Not lately, Sydney said.

Damn shame. You try to cross every *t* and dot every *i* and sometimes you can't. I tried to keep him out of it, you know.

You did?

Yes, for Christ sakes. After they saw that big dumb blond —

Captain Smalley, Sydney said. Let's use his name. At least he had one, Sydney thought. The villagers at Song Nu did not, so far as the Americans were concerned. The men, women, and children of Song Nu were as anonymous as farm animals. His head began to spin and for a moment he thought he would be sick.

Yes, Smalley. They demanded to know where our information came from. And why it came to us and why we acted as we did. They were grateful to Pablo and to you, too, Syd.

Me? They were grateful to me? So they could incinerate a village?

They needed to know for their after-action report, you see. It was important to them, in the event there were inquiries. They were relentless. So I told them on an absolutely confidential eyes-only basis. Pablo didn't fool anyone with his cock-and-bull story. The map was Claude Armand's, you were the messenger, and Pablo the retriever. And the army promised there wouldn't be any reprisals, and why should there be? Armand helped us out. Of course they were miffed because civilians were involved. They lost a man and failed to find him and needed us, and that wounds their pride. So the army said they'd try to be a little more careful with the bombing runs in Armand's neighborhood, maybe try to look out for him in other ways. They sent a team to interview him, but no one was home, no Armands, no workers. They wanted to know if he had any other useful bits of information that he might want to share in return for — whatever he needed.

Sydney's head was still. He wondered which was worse, provider, messenger, or retriever.

Pretty place they have, isn't it? The door wasn't locked so our people had a look around, sat on the verandah for a while hoping they'd return. Then they decided things were too quiet for their liking and left. On the way out one of the choppers took a hit, small arms. So they circled back and hosed things down but didn't see anyone. They said it was real Indian country. They wondered how those Frenchies survived, year to year.

They went in with helicopters?

Of course. How else?

Did they take a brass band, too?

Rostok smiled. He said, Our people were impressed, seeing how the Armands lived. None of the modern conveniences, like a TV or a dishwasher, but it looked to them like a nice life, a big house with plenty of servants, a fine green lawn, everything so quiet you could hear the clocks tick. You have to wonder what it is that drives people to a colonial life unless it's an attraction to solitude along with the servants. That, and feeling superior to the natives.

Sydney listened to Rostok's version of la vie coloniale, remembering the downpour on the iron roof, so deafening he thought it was an artillery barrage. And it seemed to him that in a certain sense the Armands were prisoners, unable to move freely, caught between the skirmish lines of foreigners, and this in a country once ruled by Frenchmen, and loved by them. Not loved in return, however. Despised, though despised a little less now that the Americans were here. He thought that on balance messenger was the greater crime. The messenger was the croupier who sent the ball spinning.

He said, How much did you tell them about Pablo?

Not the whole story, Syd. Pablo wanted his name kept out, and I kept it out except to say that he'd been helpful. Everyone knows Pab has special contacts in the community. God knows Smalley was in no condition to confirm or deny anything so I had it pretty much my own way. You had a nice mention in dispatches, too. I kept it vague and loose and the reporters are still trying to figure things out. Security's been pretty good, all things considered. Saigon leaks like an infant. Thing is, no one has any interest in telling the whole story. What a circus!

So you took the credit, Sydney said.

Someone had to. Smalley couldn't very well have walked out of Song Nu by himself, could he? It was a subtle operation, thanks to Pablo. And the credit wasn't for me, it was for Llewellyn Group. And it's ancient history now. No one gives a damn because of the changing nature of the effort. Rostok gestured grandly at the vessel in front of them.

The whiskey had been offloaded and now they were starting on file cabinets, one cabinet after another, sturdy gunmetal gray, all with combination locks. Some had two drawers, others three or four drawers. They were heavy enough so that each file cabinet required two stevedores to manhandle it down the gangway. Once they were on the quay the ground crew moved them into the same warehouse where the whiskey was. They kept spilling from the hold like fruit from a horn of plenty. Sydney counted two dozen file cabinets and then gave up, thinking instead about the paper that would go into them, the copies and the originals. Two dozen file cabinets would not hold five minutes' work from the various American commands.

We need those, Ros said. Thank God for the combination locks.

The military will have priority, Sydney said.

Maybe not, Rostok said. Maybe not this time. Maybe this time Llewellyn Group's on those invoices. I wouldn't be surprised. This isn't public yet, Syd, so keep it under your arm, but we're getting an additional ten men and. He paused there, evidently uncertain whether to finish the sentence. Then he looked sideways at Sydney and continued, I've been invited to attend mission council meeting on Fridays. Deputy ambassador heads it up, as you know. That's where the thinking gets done. It's where the effort comes together, and as of next week I've a place at the table. My name will be on the cables along with all of theirs. So, Syd, Llewellyn Group's in the first foursome.

Congratulations, Ros.

These meetings. They're principals only.

You've been waiting a long time.

Even Boyd Llewellyn sent me a telegram, en clair so that everyone could read it, even the secretaries. Boyd and I are getting along much better now. I may have misjudged him. Fact is, he can squeeze money from a stone.

So you're staying on, Sydney said.

I owe them one more year. One more year, then I'm gone.

Where, Ros?

Maybe the private sector, because we'll be doing business here for — well, years and years. Maybe an ambassadorship. You burn out, you know. You're the man who's seen too much, knows too much. So you need a period of decompression. Maybe I'll write a book describing how we did it.

Sydney looked at him. Did what?

Survived, Syd. Survived those early days of confusion and uncertainty, when we didn't know where we were going or how we would get there. We didn't know where "there" was. We didn't know what we wanted really, so we went in one toe at a time thinking the Vietnamese could do it themselves, with our support and know-how. It was an illusion. We live by illusions. Anyone who knew anything knew we'd have to come in full fig. We'd have to take over. We'd run the war and run their economy and stabilize the government and secure the countryside. We knew we could do it, we didn't have the will to do it then. But we have the will now. Those early days, we're lucky we weren't thrown out like the French were. Simple fact, we came in with too little. Not making that mistake again, he concluded, gesturing again at the freighter at quayside.

The horn of plenty was momentarily empty and the stevedores were taking a break. They were lounging, smoking cigarettes and drinking tea. Now and then one of them would disappear into the warehouse and remain for a few minutes, then reappear. When someone on board yelled a command they all rose and sauntered back up the gangway to see what else was in the inventory. Their nonchalance reminded Sydney of the cabin boys and stewards aboard the yachts on Long Island Sound, the crew immaculate in white, balancing trays of drinks or pulling on a jib sheet, never using more energy than was necessary. A fine way to spend the summer, his father had warned, so long as you don't get used to it. He realized he was homesick for the crisp New England air, and the empty beaches when the children had gone back to school.

What happens to you now, Syd?

I'll try teaching for a while. Vietnam doesn't prepare you for much, does it?

Teaching? Rostok laughed. I'd never figure you for a teacher.

You're a doer. And you're wrong about the preparation. You have some practical experience, some knowledge of the way the world works. That's what the classroom needs more of, someone who's worked close to the fire. Has watched things burn. What university will it be?

Prep school, he said. Some boys' school not too far from New York City. That's where my daughter is.

Teaching adolescent boys? What a pain in the ass. The social sciences, I suppose. That's what you started out as, a social scientist, and I'd guess our environment here has only added to your knowledge. Everyone needs some on-the-job training, practical facts added to the usual bogus theories.

Sydney looked at him, wondering whether to spoil his picture and tell him he intended to teach English. He had decided that he had nothing to bring to the social sciences, and the social sciences had nothing to bring to him. If he was to explain the way the world worked, he would have to journey to the offside made-up discredited world of novelists and poets. That would not save him any more than social science, civics, or love. But he thought it would make a harmless beginning. He smiled at Rostok and said, I'll be teaching English, Ros. No on-the-job training for that.

Tell you what, Rostok said, clapping his hands. Sydney thought that if he were more full of himself he'd explode. I have a fine edition of the works of Joseph Conrad. You can have it. It's in our apartment in Washington. I'll tell the tenants. You go in and take the set. I envy you, making the acquaintance of Almayer, Nelson (or Nielson), Captain Whalley, and Jim. Thing about Conrad is, he's an inspiration for an adolescent boy. Conrad understands the need for self-reliance and clear vision, knowing what you want and doing whatever's necessary to achieve it. Conrad has no patience with illusions. Conrad sees the storm gathering and he meets it head-on and God help anyone who gets in his way. He steers his vessel into the eye of the typhoon, knowing that God rewards the brave; and if God is absent, it's up to the man to defeat the sea. There's something of the manifest destiny in Joseph Conrad, don't you think? And he's relevant in these times because he hated the Russians. Dostoyevsky once insulted Conrad's favorite uncle. Indicated contempt for all Poles and Conrad never forgave nor forgot. So everything's personal, you see. And it's important to have confidence.

Sydney looked hard at him. Speechless was not the word.

He is our greatest novelist. Why, he's greater even than Greene!

Promise me something, Ros.

Rostok looked at him suspiciously.

You'll stay away from the Armands. You won't contact them. You won't threaten them. You won't ask them for favors. You'll pretend they don't exist.

That's a tough assignment, Syd. You see, they're *in*. They've anted up, they're part of the game whether they want to be or not. It's the sort of hand, you have to play it out. You can't leave the table whenever you want to. So if we need some help, we're going to talk to them. We have no choice, given the stakes. They're part of things, same's you or me or Pablo. It's all the same loyalty, Syd.

They did us a favor. Smalley's alive because of them.

Why — that's the reason they're in! You can't avoid the war. It's all around us. It's the oxygen we all breathe, even the Armands. You can't resign from it any more than you can resign from a typhoon. Even you. When you go back to the world you'll still be in the war. It's nature's way, and we've given our word. Yet. In the specific manner we're going forward now into our tunnel, the Armands are small potatoes. Probably we won't have the time for them, Syd. And I'm guessing they'll be content to seek a protected anchorage as the barometer falls and the wind rises. They'll need us more than we need them. And I can tell you this, cross my heart. If they need us, we'll be there.

Rostok smiled and Sydney smiled back. Sydney was still bushwhacking through the thicket of card games, typhoons, anchorages, and Joseph Conrad's Russophobia. He was certain that the Armands would continue to feint and evade, for the rest of their lives if need be. Rostok did not know that they had left Plantation Louvet and were staying with friends at a cottage at Vung Tao. They did not believe they were safe in their own house. There were so many rumors they could not sort them out, but the most persistent had them as informers whose collaboration with the Americans had resulted in the destruction of Song Nu. And they knew there was truth to the accusation. So they had driven to Vung Tao on back roads and would remain a month or more, until the atmosphere improved. But they knew also that Vietnamese had long memories and their situation could never be as it had been.

So we'll do what we can and hope it's enough, Dede Armand had said when Sydney showed up unannounced the day before, to offer what explanations he could and tell them he was going home and would be happy to carry whatever messages they had to their families in France and America.

Tell them we are all right, she said.

Will you ask my mother to send me some underwear?

Claude wants English crackers and a wheel of brie.

As for the situation, Dede went on, at some point we'll have to explain. Maybe they'll believe us, most likely they won't. She stood in the front doorway and did not invite him in. He could see three pieces of luggage in the hall, and beyond the luggage Claude Armand on the verandah talking to his foreman.

She looked at Sydney and said, Why did you do it?

Rostok did it, Sydney said. Rostok gave you away. Pablo and I wanted to get Smalley out, and forget how it was done or who did it. But Rostok — finds things out. That's what he does for a living, and he's good at it.

Always Rostok, she said.

And we were careless, Sydney said. We could have gone ahead without his knowledge, simply done it on our own accord. Sydney paused then, wondering why they had not acted alone, according to their own good instincts, and knew at once that he and Pablo did not have what Rostok had in abundance, confidence, a sense of infallibility. They did not trust their own judgment, and at the same time they did not rely on Rostok, either. They relied on the institution, the government itself, the United States. Sydney said, I believed I had to involve him.

And that was a mistake, wasn't it?

A big mistake, Dede.

You're a dangerous friend, Sydney. You come from a dangerous country. It's not good for us, you know. They won't rest. The Americans will come to call — in fact they already have. They searched the house. Rifled the drawers, looked at the photographs on the wall, helped themselves to beer. And one of them stole my Buddhas, all five. My bronze Buddhas that I've had for years and depended on and now they're in some soldier's pack, war souvenirs.

At least they did not disturb the graves of my children, she said.

I'm sorry, Dede. Sorry for — all of it.

This is the life you've made for us, Sydney. And they'll come again, when they think there's something valuable we can tell them. Next month, or two months from now, we'll have a visit from VC. They'll have questions, too, and they'll assume we know some of the answers; and we will. What do you suggest we do then, Sydney? They'll demand a larger cut of our payroll and there'll be other sorts of dues to pay. And we'll give them what they ask because what else can we do? We refuse to leave our home. No one can make us, not you certainly. Not VC if we can help it. I refuse to wander this earth like a lost soul or a displaced person.

Raised voices inside caused Sydney to raise his eyes. Claude was arguing with his foreman. He shook his head once, and again, but without conviction. The foreman took a step forward and snarled something, his finger tapping Claude Armand's chest, emphasizing each word. Then they separated and stood glaring at each other. The air was charged and Sydney believed something violent was at hand. When Claude nodded at last, the foreman dipped his head in mockery, and the Frenchman began again to explain, his voice softer now.

Goodbye, Sydney, Dede said, and closed the door.

For a long time Sydney sat in his car looking at the house nestled so close to the earth, its stucco chipped, its foundation in need of repair. The curtains were drawn. As architecture, it had no distinguishing features beyond an undefinable colonial ambiance. Foreigners lived there. It disclosed something of its past but nothing of its future. It was not an obvious place for anyone to cling to, and to love beyond life itself. Forbidden its solace, Dede saw herself adrift on the surface of the earth, a soul lost. Surely that would not happen. She would not permit it. Dede and her husband would find a means of survival. They were practical people. They were resourceful. If you wanted a thing that badly, then fortune was on your side, however unsettled the future. Sydney saw a curtain move, and close again. Who knew the shape of things to come? They were still alive after all, and Dede was with her children.

The ship stirred. Rostok and Sydney stood shoulder to shoulder watching the horn of plenty gush forth once more. They were offloading America, the arsenal of democracy, its knowledge and its wealth, its optimism and industrial might. Typewriters, blackboards, two cases of thesauruses and three of dictionaries, cartons of envelopes and notepads, pencils, paper clips, gum erasers and ballpoint pens, account ledgers, file folders, coffee mugs, paperweights and insect repellent and scissors and picture frames and desk lamps. Television sets were followed by transistor radios, then telephones, movie projectors, intercom systems, lecterns with microphones attached, and case after case of plastic rulers. An American stood to one side with a checklist on a clipboard.

Sydney and Rostok stood quietly for some time watching the offloading, and then Sydney noticed the prayer flag hanging from one of the aft portholes, no doubt an ancestor being remembered. The flag hung limply in the damp breeze, and then a gust came up and rocked it, the cloth rising and falling, rippling in the current. He imagined the prayers released, flying to whoever might need them, words of faith and consolation winging west to Laos and Burma, to Assam and Pakistan, farther west to Persia and the Anatolian plateau, gathering speed across the Aegean to the Po valley and on to dry Iberia, still strong and confident as they swarmed across the Atlantic to the New World.